MW00944036

OUT OF A BARREN PLACE

… and a Little Child Shall Lead Them

A Novel

By

Shirley McCullough

Copyright © 2007 by Shirley McCullough

OUT OF A BARREN PLACE
by Shirley McCullough

Printed in the United States of America

ISBN 978-1-60266-272-8

All rights reserved solely by the author. The author guaran-
tees all contents are original and do not infringe upon the
legal rights of any other person or work. No part of this book
may be reproduced in any form without the permission of
the author. The views expressed in this book are not neces-
sarily those of the publisher.

Unless otherwise indicated, Bible quotations are taken from
The New King James version of the Bible. Copyright © 1982
by Thomas Nelson, Inc.

This is a work of fiction. Names, characters, places and
incidents either are products of the author's imagination or
are used fictitiously. Any resemblance to actual events or
persons, living or dead is entirely coincidental.

www.xulonpress.com

Blessings —
Shirley McCullough

Acknowledgements:

First I want to thank my husband, "Red," for his patience, support and interest in my story. An interest so strong he drove me deep into the Arizona Strip so that I could see it first-hand.

I also want to thank our extended family and numerous friends who encouraged me along the way, with a special thanks to my daughter, Annette Steiger, who assisted, insisted, and persisted in getting this book published and for the many hours she dedicated to this effort.

Finally, to my dear editor, Max James, who believed in my story more than I did, and whose great effort, dedication, and expertise have made this possible.

Shirley

"Shirley draws her readers through a gamut of emotions as she sees to the heart of her characters. Her elegant descriptions have a poetic, musical quality."
    — MAX JAMES, Editor *Out of a Barren Place …and a Little Child Shall Lead Them*

Former journalist of the US Navy Public Information Office under Commanding Officer and mentor, William J. Lederer

Assisted author Herman Wouk in researching PIO's history archives. Much of this research went into *The Caine Mutiny*, Wouk's first Pulitzer Prize-winning novel.

Former editor of *Corona Daily Independent*, Corona California

Editor of the four *Bounce Back* books, a series compiled by his wife Diana James.

Former President and founder of Christian Writers of Idaho.

Shirley McCullough met Max and Diana James through Christian Writers of Idaho.

OUT OF A BARREN PLACE
… and a Little Child Shall Lead Them

By Shirley McCullough

CHAPTER 1

Darcy did not cry. It was over. Peter Callahan, professor of music, was dead. Cal, so lean and tall, so tan and blond, and handsome as Adonis, no longer existed. His lyrical voice was hushed forever. Still, she didn't cry. Not Darcy Callahan. Stoic as stone, she managed a feeble smile for the gathering of friends. She ignored the organ music, the wilting flowers, and the sweltering heat that had turned her impeccable suit into a mass of soggy black linen. Nothing could thaw her heart, not even Cal's favorite song, his final request in this ritual that he had arranged for himself.

As friends hurried from the campus chapel, Darcy entered widowhood with perfect composure. She didn't merely hide her feelings; she denied they existed.

"Darcy, won't you let us stay with you for a while?" a voice from behind her called.

Matt and Janet, her close neighbors, had hovered nearby the last few days. It was Matt who had notified Darcy of the accident, who stayed with her at Cal's bedside during those last horrendous hours, and who delivered the eulogy today. Matt seemed to understand Darcy's dry-eyed response to Cal's death; maybe someday she would too. For now, she wanted only to be alone. There was so much to do to remove all traces of Cal.

"Thanks so much, but I'm okay."

Her voice was steady. Lifting her chin, she waded through the suffocating Las Vegas heat waves that snaked upward from the pavement, and hoped no one noticed her clenched jaw. At home she peeled off her clammy clothes, tossed her wedding ring into her jewel case and hit the shower. Minutes later, cool in a baggy jumper, she braided her hair and began to clean the closets.

Whatever else Darcy was, she was methodical. Every project began with a list written in her mind. Cal's finest clothes would go to the consignment shops along with his art collectibles. Others were destined for the university drama department's costume collection. Sorting through a drawer crammed with Cal's portraits, she wrapped the oldest one in white mesh and tucked it into a shopping bag with other items. The others went through the shredder. She had already listed the house for sale. By the middle of June she would leave it all, including Cal, behind. Gladly.

*   *   *   *   *

Darcy pulled the dry desert air deep into her lungs. June at last, and she was on her way to Elko, Nevada. Life in Las Vegas was behind her. She was on her own. No turning back. No more apologies. Then an unbidden thought: *No Cal.* It all seemed like yesterday, or a generation ago. No point in thinking about that now.

By force of habit, and to divert her thoughts, she went over her list again. The house had sold quickly. Cal's possessions, including his sports car, were gone, and his debts paid. The baby grand piano, the jewel in Cal's crown, now adorned the home of other music lovers. Little remained to connect Darcy to Vegas—or to Cal: the lone portrait, her wedding ring in the jewel case, the locked silver box from their Mexico City honeymoon (she'd decide what to do with its contents later on when her mind cleared). And memories, some concealed just beneath the surface of her consciousness, others buried much deeper, where they belonged.

Her personal belongings fit easily into the pickup truck's shell: her computer, books, cameras, and a few boxes she would decide about later. Her clothes too, but she would replace them after she checked out the styles in Elko. Following her friend Carol's suggestion, she had applied for a part-time teaching position next fall in the high school music department there, and had arranged to have her mail forwarded to Carol's address in Elko.

She and Carol were longtime best friends in Las Vegas before Carol moved to Elko, and they had continued the relationship by phone and e-mail. Carol was unable to attend Cal's funeral due to a prior speaking engagement at a professional counselors' conference, but had phoned Darcy the day before to offer her condolences and to tell her about the teaching position in Elko. A week later she was in Las Vegas on business and they had met for lunch. Darcy thanked Carol for the heads-up on the teaching job, and informed her that she had applied and had arranged for an interview appointment on June 16 in Elko.

Determined to make a complete break from Las Vegas, she told Carol, "When I settle in Elko, no one except my employer needs to know that I came from Vegas. Oh, Vegas is a fine city, but I'm sick of seeing people's eyebrows raise when I mention living here."

Carol's answer surprised Darcy. "It's not about where you live. It's your beauty, both inside and outside."

Darcy's mouth turned down. *"Inner* beauty? Ha! Haven't heard that one for a while. People aren't interested in that. If you're from Vegas, they stare at the surface and jump to conclusions."

Carol protested. "But it's not because you're from Vegas. It's your movie star figure, that glorious long blond hair and those great looking legs that make people think you're a showgirl."

"Carol, just listen to yourself! You mention so-called 'inner beauty,' and then you go on to describe me from the outside. Just what I need! To be thought of as some kind of trophy..." She stopped short.

"Trophy?" Carol gasped. "Oh, Darcy, please forgive me! That's not what I meant at all. I didn't mean to go there. I'm so sorry."

After a heavy silence, Carol continued. "I guess what I intended to say was... yes, you do have inner beauty; it's just hard to put into words. Face it, though—you're strikingly beautiful on the outside, too. You have to accept that. I once heard Bob talking to one of his buddies about your 'knee-buckling beauty' and that didn't bother me at all, because it's true. Maybe that's why people might think of you as a show-girl. Even with your crystal tongue, they just don't figure you for a music teacher."

"Crystal tongue?"

"Yes. When you say words like 'kettle' or 'pretty,' you pronounce the T's separately. It sounds so... so *English!* And so *proper!*"

"You know I've never set foot in England," Darcy retorted. "I got that 'crystal tongue' from my grandmother, who reared me—I suppose it just rubbed off on me. I use as much slang as anyone does. If I didn't, I'd sound like a foreigner. But here's what I'm complaining about: It's crazy how people think everyone who lives in Vegas is involved in the casino or the shows. Most of them don't even know about the university."

The two had debated the subject before. Now that Darcy was moving to northern Nevada to be near Carol and her husband, she remained adamant. She was from southern Nevada. Not Vegas. *Not* a showgirl!

"We definitely want you to move up there," Carol said. "But are you sure you want to pass up that position at the university? You're a shoo-in there, and you deserve it."

"I've already turned it down," Darcy answered, a bit too sharply. "I don't want a full time job. I can earn more with my ghostwriting jobs. Mostly though, I want out of this place." Her voice softened. "What I mean is... I'm ready to relocate."

"Well," Carol replied, "You make a pretty good case there. But are you sure it's about the Vegas syndrome? Isn't it more about Cal?"

Darcy drew a long breath; looked down into her teacup, then back up at Carol. "Girl, I should have known. You're so perceptive! No wonder you're such a successful counselor."

Carol smiled and shrugged modestly. "Thanks for the compliment. And you're a wonderful music teacher, from all I've heard. Part time teaching jobs aren't all that easy to come by, but I'd say that with your background, yours is practically guaranteed."

Darcy's reputation had preceded her, thanks to Carol, and she had forwarded an impressive résumé. She taught several instruments as well as voice. If or when she learned that the job was hers, she could sign the contract and then do anything she wanted until late August.

Now she asked herself why she was sitting here in a pickup truck in Mesquite, Nevada, a stone's throw from the Arizona border and only thirty-eight miles from St. George in southwest Utah, torn by last minute indecision. She had five days left before the interview. Should she go straight to Elko, or indulge herself for a couple of days alone at the guest ranch she'd read about? If ever there was a perfect time for a desert retreat, this was it.

Just as she had once left her teen-age self, Drucilla
O'Rourk, back east, she was now leaving the old Darcy in
Vegas. After eight years as Cal's wife and two months as his
widow, she vowed that from now on this was her life, and
she'd live it on her terms. All she wanted was to be herself,
Darcy Callahan—whoever *that* was.

She would go to the guest ranch.

* * * * *

Satisfied with her decision, she called the Cottonwood
Ranch and made a reservation, then phoned Carol to tell
her about her change in plans. For what seemed like the
hundredth time, she read the brochure. She squinted at the
rumpled page with its map of the extreme northwestern
corner of Arizona.

Still unsure, she read the directions again. "Bring the
family to Cottonwood Ranch in the beautiful Arizona Strip.
This remote getaway is nestled in the shadow of the Virgin
Mountains in northwestern Arizona. Take the St. George exit
off Interstate 15 and follow the road leading south from there
into Arizona. Look for a sign pointing to Cottonwood Ranch.
Turn onto the picturesque dirt road and look for a second
sign that will point you to a leisurely drive to the ranch."

The roar of the truck charged her with a sense of adven-
ture as she pulled onto Interstate 15 heading northeast to St.
George. It was relaxing to drive out here away from city
traffic. No need to worry about road signs on the Interstate,
since there was only one highway. It was now late afternoon,
but she was confident that she could make it to the ranch
before nightfall.

Sooner than she expected, the St. George exit appeared.
She swung the truck eastward, then south on the road that
would take her into the Arizona Strip. Minutes later, as she

crossed into Arizona, the blacktop gave way to a wide dirt road that led her into sagebrush country.

No traffic; the world was hers. She punched the CD player. Rubenstein playing Chopin. Cal did not care for Rubenstein——too mellow. Cal detested Chopin—too romantic. She turned the volume up and hummed along.

Cruising along, she allowed her gaze to wander beyond the profusion of wildflowers to the steep, dark Virgin Mountains that framed the desert. Years earlier, when she moved to Las Vegas from the wooded hills of West Virginia, she had felt uneasy in the vast expanse of the Southwest desert, where her gaze in any direction met not one building or tall tree. She could laugh at herself now, at how she'd expected the desert to have nothing but cactus and rattlesnakes. She'd hated the dull color and the tangy smell of sage back then. Now it reminded her of freedom. Leaning forward, she searched ahead. No fences. The air was still; nothing moved. Here was the peace and quiet, the freedom she wanted.

The Arizona Strip certainly couldn't be confused with the Vegas strip, she mused. This wild area, isolated from the rest of Arizona by the Grand Canyon and described by some as frontier country (not more than two people per square mile), was the subject of an ongoing debate. Some people thought it should have been designated as part of Utah or Nevada, rather than Arizona. To Darcy's eyes, it was an alien world, empty and inviting. Could she find the ranch? Well, other city people had. She could, too.

The setting sun and a blood-orange row of low clouds hovering over the mountains cast a pink tinge on the desert. Overhead, dark gray clouds threatened rain. She felt a stab of anxiety and accelerated. The truck's rear wheels bit into the dirt road, throwing a shower of dust into the air behind her and bouncing her in the wide seat. She tightened her seat belt and held her speed.

Darkness was beginning to set in when she saw a sign ahead. She turned on the headlights and slowed the truck. "Cottonwood Guest Ranch," the sign read, with an arrow pointing right to a dirt road. She turned and followed the bumpy road slowly. After another eight or ten minutes, another sign loomed in the headlights. "Cottonwood," she read aloud. "This must be the second road the brochure mentioned." She made a right turn at the crossroads onto what looked more like a dusty trail than a road.

Leaning forward to scan the trail ahead, she didn't see a broken-off section of the original sign lying at the foot of the signpost. It said "Ranch," and an arrow pointed *left*.

* * * * *

For mile after mile, Darcy gripped the steering wheel, scarcely able to control the truck. *Leisurely drive! Picturesque road! Ha!* This trail was nothing more than a pair of dry ruts through a convoluted sagebrush desert. Her breath felt ragged in her throat.

The loose soil turned rocky. The truck dodged from side to side. Deep gullies and arroyos opened up ahead, forcing her to ease off the edge of the trail. After several minutes of twists and turns she could see neither ruts nor trail. Her heart pounded. Her mouth was as dry as the lifeless soil. She was alone out here, and hadn't the slightest idea where she was.

She stopped the truck, flicked the headlights off, and stared into the darkness. Clouds covered the moon and stars. No way to tell north from south, east from west. In desperation, she kicked off her sandals and climbed to the truck's hood, then slid onto the roof. Turning full circle, she searched in vain for a yard light, a window, a headlight. She would have welcomed the flashy lights of Vegas at this moment. Her senses detected nothing but blackness and the rustle of the sage.

Don't give in to fear, she told herself. *There's someone around here. Where there's a ranch, there has to be ranch hands.* Back in the truck, she shifted into four-wheel drive, and drove blindly again through the high brush in search of the trail. At length she came upon a trail of tracks, only to find that they were her own tracks. She had gone full-circle!

As she drove farther, small rocks thumping on the truck's underside grew into threatening boulders that forced her to stop. Beyond the boulders, the headlights fell on emptiness.

Tension stung her neck and shoulders, as if she had spent hours at the keyboard. She'd have to turn around. She grabbed a flashlight, got out of the truck, and walked around the boulders. Straight ahead the terrain fell away sharply; and to her left and right she saw nothing but large rocks. She couldn't turn around here, at least not until daylight. Alarm tightened her throat. *Get a grip, Callahan. You're resourceful. You're tough.*

With all the resolve she could gather, she walked a wide circle around the truck, flashing the beam from side to side. Her breath came in deep gulps. No tracks, no trail here; nothing but little scurrying sounds in the brush. Heavy raindrops began falling. Suddenly giving in to panic, she turned and ran toward the truck, her feet slipping and sliding with each step.

She dived inside the truck just ahead of the rainstorm. She tried to relax. She'd been rambling for what seemed to be hours. *No problem!* She told herself. She would fight this fear the same way she handled stage fright: by talking to herself, by whistling a happy tune as the old song goes. She closed her eyes, forced her breath into a slow rhythm, and set her mind to work forming its habitual nighttime list. She would stay until daylight, then follow her tire tracks back to the highway. She was hungry. Again, no problem. She opened a granola bar, ate half of it, then—feeling better—curled up in the bucket seat, cradled under her light flannel jacket.

Raindrops thrummed a lullaby on the truck's roof. The plaintive nesting sounds of the doves had quieted hours ago. A wolf—no, only a coyote—yelped in the distance. She reached over, locked the doors, and settled in for the night. The wind buffeted the truck like a rhythmic tide. The rain would relax her mind and lull her to sleep. Tomorrow the dust would be settled, the air would be clear—and, she hoped, her tire tracks would still be there.

* * * * *

Darcy felt the sun warming her face before her eyes opened. Looking out, she was shocked to see how far she had climbed up the mountainside. Her stomach growled. The thing to do now was to find out where she was and how she could get to the guest ranch or, barring that, back to the highway. She stepped out of the truck and slammed the door.

Stomping around the boulders, she stopped abruptly. A mere twenty feet ahead was a steep cliff with a forty-foot drop. Her hands flew to her mouth. She held her breath and felt her heart pounding in her ears. Thank God she'd stopped when she did, or she'd be at the bottom of the cliff!

Stunned and shaken, she turned her back to the cliff and sank onto a rock with her head on her knees. She had to think this through.

At length she looked up and blinked in disbelief. There, staring into her face, was a pair of the deepest blue eyes she had ever seen, bottle blue eyes in the mud-streaked face of a child. Tousled blond hair framed a chubby, lightly freckled face. Judging from his grubby tee shirt and overalls, he must be camping. Relief surged through her. There must be a camp-ground nearby with someone who could get her oriented.

Smiling, she spoke. "Hello, there." Darcy half expected the boy to run. A swift glance told her no one else was around.

"Hi." A hesitant smile flitted through his eyes and onto a wide mouth. As he moved closer, his voice softened to an earnestness that surprised her. "I'm sure glad you came."

"You are?" Puzzled but slightly amused, she asked, "Why? Were you expecting me?" Silly question. Of course he wasn't expecting her! Unless.... "Is this the Cottonwood Ranch?"

"I don't think so. I guess it's just my dad's place." His eyes questioned hers. "Did he tell you to come?"

"Who? Your dad? No. Nobody told me to come." Then, "I think I'm lost."

The boy squinted into the sun. "Then how'd you know you were s'posed to come?"

She'd better choose her words carefully. This kid thought she was someone he expected. If she embarrassed him, he might run off, and she needed him to stay around until she got her bearings. Her gaze scanned the countryside. No campground or cabins. Taking her time, she stretched her arms and looked around. "Who do you think told me to come?"

"God."

Darcy's raised eyebrows prompted him to explain.

"See, I told God that I wanted someone to come and go with me to Clark's place. So I waited a long time, and last night I saw your headlights." His head nodded with importance and assurance. "And *that's* how I knew he told you."

Darcy stood speechless. The kid obviously believed what he said. But why did he need her? Where were his parents? And what did he mean about telling God? That sounded like praying. She knew very little about praying, and less about little boys. She walked slowly toward the truck, hoping to find her voice.

"You mean you wanted someone to come, so you asked God?" she asked. "Like in a prayer?"

The child's streaked face broke into a wide smile. "Uh huh. That's what I did."

19

She took another deep breath. "So you asked God to tell *me* to come and take *you* somewhere?"

"Yeah, to Clark's place."

Unsure of what to say next, she sat on the running board and changed the subject. "My name is Darcy. What's your name?"

"Jamie." He hesitated, then added. "See, it's really James Chadwell Granger, but my mom and my dad call me Jamie. Sometimes they call me Chad. I'm six."

The blue eyes now held an expression of expectancy, as though she should make the next move. His chubby hand, grimy with dirt and traces of peanut butter, ran over her truck's gray fender. "You sure got a real nice truck."

Darcy stifled a chuckle. For some reason she couldn't define, she felt herself warming to this kid.

"Thank you. It's a four-wheel-drive," she said. An awkward pause followed. She was stalling for time. Maybe he was, too.

"Yeah. My dad's truck's that kind, too." Darcy listened in astonishment as he commented on the special features of her truck, and was satisfied to notice that it compared favorably with his dad's truck.

"Where is your dad's truck? Are your parents around here?"

He pointed toward some heavy brush over to her left. "The truck's over there. And my mom and dad are up there." He pointed up to a tree-lined slope. "Under the rocks."

"You mean they're up there sitting by the rocks? Like on a picnic?"

"No. They're up there in the place where the rocks fell down."

Darcy felt her skin tighten on the back of her neck. She cleared her throat. "The rocks fell down?"

"Uh huh." Jamie's voice lowered to a whisper. "I wish they didn't."

20

"Why, Jamie?" A sense of dread crept into her thoughts. "Did something bad happen?"

He nodded slowly. "See, the rocks came down, and my mom and my dad were there."

She didn't want to ask, didn't want to know. "What I mean is—did the rocks hurt your mom and dad?" She knew the answer before he spoke.

"Yeah." His eyes glistened as tears welled up. His small chin trembled. "The rocks rolled down and covered 'em up."

Darcy was grateful for her ability to control her voice in a time of crisis. "Are you sure the rocks covered them up?" *Kids' imaginations sometimes....*

"Uh huh. I *saw* the rocks fall down." He looked up, as if to explain. "See, I saw my dad comin' home for supper, and my mom was walkin' out there to be with him when it happened."

Darcy couldn't think of an easy way to ask. "When was that, Jamie? How long ago?"

"About, uh... I don't know." Then he brightened. "I made the days on the calendar. I think it was about a week ago."

"And where do you live?" she asked.

"Up there," he replied, pointing up toward the same slope where, he had said, the rocks came down. "We have a house. You wanta see it?"

Her breath eased out. "Yes, Jamie, I would like very much to see your house." *And get some breakfast, and some directions. Most important of all, though, to find out if he's telling the truth about his parents, and if so, to figure out what to do.*

Amazingly she felt no fear, no frustration, now that she wasn't alone. A talkative six-year-old could be great company, and if his story turned out to be true, his needs would far eclipse her concern about finding the guest ranch or getting to her interview appointment on time.

The boy reached toward her. She grasped his sticky hand, grabbed her handbag from the truck and slammed the truck door. Her spirits lifted. He seemed to know where he was going, and holding his hand felt good—she sensed an attitude of trust on his part. Somehow, something good would come out of all this, she assured herself.

They had gone only a few steps when he stopped and picked up a twisted limb of dry brush, holding it behind his waist. "We do it this way, he offered. You can drag it and I'll walk in front. Then he added a bit of pint-size importance: " 'Cause *I* know the way."

He handed her the brush, then turned and walked ahead. "It wipes out our footprints." His manner was so matter-of-fact, Darcy wondered if he had seen the question in her eyes.

"Why do we need to wipe out our footprints?"

He shrugged. "It's how my dad does it."

Following her small guide, Darcy stole a furtive glance around. Could she find her way back to the truck? Looking over her shoulder, she could barely distinguish her truck's gray color from its sheltering boulders and tall brush. Her gaze scoured the hillside for a landmark as Jamie chattered about the things that he would show her, his house and his toys. Her mind wandered until he stopped abruptly in front of a brush pile.

"There's my dad's truck," he announced. His face beamed.

Darcy looked in the direction he pointed. She saw nothing but a bramble pile.

"Where? I don't see a truck." He must have been playing a joke, and she was not in a joking mood. She was hungry and in need of a restroom.

"Right here." He stepped up to the brush pile and banged on something hard—something with a metallic sound.

As she stared at the brush, her mind slowly assembled images like pieces of a jigsaw puzzle until a picture emerged.

There beneath an olive-drab netting stood a truck painted in dull tan and brown tones. Tan canvas shrouded its windshield. Its wheels and bumpers hid behind limbs of juniper and sagebrush. Strips of dark fabric concealed its mirrors, reflectors and door handles—anything shiny.

Darcy felt herself shiver. This thing was not only hidden—–it was *camouflaged,* like an army truck on a battlefield. Without the boy's help, she wouldn't have seen it if she'd stared at this brush pile for a week. This place was obviously someone's hideout. Whose? Drug dealers? Some kind of fanatic doomsday cult? A militia group? What had she stumbled into? What kind of wacko...?

Then, unaccustomed to praying, her thoughts asked, *God? How did I get into a place like this?*

CHAPTER 2

Jamie chattered incessantly as he scrambled over rocks and around boulders, following the curve of the hillside. Stumbling along behind him, Darcy looked out at the spread of flat land below. Only a few struggling clumps of brush grew between the stones scattered across the desolate valley floor. Surely this couldn't be the Cottonwood Ranch. At least on this rocky slope she didn't have to drag that silly tree branch. As for those scurrying sounds, they were made by nothing more fearsome than tiny lizards and birds that were as afraid of her as she was of them. She tried to listen to what the boy was saying.

"We can't go to Clark's till tomorrow," he said.

She slapped at the tiny gnats swarming around her eyes. "Why not?"

"Cause the calendar has one more empty place. We only go when it doesn't have any empty places."

"But what if you need to go sooner? Can't you go when you want to?"

"Nope. Sometimes Clark isn't there."

"I've been meaning to ask—just who *is* this 'Clark' person?"

"He's a friend of my dad's. We get our groceries there."

Sweat trickled down her neck and back, and her skin itched from the prickly brush. What she needed most, next to a good meal and some adult information, was a hot bath and clean clothes. Suddenly she let out a high-pitched squeak and stopped in her tracks. Jamie paused. "What's the matter?"

Darcy's eyes were wide open. "I didn't lock my truck. Everything I own is sitting out there in full view in the camper shell. I should go back and lock it."

Jamie's eyebrows peaked into question marks. "My dad didn't lock his truck."

Her escaping breath hissed through her teeth. *Of course his dad didn't lock his truck. He hid it like a secret weapon!* Instant thoughts flashed through her mind like pages of a science fiction thriller—thoughts of secret air bases, stealth aircraft testing and flying saucers. She looked at her watch. Eight a.m. She had plenty of time, but something pressed her to hurry—to get away from this strange place.

Their shoes now crunched across gray rock. Insects whirred and chirped in the brush. No palm-lined Vegas streets, no flawless golf courses tamed this part of the desert. Surprisingly, this natural terrain calmed Darcy's spirit, though the dust filled her nose and eyes. Living in the desert meant accepting dust as part of the air. She followed Jamie quietly.

The hill had turned into a gray cliff rising above a steep slope. Her gaze played over its surface. She noticed varied shades of gray: green-gray, yellow-gray, even silver and blue-gray. Dark old junipers with gnarled trunks wound around gray boulders like giant bonsai, if there could ever be such a thing. Scrub oak, desert mahogany and rabbit brush grew between the ledges, their shadows giving the face of the cliff a texture both hostile and inviting. Gray rocks— some as big as houses—had rolled out onto the valley floor, tossed by the same force that had sliced this mountain eons ago. Squinting at the top of the cliff, Darcy could make out the shapes of trees. Some kind of evergreen, she supposed. Her foot slipped on a loose rock and she nearly fell. Jamie stopped suddenly and she bumped into him and sent him sprawling.

"Our house is right here," he said, brushing his dusty clothes. "We have to bend down and walk under this bush."

Crouching and scraping along behind, Darcy followed him through a tangle of chaparral. When finally they stood up, she found herself looking at the entrance to a narrow canyon, a mere crack in the earth reaching far back into the cliff, the canyon invisible beyond that thicket. The lower half of its steep walls sat in dark shadows. To her left, the cliff rose high, its upper half golden in the sunlight, dotted with shrubs. The right side sat lower and not as steep or rocky. On its flat top, a tall rock pillar pointed at the sky. The canyon extended below the dirt path where they stood, its bottom a jumble of rubble and dense foliage. Wordlessly, she followed him into the canyon, scrambling over rocks, feeling and hearing the loose rubble give way beneath her feet and tumble to the foot of the cliff.

"We're here."

Jamie's words yanked her thoughts back. She stared at the secluded place. If the boy's parents lived here, they had a good reason. They were hiding.

"We are? I don't see a house." She saw nothing here but rocky cliff walls.

"See, here's the door." Jamie pointed toward the gray stone wall. Again Darcy stared at the wall, then back at him.

"Door?" She hated parroting his words, but there was no door here. Then, summoning her patience, she suggested, "Why don't you show me the door?"

"Okay." Jamie seemed undisturbed at her blindness. She held her breath as he walked up to the face of the rock wall and stretched out his hand.

Darcy gasped. There was a door! Right in the cliff, with a gray weathered screen door blending it into the shadowed stone. Stunned, she watched as the child opened the door and walked inside, then turned with a grin.

"This is our house. Do you want to come in? We can have lemonade."

Darcy stood there saucer-eyed, gaping at Jamie's "house." It was nothing but an opening in the cliff. A cave! She stepped back as images of disgusting creatures slithered across her mind. What kind of people would live in a cave in this century? And why?

On closer inspection, she saw that its front had been enclosed with rubble and cement, nearly indiscernible from the cliff wall. A stone slab protruded into a porch-like roof that shaded and disguised the doorway. The space where she stood was paved with flagstone, like a patio. It had been recently swept. Too astonished to speak, she walked dumbly through the door. Light flooded the interior.

"You can sit here." Jamie motioned toward a wicker rocking chair. Though she scarcely heard a word, she noticed his manners were not those of a backwoods family. Swiveling her head to look around, she lowered herself onto the chair. A rocker! Inside a cliff! Forgetting her own manners, she peered at each detail. It was not exactly a house, but it seemed like one—a very nice one—rustic but comfortable. The spacious cave was cool and quiet. Several rag rugs brightened the rock-paved floor. Colored pictures decorated the rough walls. A pair of folding lawn chairs, softened by corduroy pads, flanked a makeshift end table that held a lantern and a Bible. Jamie sat in a child's chair covered with removable terry cloth. One hasty glance told Darcy this house had no electricity, no plumbing... no phone.

"This is a very nice house," she stammered. "Do you live here all the time?" Maybe it was only a summer place, but it was the home of real people, not kooks. A natural cave, warm in winter and cool in summer. It made sense. It had all the marks of a lady, like some of the pioneer homes in the history books. Curiously, her fear had vanished.

"We live here all the time," he answered, "except for when we go to Clark's." That didn't tell her much.

Darcy continued to stare around the room. There were no cobwebs, only a thin layer of dust. A small wood-burning cook stove took up one wall. Above it, a stove hood with a series of ducts along the ceiling provided a smoke exhaust system to the outside. In front of the stove stood a table covered by a flowered cloth. Alongside, she saw a tall unit of wooden shelves stacked with brightly colored dishes and storage boxes. The top shelf held a squat blue cream pitcher filled with wilted flowers. A guitar hung on the wall.

She stood up, and only then noticed the window. More accurately it was a flat windshield, frame and all, from an old car—late 1920's she guessed. The kind of windshield that could be cranked open. *A window in a cave! Just like the Flintstones.* The glass was clean and hung with blue checked curtains. Looking out, she saw a canvas awning designed to be lowered over the window at night. A rusty mesh screen kept insects out and dulled the glare of the glass. Sunlight flooding the front half of the room bounced to the back of the chamber through two well-placed mirrors. On the opposite side of the room stood a double bed covered by a delicate handmade quilt. A tall dresser filled the space between the bed and a plaid curtain that separated the front of the cave from the back. Below the window she saw a bookcase jammed with familiar magazines and children's books. Darcy looked closer. A series of home schooling texts caught her eye, especially the dog-eared first grade volume.

She turned to Jamie. "Are these your books? Do you have school here?"

"My mom and I did school," he said softly. "Sometimes my dad, too."

Something in his tone triggered another shiver. While she inspected the room, the child stirred a dry lemonade mix in a plastic pitcher and poured it into tall glasses. She hesitated briefly, then sipped. It was cool and tasty, and the glass was clean enough. Not certain how she should approach the subject, she asked, "Jamie, where is the place where the rocks fell down?"

He pointed out the door toward the deep end of the canyon. "Out there— by my dad's mine."

Darcy's hand flew to her forehead. Relief flooded her mind. *A mine! Of course, they're miners, not crooks or drug dealers. That explains the secrecy!*

"When did you say that was, Jamie? How long ago?"

"It's on the calendar. I made the days on the calendar.

The calendar! Maybe she could tell from that. Jamie climbed onto a chair under a wall calendar with Bible pictures. "See, I made a big X every night, just like my mom did." He counted aloud eight squares with a dark penciled X. The previous squares had been marked with a lighter touch. One square remained unmarked. The space for June 13 was marked "Clark." Today was June 12.

Darcy felt a chill. *Eight days! Has he been out here alone that long?*

"Jamie, have you had anything to eat?"

He nodded. "I made chili."

Her mind registered what her eyes had ignored before. On the kitchen table sat a jar of peanut butter, a cracker box and a cluster of empty cans. *Chili con carne.* She counted eight cans with tops scarred by a can opener in a child's hands. There was no saucepan or bowl.

"Did you heat the chili on the stove?"

"No." His face took on a stern expression. "See, I'm not allowed to make a fire." Then, opening a child's backpack, he brightened. "I put some stuff in here for if I had to walk to Clark's. It might take me two days."

Darcy's heart melted as he pulled out two more cans of chili. A quick glance around the kitchen revealed an enameled dishpan with a stack of spoons soaking in cold soapy water. Inside her breast, she felt as useless and empty as those cans. From somewhere in that void came a phrase from an old song—something about a motherless child. She wanted to cry for Jamie, for his parents, for herself.

"Maybe you should show me the place where, uh, the rocks came down."

He slid off his chair without a word. She followed him out the door, along a rocky path into the canyon. Nothing could hide the sight she'd dreaded—the pale gray scar high on the canyon wall and the jumble of sharp rocks below—a landslide as wide and deep as a schoolhouse, as silent as a shadow. Numbed, she could only stand there trying to see in her mind what this child had been through in the last eight days.

Jamie pointed to a dark spot high on the cliff that was, she supposed, something like a tree house. "See, I was up there at my mine, and a big noise happened. My mom and my dad were running back to the house. They yelled at me to climb up to the top." The blue eyes glistened. He blinked rapidly. "And the rocks came down and covered 'em up."

Darcy's arm went around his shoulder. He leaned close, not resisting as her face touched his tousled hair. Thoughts whirled through her mind: *What shall I do now? I'm lost, and the people I've counted on to direct me back to civilization are dead. And Jamie, this sad beautiful child, trying so hard to be brave, thinks God sent me to make it all better. Now what?*

Again her mind began to form a list. *How do people help when there's a death? A funeral—I can do that—music, flowers, eulogy, food. Food! People bring food.*

The thought of food reminded her: "Do you think we should have something to eat?"

"Sure. We got lots of stuff in the cellar." His head nodded gravely. "And it's okay if *you* make a fire."

She hoped he didn't want chili.

As they walked back along the path, Darcy asked. "Is there a bathroom nearby?"

Jamie pointed to a small outdoor privy nestled under a juniper tree. Darcy excused herself and walked down the gravel path to the little hut. When she returned, he had dipped water from a bucket into a shallow pan. "We wash up in the wash pan."

Scrubbing off the grime in this cool soapy water was refreshing. "You'll have to show me where to get more water, and find some food."

She followed him to the spring, a tiny stream that trickled straight from the rock, collecting in a plastic bucket, then overflowing into an old wooden barrel. She lifted the bucket as he explained. "This is the drinking water. It's the cleanest. The wash water's in the barrel."

She listened to his list of favorite foods as they trudged along. He took her into a small corridor between cliffs just beyond the cave-house and pointed to an opening in the cliff wall that could be seen only from there. "Here's the cellar."

Again she stared at a rock wall, but this time she could see the door. Jamie grunted as he tugged at the heavy door.

The cellar, a cool cave, was larger than the house. The space, illuminated by daylight that was augmented by lanterns, was as organized as a supermarket. Shelves lining the walls held modern plastic food containers. Darcy stared in amazement. "Look here," she said, "We have macaroni, and spaghetti, and chips, and potatoes…and canned tuna and chicken. Here's some canned beef. Would you like beef?"

"Sure." He bounced from one foot to another. "We can cook it in noodles. That's the way my mom did it."

Okay, she thought. *I can handle that. I'm hungry enough to eat dirt.*

32

She gathered a small jar of berry jam, a can of green beans, and a tin of canned beef, then exclaimed, "Look! Peaches in glass jars!" Darcy hadn't seen home-canned peaches for years.

"My mom made peaches at Clark's house," Jamie said as they carried the food cans and jars back to the cave-house. There, he watched as she emptied the beef into a saucepan. Darcy hoped she could start a fire in the stove. There was plenty of firewood. Jamie found the matches and crumpled some paper. "My dad would put some paper in, and then he put the match in and made the fire start fast so it wouldn't smoke."

Smoke! If smoke could reveal their location, then smoke might help someone find this place. She lit the fire.

The hot food, prepared with Jamie's help, smelled delicious. Darcy rinsed and wiped the plates and set the table while Jamie scrubbed his hands and face.

"Let's have some lunch," she announced ceremoniously.

"But first we say grace," Jamie added. Without further comment, he took her hands in his, bowed his head and recited a child's blessing.

> "Thank you for the flowers so sweet.
> Thank you for the food we eat.
> Thank you for the birds that sing.
> Thank you, God, for everything. Amen."

A lump welled up in Darcy's throat. She wondered if she could swallow. "That was very nice," she said. "Did you say grace when, uh, when you ate your chili?"

"Uh huh. We always do grace." They filled their plates and ate with hearty appetites. They ate it all and followed it with peaches and stale chocolate cookies from the cookie jar.

She was still hungry. "Jamie, where's the bread box?"

"We don't have one anymore," he replied. "My baby sister's in it."

Darcy stiffened, but managed to find her school-teacher voice. "Your sister is in the bread box? Hmm!" She dared not ask; she couldn't handle another surprise, like the hidden truck or the door in the rock.

He went to the shelf and lifted a half-loaf of homemade bread wrapped in a clean towel. Darcy checked it for mold; finding none, she sliced the stale bread and spread it with jam. They ate in silence. She wouldn't mention the bread box again.

But he did. "My baby sister's over there." Jamie pointed out the window toward the opposite side of the canyon. "There's a big rock over there. That's where she is."

No matter how exhausted Darcy was, there was no way to avoid this conversation. She couldn't ignore him. "Why is your sister over there?"

"She's just there. She's dead over there. She's in the bread box. My mom said she's up in Heaven with Jesus."

His explanation struck fear to her heart. "Do you mean, she's buried there? In the bread box?"

"Uh huh. See, my dad put her there when she died." He thought for a few seconds, then added, "I think I was just a little kid then. I can show you the place where she is."

Despite her misgivings, when the meal was finished she found herself following Jamie once more along the path. They crossed the canyon and climbed up a steep wall, then around a large juniper to the flat mesa. Here the dirt was loose and soft. At one end of the mesa the tall rock she had seen from below towered above the shrubs and boulders.

Here was a landmark she needed. Right now though, she needed to listen to what the child was saying. She wasn't going to get away from this place today, anyway. No problem. She would sleep in the cave tonight.

34

"Here's where my baby sister is," Jamie said. "My dad made a special place for her." He pointed to an area sheltered by a dense juniper where the earth had been flattened and groomed. At one end stood a tiny white cross entwined with a dainty pink wreath, a miniature grave.

Darcy's eyes filled. She was glad Jamie was still talking. "And when my dad put her here, God gave us a present."

She swallowed. "A present?"

"Yeah. My mom says it was to comf... uh, to make us feel better. I can show you our present."

Tongue-tied, she followed him back to the cave and watched as he climbed up on the dresser and brought down a white porcelain box decorated with carved roses and trimmed in gold. How strange it seemed in these surroundings.

"See?" He held up a delicate necklace, one diminutive coral bead strung on a fine gold chain. "God gave us the little pink thing, and then Clark made the chain. My mom wore it on Sundays."

Darcy felt too tired to hear an explanation. "Very nice," was all she could say. No—wait! She had to ask: "Jamie, does it make you feel better to see your sister's special place?"

"I guess so." He must have been reading her mind. "Do you think we could make a special place for my mom and my dad?"

She tousled his hair. "That would be nice," she said.

* * * * *

It was early afternoon, and the sun warmed the mesa when they reached it for the second time. Darcy carried a shovel from the cellar. No need to dig a hole. Just let Jamie smooth a place, and maybe put some wildflowers on it.

After she gathered a bundle of flowers, she sat close by on a high point above the mesa. Here, in the shade of a juniper, she rested her legs and watched the boy scrape a flat place near his sister's grave. Her vantage point offered her a panoramic view. To the east she saw the dry valley below. On the opposite side she could see only foliage, rocks, and cliffs; how truly hidden the little home site was!

Looking down into the canyon, she saw the ugly landslide on the far side of the spring. A dark stain on the face of the cliff revealed the plentiful water supply that existed long ago. Beside the spring, blended into the gray stone, stood a weathered wash bench and a rusty sheepherder stove. Jamie explained how his mom "cooked the wash water in the winter," and how in summer a solar water heater saved on firewood. An old-fashioned washboard and a hand-cranked wringer on the galvanized tub was the most modern part of this laundry. She smiled at the ingenious way the hot water was siphoned through a hose to the tub, or to a bucket above a canvas-curtained shower stall. Nothing seemed desolate. This was a happy place.

She handed Jamie the bouquet of wild flowers. He placed them on the groomed site, then quietly examined his work. "Does this look good? Do my mom and dad like it?"

"I'm sure they do."

"One time my dad said a prayer. Should we say a prayer?"

Uncertain, she stalled. "If you want to. Do you know a prayer?"

"Uh huh. I know one," he answered. Darcy swallowed the lump in her throat as Jamie, with the confidence of six years, bowed his head. "Now I lay me down to sleep...." She didn't hear the rest. The lump wouldn't stay swallowed. Of all the pompous prayers she had heard, none had ever touched her more deeply. Luckily the flowers made her sneeze, giving her a reason to dab her watery eyes.

"Look." Jamie bent down and lifted something from the soft earth. "See this?" He handed her an object encrusted with dirt. It was a heavy turquoise pendant—some kind of charm— strung on worn rawhide. "Is this our present from God?"

"It's *your* present from God." Completely wrung out, her voice squeaked.

"Oh." He was quiet for only a minute. "What do we do now?"

Darcy was at a loss for an answer. How could this happen? What kind of God would allow...? Suddenly she stiffened. *Wait! What's that noise?*

A rumbling, whooping sound prompted her to stand up and look around. Following the sound to its source, she spotted a helicopter flying low over the valley. *Someone's coming. So there is a reason for hiding!* She pushed Jamie roughly to the ground.

"Stay low, Jamie. Don't stand up." Squinting through the juniper brush, she watched the blue aircraft circle and land on the rocky valley floor beyond the mesa. A cloud of thick dust billowed eastward. "It's a helicopter," she shouted. "Has it ever come here before?"

He shrugged and shook his head.

"Let's keep down," she said. "We don't know who it is."

From his position, Jamie couldn't see the aircraft. Darcy stretched her neck to peer through the shrubbery. The motor whirred and stopped. When the rotor blades ceased turning, the pilot stepped out and, keeping his head down, walked around to the passenger door. A tall man in a baggy jump suit, his face was partly hidden beneath reflective aviator's glasses and the shadow of his gray Stetson. Tugging at the door, he leaned in and helped someone from the craft, a frail man, bent with age. The man accepted the pilot's supportive arm, and they walked slowly across the rocky earth, straight toward the mesa.

Darcy's throat went dry, and her thoughts raced. *We're trapped up here. Who are those men? Claim jumpers? Drug dealers? What better place for a drug deal than here? If they're good men, maybe they can help us. But what if they're not? Could they be the reason Jamie's parents were hiding? Were his parents dealers?* She crouched and slid behind the juniper with her fingers to her lips, signaling Jamie to stay quiet.

She watched as the men labored up the slope of the mesa and stopped at the crest. Peering through the brush, she could see the older man's wrinkled brown skin. His long gray hair was wrapped into a bun and tied with hand spun yarn. Darcy had seen that old Navajo hairstyle years ago, but only in ceremonies.

Leaning heavily on the pilot's arm, he climbed to the base of the tall rock, took a deep breath and sat on the ground. He faced eastward, partially away from Darcy and Jamie's hiding place. The pilot put his fingers to his mouth, indicating that the man should whistle when he was ready to leave. He then hurried down the slope toward the helicopter, where he stood facing away from the mesa.

That pilot was very courteous, Darcy thought. Fascinated, she watched the old man remove his shirt. His body looked like a mummy that had been shrink-wrapped in tortoise shell plastic. An old bone necklace and breastplate covered his thin chest. Some type of ceremonial wear, she concluded.

She glanced down at Jamie, motioning for him to crawl up beside her. Her arm went around him as they watched in silence. After a lengthy meditation, the man lifted his wrinkled arms and began to chant in a strange language, swaying with the rhythm of his song. His voice, as it rose and fell in volume, cracked with emotion, yet was strangely soothing. The scene reminded Darcy of a painting she had seen titled *My Soul Cries Out.*

"Is he crying?" Jamie whispered.

"I think so." Darcy immediately wished she could erase her words.

Too late. Jamie didn't miss anything. "Why's he crying?"

38

"Well, I think this must be a special place for his people, where...." She wanted to bite her tongue.

The blue eyes widened. "Is this his special place, too? Are his mom and dad here?"

How could she explain? How could she comfort him? Nothing was more important to her at that moment. "Maybe this is just a place where he comes to, uh, remember them." The wildflower pollen burned her nose and made her eyes water. She pressed a finger beneath her nose to squelch a sneeze.

Jamie's eyes studied her face. Slowly his smooth face crumpled. Torrents of tears flowed down his round cheeks. He leaned toward her and buried his face in her bosom, his body convulsed with silent sobs. Darcy's embrace tightened as eight days of unshed tears burst out, soaking her shirt. Her throat ached until, at last, her own tears dropped from her cheeks onto his tousled hair. If there was a God in Heaven, He could not ignore these strangers linked by grief.

The sun was blasting on their backs when their tears dried. The old man's chant had softened. Darcy forced herself to think. Should she make contact with these men? Could they show her the way to Clark's house? She hated this confusion, this indecision.

"Jamie," she whispered. "Are you sure you know the way to Clark's house?"

"Yeah" he answered between stifled sobs. "Up beyond the lilies, past the red-eyed toad." He sobbed again, new tears smearing mud over his face.

Her scalp tightened. That didn't help; it sounded like a nursery rhyme. What about real directions?

"It's what we say when we drive to Clark's." He repeated the lines, adding something about a needle.

She stifled a groan of despair. How could she follow these directions? Still, he had been right about everything else: the truck, the house, the "special place" for his baby sister. She would just have to trust him once more.

Silence washed over them. The man had stopped chanting. Crawling higher, hidden by thick brush, she watched as he scraped a shallow depression, placed an object in the soft earth, and covered it with a stone. She answered Jamie's question before he asked. "I think he's leaving a present."

Suddenly a sharp whistle drowned her words. She stretched her neck to look. The pilot turned and started toward the mesa. "Get down, Jamie," she said.

If he stays below the chaparral, he won't see us, or the canyon, or the landslide, she thought. With Jamie's face buried again in her shirt, she squinted through the brush. The pilot reached the top and helped the man to his feet, then stood looking over the valley while the old fellow worked the cramp out of his legs. As he waited, the pilot lifted his hat and ran his fingers through a thick shock of reddish-blond hair, then gently helped the old man down the steep slope and into the helicopter.

They couldn't be anyone's enemies, she decided. She'd ask for their help. She stood and yelled, but her decision had come too late. The men did not see or hear her. The helicopter blades whirled and the engine purred while the pilot completed his checklist and brought the aircraft up to temperature. As it roared and lifted off, the downdraft from its rotor blades swept the desert floor clean, leaving behind a low, curved ridge.

Back at the cave, Darcy felt nothing but deep exhaustion. She napped while Jamie played quietly with his toys. When she awakened, dusk was setting in. It was getting late, and time was wasting. She lit the lamps and relaxed in the rocker while Jamie took his bath, then took one herself. The solar heater held ample warm water for baths and shampoos, and she found clean clothes in a dresser drawer. Afterward, Jamie introduced her to the charcoal grill and the Dutch ovens. "It's so the house doesn't get hot, and it doesn't smoke," he explained.

When supper was over, Darcy leaned back in the rocker. Evening had never been so welcome. She went over the supply list she'd found tucked into a chipped black and white pot on the shelf. Along with staples such as yeast and flour, the list included items she would never have thought of: dried fruits, powdered eggs, as well as batteries, lantern fuel and candles. She'd read somewhere that a person's life-style could be determined by their grocery list. Now she believed it.

Jamie read to her from his schoolbook, and she read *The Velveteen Rabbit* to him twice. Finally she smoothed his hair and was about to suggest they go to bed, when she noticed a white scar under his hairline.

"What's this?"

He shrugged. "That's where Cougey tasted me," he said, matter-of-factly.

Darcy laughed. "Who's Cougey?"

She stared in disbelief as the child pulled back the curtain that formed his bedroom wall. On the wall of the cave, over his narrow bed, hung a cougar skin rug. Its mouth was open in a snarl, its fangs and eyes gleaming.

"Him." Jamie's hand stroked the tan hide. "See, he tried to eat me when I was little, but my dad made him quit. Dad said Cougey tasted me and spitted me out, but Dad was just playin' a joke on me. You want to pet him?"

Then, without waiting for her answer, he changed the subject. "I've got a picture of God, too."

She couldn't respond. The boy was now pointing at a magazine photo hanging over his bed, a picture of a red hen with three fluffy baby chicks peeking out from under her feathers. Her voice became a squeaky whisper. "Is God a chicken?"

Jamie pondered his answer. "See, my mom said that God is like this hen. That was when she showed me my baby sister's special place." Then abruptly he bounced over to the bookcase, "and my mom said, Jesus loves all the people and he died for them, even the ones who don't love him back, and she told me that if we do love him back, when it is our turn to die we get to go to heaven and live with him." Jamie became silent while he searched through the books.

Darcy felt nothing but relief. She didn't understand or care. If he was making up stories, that was okay, too. He came back to her chair carrying a sketch pad.

She watched, half asleep, while he showed her his father's drawings. He leafed through the beautiful colored sketches of Jamie's mom at the clothesline, picking flowers, rocking Jamie in the wicker chair. The last one showed her strumming the guitar.

She listened to his childish account. "We sang songs every night. Then on Sunday, my dad didn't work in his mine, and my mom wore her flowered dress and she cooked a real good dinner and a cake, and we sang these songs." Wistfully, he handed her a worn red hymnal. "Do you have a dress?"

Darcy nodded.

"Do you know the song about the wings?" She shrugged. His voice took on a solemn tone. "It needs two people to sing it."

Somewhere in the back of her mind, Darcy felt a new sensation tugging at her heart. Something about the way Jamie's parents talked to him, making up funny rhymes and stories, dealing with death in a non-threatening way. *If only someone had talked to me that way when Grandmother died. If I ever have a child....* Her thoughts trailed off.

"You know what?" Jamie's constant talking gave her an excuse to stop thinking. "My mom's hair looked like yours."

Darcy looked closer at the drawing. "Right." They had the same thick blond braid.

"But my mom's eyes were blue. Yours are brown."

"What's your mom's name?"

"Sarah. And my dad's name was Jim. Jim Granger."

"Those are nice names." Though she didn't notice, subconsciously her mind registered a change. More and more now, Jamie spoke of his parents in past tense.

She listened as he sang *Jesus Loves Me*, and said his prayers. Weariness almost overwhelmed her as she slipped into pajamas from Sarah's drawer and collapsed into the double bed. Her mind began making its list. She had to get Jamie to Clark's house, and then get to Elko. Would Clark be there? What would become of Jamie?

A coyote yipped. "Darcy, my dad said the coyotes sing night music to us." Jamie's voice sounded distant from his place behind the curtain.

"That's nice." Wearily, she let her thoughts drift back over an exhausting day of surprises and tears. Thoughts of the loving couple in whose bed she now lay. Thoughts of this funny little blue-eyed kid who asked God to send her, who had been tasted by a cougar, whose sister was in the bread box... and whose God was a chicken.

"Darcy," he called out sleepily, "I'm glad God told you to come. I'm sure glad you came."

"I'm glad too, Jamie. Good night."

Despite her scrambled plans, she had never been more sincere. She drifted off to sleep, unaware that for an entire day she had not once thought about Cal.

CHAPTER 3

Morning dawned bright and sunny. Turning from the wash pan, Darcy faced the sky. The sun's rays beamed in all directions from behind a fat cloud, tugging her thoughts back to the long ago morning when she had asked Grandmother, "If the cloud moves away, will we see God's face?" Grandmother frowned and turned aside. Darcy never asked her about God again.

At Jamie's request, she cooked a big breakfast of oatmeal with raisins. She reviewed her plans. This afternoon they would go to Clark's house and Jamie would stay there. Then she would get her bearings and head for Elko.

She listened to Jamie's excited schedule for the day. "Before we leave I can show you my dad's mine, and we can bring some wood. And I can show you my mine, too. I can see almost the whole world from up there."

"Shouldn't we get started? I thought you were raring to go."

"On the days we went to Clark's house, my dad made us wait till the sunshine got down to the cellar door. We're not s'posed to get to Clark's till after dark."

It didn't make sense, but she let it go. Maybe she'd be able to unravel the mystery, this need for secrecy, when they got to Clark's.

While Jamie entertained himself outside with his toys, she took her time cleaning the dishes, then allowed herself time to scrutinize this home more closely, in case she wanted to feature it in an article someday. The walls and ceiling were cloaked in tan canvas—to prevent dirt from sifting down, she reasoned. A blue plastic tarp covered the wall behind Jamie's bed. His cowboy bedspread held a menagerie of stuffed animals. The cheerful effect contrasted sharply with the drabness outside. Clever people, she thought, admiring the couple who had managed to turn this cave into a cozy home. The twin mattresses stitched together to cover the wide bed had puzzled her until she realized that everything in this house had been carried in on someone's back.

After spending most of the morning leisurely tidying up the cave-house and helping Jamie to store his toys, she fixed a light lunch. After they ate, she said, "Okay, let's go see your dad's mine."

She followed Jamie as he bounced along the rocky path past the spring, down to the canyon floor below the rockslide and up to the mouth of another cave.

Through the mine's entrance, a yawning hole in the stone wall, she saw a stack of split firewood and suspected that Jamie's father spent more time gathering wood than in mining. He must have done some mining, though; in front of the opening stood an old weather-beaten rocker box, like one she had seen in a museum.

Jamie answered Darcy's question before she asked: "My dad went inside there and dug a whole bunch of dirt. And then he brought it out here in his wheelbarrow and then he put some of it in this thing." He pointed to the rocker box. "And then he poured water on it and rocked it like this." His small arms strained to rock the heavy wooden structure from side to side. "And after that he opened this little door and let the water run out, then he picked some stuff out of the bottom."

Darcy's curiosity soared. "Did your dad get lots of stuff? What did he do with it?"

Jamie's forehead bunched into a frown. "I don't know." Then his face brightened: "We'll ask Clark."

Darcy peered into the bottom of the box. No gold nuggets, no gold dust, nothing but dry mud. She walked farther into the mineshaft. Here hung an assortment of jackets and slickers and an old metal miner's hat with a light on the front. A bench held an array of picks, shovels and kerosene lanterns. Axes and a chain saw leaned against the wall of the tunnel. No iron rails or ore carts. No dynamite. A man's footprints and wheelbarrow tracks led into the darkness. He must have brought all the ore out by brute strength.

She straightened to see the edge of the sunlight on the cliff wall. It almost reached the cellar. According to Jamie's dad, it was time to leave.

"OK, Jamie, it's time to go," she said. "We'll have to take a rain check on your mine." *What am I saying? Oh well, who knows? It could happen.*

After gathering Jamie's clothes and a few toys from the cave-house, they headed out. Jamie eagerly bounded ahead, leading the way back to the truck. She lagged behind and lost sight of him briefly. Her anxiety grew with each step along the trail. Was her truck still there? Would she be able to find it? If not, would she be able to drive Jamie's dad's truck out to Clark's? Did she have enough gas? Did Jamie really know the way?

"Here's your truck," she heard Jamie cry out. He was cleaning the windshield when Darcy puffed up beside him. She had walked past his father's truck without seeing it. She renewed her decision to trust Jamie's directions when he led her to a hidden stash of gas cans and helped her fill the tank.

As Jamie speculated about all the good things they would have for supper at Clark's house, Darcy tried to plan how she would tell that family friend about Jim and Sarah. She

47

wondered how he would feel about having this kid dumped on him while she went on her way. Would he be able to get in touch with Jim's and Sarah's families?

"Do you have any other relatives? Any uncles and aunts?"

"I guess so. My mom said my uncles and aunts are all in the Bible."

Darcy decided not to pursue that. "Okay, Jamie. Now, tell me which way to go." She eased her truck out of its tight place between the boulders and they moved out. She noticed only a faint trace of her earlier tire tracks, then lost them entirely as Jamie pointed the way around the base of a cliff and into open terrain.

Anxiety gripped her. "Are you sure you know the way?"

"Sure. It's real easy. Here's how my mom taught it to me." He began reciting a rhyme in his high singsong voice:

> "Up beyond the lilies, on the twisty road,
> Turn around the feet of the red-eyed toad.
> Aim for the needle so tall and dark
> Then down to the road that goes to Clark."

"Okay." Darcy thought she was handling this bit of information quite well. "Can you show me the lilies?"

"Not yet. They're way up there in a big green place. Dad called it a meadow." He peered ahead quietly for a while, except to call out for changes in direction. Finally, as they rounded a hilltop, he pointed.

"There it is! There's the meadow!" he exclaimed. "And see those little white flowers? They're lilies. Stop here." He jumped out, picked up a brushy limb and tied it to the back bumper.

"How did you do that so fast?" He would have an answer.

"Easy! My dad left some small ropes."

48

"Okay. Now where's the toad?"

"It's way over there." He pointed across the wide meadow. "I'll tell you when I see it. But we have to drive around the edge of the meadow, 'cause it's wet and soft in the middle."

Darcy chuckled as she steered around the meadow according to the boy's directions, but tightened as she pondered what might have happened if she'd driven straight across the meadow. He was a good little navigator. She was beginning to feel safe with him guiding her.

Minutes later, as they reached the far side of the meadow, he yelled. "There it is! There's the red-eyed toad!"

"How can you see a toad from here?" Darcy asked with unaccustomed composure. Suddenly, before Jamie could point it out to her, she saw a looming dark gray boulder shaped for all the world like a huge warty toad. In the place where its eyes should be grew something red, some kind of lichens or shrub. She yelled with delight. "I see it! I see it!" She promised herself that she would never doubt the kid again.

"This is the good part—here's where you *gun* it!" Jamie squealed.

She felt no qualms about following his grinning instructions. Turning in a tight circle around the "toad," she pressed hard on the accelerator. The truck shot up onto a previously unseen plateau where, once again, he told her to stop.

She waited while Jamie jumped down and untied the limb that had obscured their tracks up the embankment. They had come off the desert, around a meadow, and were now in a forest of small pungent trees. Her gaze lifted to the top of the mountain to a stand of pinion pine. In the distance a range of peaks formed a jagged skyline.

"Now," Jamie said, pointing to a pinnacle on the distant purple mountains, "See that needle? That's where we aim."

"That far?" She looked at the gas gauge. "That's a long way off."

He laughed. "No, we don't go *there*. We just aim at the needle. You know, *point,* like a gun. That's how we find the road."

Relieved, she aimed the truck at the needle and was not surprised when, a few miles up the grade, a road came into view. Not a real road; it was only a packed-down set of tire tracks with low brush growing between, but nevertheless a welcome, faint sign of civilization.

"OK. You got us to the road. Now what?"

"We stop at the flat place and swim in the water and eat cookies. Then when it's dark, we go to Clark's."

Darcy didn't ask. Somehow it all made sense. Or it soon would. Or it didn't matter. They stopped, he swam, they ate; and only after darkness fell did they start off again.

The tracks eventually led onto a wider trail down the mountain. A nearly full moon in a clear sky brightened the scene. Jamie leaned forward. "Here's where we turn the lights off."

Lights off? She stopped the truck, snapped off the light switch, and peered ahead. In the moonlight a small settlement lay before them at the foot of the mountain. Two rows of long low buildings stretched out toward a two-story structure. Other buildings stood in the distance: one large house and several small houses with lighted windows.

So this was the place where Clark lived, the place where she would leave Jamie. Her eyes stung at the thought. She drove slowly down the slope to the valley floor.

"We turn here." Jamie pointed to the left. She turned off on a road that ran beside the big two-story building. "Now, turn to the right here. That's Clark's garage."

She turned and stopped the truck. Straight ahead stood a garage built onto the back of the large barn-like building she had seen from the hill. The overhead door was open and a dim light shone on a man bending over a workbench.

"There's Clark!" Jamie bounced up and down on the seat. "Just drive right in and he'll shut the door."

Shut the door? Anxiety clutched Darcy as the man straightened up and stared at her truck. "He doesn't know this truck, Jamie. You'd better run in so he'll know it's you." She didn't have to tell him—he was already running toward the man before she finished.

"Hey there, Jamie!" The man's voice carried over the sound of the idling motor as the boy ran into his arms. Immediately, the tension drained from Darcy's shoulders. There was no doubt this man was real, and glad to see Jamie. Now she had some explaining to do.

The garage door closed behind her as she stepped out of the truck into the dim light. The man's face almost glowed with joy. *Oh, no!* She thought. *I shouldn't have worn my hair in this braid. Jamie says I look like his mom.*

"Hey, Sarah! Where'd you get the new rig?" The man walked toward her. She wanted to turn and run. He stopped in mid-stride, then stepped backward. His eyes darted back to the truck.

Darcy slipped the ignition key into her vest pocket and stepped forward. "I'm Darcy Callahan, and I'm sorry to intrude this way."

After a slight hesitation, he extended his hand and introduced himself as Clark Tygard. During her brief explanation she watched the expression on his weathered face change from beaming delight to confusion, to slack-jawed shock, finally collapsing into deep lines of grief. Jamie's hand slipped into Clark's.

"Well..." Clark's voice wavered, "Let's go in and have some supper." He stepped out of his greasy mechanic's overalls. Then, starting to turn, she paused as he smoothed the gray fringe on his neck, removed his cap and ran his fingers through his hair. A thick shock of reddish-gold hair.

Darcy froze. He was the *pilot!* The helicopter pilot who was so kind to that old Navajo man out by the cliffs. Something inside restrained her from blurting out her recognition—a sense of caution, perhaps, or maybe a tinge of guilt at having played *voyeur* while the old Navajo was going through his sad ritual by the tall rock.

She followed in silence as Clark led them to his upstairs apartment. Jamie hurried ahead to open the door. "We always get a real good supper at Clark's house," he said proudly. An aroma of roast chicken with bread and herb stuffing filled the room.

A sudden, saddening thought struck her: This dinner had been prepared for Jim, Sarah, and Jamie. Not for her.

Despite her stress at the thought, Darcy felt ravenous. "Sure smells good," she said. "Your wife must be a good cook!"

Again Clark paused, as if wondering what to say, then turned to her. "Actually, I'm a widower. Been over six years since my wife died." He nodded sideways toward a small hutch. "Taught me some good tricks about cookin', and I learned some more out of necessity. Had that chicken goin' in the oven for a while—should be just about ready. Maybe you'd like to freshen up?"

She hardly heard his question. An unexpected shaft of pain stabbed her chest, sorrow for people she had never met. She glanced at the hutch where a photo of a smiling woman faced the kitchen table. *He looks at her picture while he eats alone,* she mused. *It's so... sad.*

She looked back at him. "Yes, thank you. I could use some freshening."

"My mom always took a hot bath in Clark's bathtub," Jamie chirped, " 'cause he has lots of hot water and some good smelling stuff. Do you want a bath, Darcy?"

She glanced at Clark, caught his smiling nod, then said, "Later, Jamie. Right now I just need to freshen up. Maybe you should wash up, too. I'll race you."

With a squeal of delight, Jamie streaked to the bathroom. It was no contest—he ran, she walked—but how better to get a kid to wash up? She helped him scrub behind his ears and neck, then pronounced him clean enough until bath time and sent him back to the kitchen.

When she returned to the kitchen the places were set and Clark was placing the food on the table. Dinner tasted as good as it smelled. Darcy was impressed by Clark's culinary skill, and by the way he moved easily around his small kitchen in his rolled sleeves. Well organized too, she noticed; not a minute wasted looking for things. She had to stifle a grin, though, when he reached behind his white grocer's apron and wiped his hands on his hip pockets.

She was glad for Jamie's non-stop talking during dinner, glad for a moment to relax and turn the listening over to someone else. Clark encouraged the boy's discussion about dinosaurs by asking questions.

Darcy noticed how he sometimes spoke in a type of verbal shorthand, leaving the first word off of his sentences. She had worked hard to teach her students to avoid doing that, but for some reason it sounded appropriate here.

After dinner she washed the dishes while Clark drew Jamie's hot bath and gave him new pajamas. "Way you're growin', I figured you'd need some new ones," he told Jamie. After his bath and a second helping of ice cream, Jamie sat on the floor watching a video about dinosaurs.

Darcy went downstairs and quickly gathered fresh clothes from the truck. Back upstairs, she drew the water and sank into the deep tub. She heard the sound of pots and pans, and then Jamie's voice: "...Then after the rocks came down, I told God I wanted to go to your house."

Clark's voice was now under control. As she listened, Darcy thought it seemed to come from a much larger chest than his. It was rich, and resonated with kindness, the same kindness he had displayed out there on the mesa. He spoke to Jamie in a near drawl, each word taking longer than her clipped English ones.

"You sure were a brave man, Jamie. Your mom and dad would be real proud of you," she heard him say.

The melodious voice rumbled on. For some reason it reminded her of the old cast-iron furnace in Grandmother's basement, the way it growled just before the warm air flooded the house.

Sinking deeper into the fragrant suds, she closed her eyes and, in the habit of a writer, tried to remember his face. If she had needed to write a description she would have found it difficult, since he possessed no outstanding feature. His nose was long and a bit humped across the bridge. Fine wrinkles framed his eyes; kind eyes—gray, she thought. His body was lean and angular and he moved as if his joints were made of rubber bands. Below his unruly, reddish-gold hair grew a fringe of gray hair and sideburns in need of a trim. He wore a western style shirt and slim jeans with a belt that rode at a slant on his hips. A plain gold band gleamed on his ring finger. The overall effect was not of handsomeness but of strength, pleasant and comfortable.

This home would be comfortable, too, for a boy. In her mind she itemized the features of the living room: hardwood floors, a plaid sofa with wooden arms wide enough to hold a coffee mug, a leather recliner and a table stacked with books and magazines. The only decorations she remembered were a small Navajo rug on one wall, a maple hutch housing a collection of bone china cups and saucers and, of special interest, a small black and white pot on top of the hutch.

Her gaze wandered over the bathroom towels, all of them in brown and beige tones. Masculine colors. But the bath salts he had left out for Sarah were definitely feminine. At last she could close her eyes and relax all the way to her bones. Jamie would be in good hands with Clark.

But would he? She wondered if Clark would always be this way with Jamie, or would he retreat into his own thoughts, the way Grandmother did? She pushed that question from her mind.

Her bath water cooled before Darcy awoke with a start. Flustered, she dressed and hurried to the kitchen. Clark stepped through the doorway carrying a box of butter from his grocery store downstairs, then stopped and stood still while Jamie said his prayers and stretched out on his sleeping bag on the sofa.

Clark turned the lights off over Jamie and nodded toward the kitchen table. "Now, Mrs. Callahan, let's have a cup of coffee and talk this over."

Darcy felt her shoulders stiffen. She forced a smile. "Please call me Darcy. I'm a school teacher, and I get enough of being called Ms. Callahan. I've been widowed since April, and I'm on my way to Elko to apply for a teaching job at the high school there." She told him briefly about losing her directions and wandering through the sagebrush and field of boulders before meeting Jamie. "And now, I should be getting on my way, if you'll give me some directions to Elko. I'm sure they'll be better than the ones that got me lost."

"Elko! Good night, Lady! You can't start off across the desert until I check your truck over for damage."

Darcy blushed. Little did Clark know how she had abused her truck when she panicked out there in the sagebrush. "Oh, I didn't think about that. Is there a motel nearby?"

"Nope, but Jim and Sarah claimed my guest room was just as swanky as the Waldorf." He grinned. "Never seen the Waldorf, and don't think they did either; but I took their word for it." Something jarred Darcy's thoughts: *Stay overnight in a single man's house? Grandmother would disown me.*

He paused a moment, then spoke in a softened voice. "Jamie sure will be upset if you're gone when he wakes up."

Clark's rational concern for Jamie put Darcy's mind at ease. Besides, she was ready for some grown up conversation. There was so much to tell him: the landslide, the mine, the helicopter (maybe), and the red-eyed toad.

"That would be hard on me, too," she said. "Maybe we should talk. Clark, why don't you tell me about Jim and Sarah."

Clark nodded his head, took a deep breath and let out a long sigh.

"Tonight was supposed to be a real celebration for them," he began. "I had so much good news to tell them." He took another swallow of coffee. "It's a long story."

"Were Jim and Sarah hiding?"

"Yes."

"But why? They obviously were good people—surely they couldn't be running from the law? What was Jim's problem?"

He paused, as if wondering if he should go further.

"Not Jim... *Sarah*. She was in danger!"

CHAPTER 4

*S*arah! *Danger?* That didn't fit Darcy's first impression of Sarah.

"Sarah was a legal secretary for a big law firm in Salt Lake," Clark explained. "One of the lady lawyers there had died in a freak car accident. Next day, Sarah had to work late to transcribe some dictation left on the dead woman's recorder. Had somethin' to do with a Vegas gamblin' ring. She took the tape off the lady lawyer's recorder to her office and played it on hers. It was on a Friday, and Jim and I had spent the day packin' his truck to move into a new apartment they'd rented.

"On the tape she heard voices that uncovered some illegal activity goin' on in the firm. Came right after the dictation. Two men barged into the lady lawyer's office and angry words flew—guess the lady secretly pushed the record button when they came in. By their voices, Sarah recognized the men as junior lawyers of the firm. She put two and two together and concluded the woman's death was no accident—the two junior lawyers had threatened the lady lawyer; and sure enough, the woman died in a mysterious car wreck that night on the way home.

"Sarah made a duplicate copy of the tape and called us. After that she stepped into the hallway, intendin' to take the tape upstairs to her boss, a senior member of the firm. Down the hall she saw the same two men she'd heard on the tape, tryin' to break into the dead woman's office—only this time she noticed a third man. By his appearance and demeanor she reckoned him to be a private eye or even what they call an 'enforcer.' She ducked back into her office—she was in danger if they found out what she'd seen and heard."

He paused. "As you can imagine, Sarah went ballistic. Got on an inside line to her boss's office upstairs and told him what she'd heard and seen. He told her to stay put while he called 911, and then he'd come down. He did, and when the detective arrived her boss asked him to take her statement there in her office. She played the tape, gave the copy she'd made to the detective, then wrote out and signed the statement. The detective told her the police would find the men and bring them in for questionin'.

"Sarah sketched out a profile of the third man and handed it to the detective. Somethin' strange, though. Several times while she was sketchin', she looked up and caught what she thought to be furtive and knowin' glances between her boss and the detective. You can be sure that put her on her guard.

"Jim and I arrived just after the detective left. Her boss suggested that Jim and Sarah stay a few days in his summer home to calm her nerves, but Sarah flashed a warnin' glance to Jim. He thanked the boss for his offer but declined it. Only found out later from Sarah why she'd warned him."

Darcy was fascinated by the story. "Did they move into the new apartment?"

He rubbed his chin. "No. Actually, Jim and I just panicked. Only thing we could think of was to get Sarah out of town and come down here. She was four months pregnant with Jamie and didn't need the stress of dealin' with this crime. Already had the truck packed, so we brought it down here. Good thing we did. Found out later someone was lookin' all over for her."

"How did you know that?"

"Well, our first inklin' came when the Salt Lake newspaper carried a story about the lady's 'fatal accident,' but made no mention of a murder investigation. At first we thought the police might be deliberately holdin' that part of the story from the press while investigatin' it, but we couldn't be sure. Maybe that detective was holdin' back the evidence and the killers were out lookin' for Sarah. That idea spooked Jim and Sarah. They decided the safest thing they could do was to go hide out at their cabin. I agreed with them."

"And the second inkling?"

Clark went to the hutch and pulled out a poster. "What do you think of this?"

She squinted at two grainy photos on the poster that showed a woman with long blonde hair standing beside a handsome man. The caption read, "MISSING!" The other photo showed a bearded man in a dark hat and sunglasses. Its caption read, "SEEN IN THE COMPANY OF THIS MAN."

She looked closer. "Is this you behind the beard?"

"Yeah. That's why I don't wear it anymore. These photos were taken at an office picnic. But look again. Not at the pictures, but at the poster itself. Look authentic?"

Darcy squinted again. She hadn't thought about authenticity. She shook her head. "I can't tell. I don't know much about wanted posters. Why?"

"Because it's not an official law enforcement poster. Somethin' the killers made up. See, they even have a phony insignia here. Smart enough to keep it out of the post office. But ordinary folks who see it in rest rooms and coffee shops just assume it's the real thing."

He jabbed his thumb toward the north. "I spotted this one at a gas station in Provo, a week or so after Jim and Sarah left for the cabin. Thought it was real at first. And believe me, I shaved my beard and bought a light colored hat before I left town!"

Darcy looked again. The poster described Clark as an older man with gray hair. With his hat on and only the gray fringe of his hair showing, he looked like a middle-aged grandfather, but now, looking at him in person, she could see that he wasn't much older than she was.

"Sarah was so pretty, and Jim so handsome," she said.

Clark pulled a bandanna from his pocket and blew his nose. "Good people. And so much in love—what my wife called, 'joined at the heart.' I can tell you, they were happy hidin' at the cabin." He wiped his eyes on his shirt sleeve.

Darcy stared at the floor. She'd never seen a man cry. This man loved that couple. How could she distrust him? He seemed willing to believe *her* story.

Her mind was still filled with questions. "Did they know about the, uh, cabin?"

Clark nodded. "You mean the lawyers? Yeah, Sarah had once casually mentioned to her boss and the other attorneys in a staff meetin' that they had a cabin in the Arizona Strip, but never told them precisely where it was. Suppose it'd be easy for them to look it up in the records under Jim's name, except Jim for some reason never recorded the deed in his name. Still listed in the records under the name of Jim's granddaddy on his mother's side, whose name even I don't know. All the lawyers know is that it's somewhere in the Arizona Strip."

"Well," Darcy said, "that would explain all about the secrecy and the camouflage. So Jim owned the mine and wasn't just working it for someone else?"

"Oh, sure! Jim owned the cabin *and* the mine. The cabin's next to an old patented gold mine he got from his granddad. As a kid, Jim stayed with his granddad. It's somewhere up there." He motioned toward the mountain to the southwest. "Well, you know where it is. I've never seen it."

Darcy stiffened. *He's lying. Why? I saw him there yesterday. He won't trick me into telling him anything.*

She hoped her eyes hadn't narrowed with suspicion. She had developed a keen ear for speech patterns. Underneath Clark's homey drawl and colloquialisms, she detected the voice of an intelligent, educated man. Was he really just a desert rancher?

She had to keep him talking. "You said Jim owned a patented mine. What's that?"

Clark tilted back in his chair. "A patented mine is on deeded land, where the miner actually owns the land, not just the mineral rights. Jim's mine doesn't amount to much, but I'll explain that later. Anyway, Jim was a trucker and owned his own eighteen-wheeler. All paid for. Boy, they were proud of that rig. Always kept it shined up."

Darcy noticed how his jaw lumped as the muscles tightened.

He cleared his throat. "So after they decided it wasn't safe for Sarah to return, they signed the rig and Sarah's car over to me so I could sell them and buy supplies to keep them goin'. What they didn't know is that I still have the car and the truck in one of my hangars. Too easy to trace if I tried to sell 'em. Their furniture is there, too—that is, what they didn't take to his cabin.

"So you've been carrying their expenses all this time? That's sure generous of you."

He shook his head and shrugged. "Only thing I could do. Jim was like a brother to me, and I knew he'd be good for the debt. Besides, I could recoup my expenses anytime if I had to."

He paused. "They took my old pick-up truck to the cabin. Figured they could wait until the killers got caught. She assumed the police investigators could find plenty of evidence to corroborate her statement. So they hid out at Jim's mine. Said it had a pretty nice cabin. Came out here every two months for supplies. I have a grocery store downstairs, so it's easy for me to gather what they need ahead of time. I suppose you found Sarah's list."

"Yes, I did," Her mind raced: *A grocery store for such a sparse population?*

She had to say something appropriate. "I'm so sorry you lost them. You were obviously good friends."

He cleared his throat again. "Yes, we were. Jim and I were buddies in Desert Storm. I was a pilot—still am, matter of fact. He was crew chief on my helicopter. I had a couple of surprises for him, and one I planned to tell him was that I've sold my planes and my crop dustin' business in Utah and bought a chopper. It's old but in good shape, so it's a good deal. Figured Jim could go into the flyin' business with me when the coast was clear. He'd-a been thrilled."

He wasn't hiding the fact that he had a helicopter. So why was he lying about never having been at the mine? She searched for a lead. "You had a plane? Is there an airport near here?"

"Just a small dirt landin' strip. Most remote ranches like this have one. This old ranch belonged to my folks." He leaned back in his chair. "I inherited it, and I raise a few horses and run a few head of cattle. Years ago, durin' World War Two, the military built a small trainin' base out here. Didn't use it much. Those old tarmac runways are long gone—too expensive to maintain. The buildin's you saw as you drove in are what were left behind. Not bad buildin's. My dad always kept 'em up. This one was the officers' quarters."

He flashed a lopsided grin. "This apartment was probably home of the commandant. Long time back. I moved out here and fixed it up after my wife died."

Darcy shifted in her chair. He was widowed, too—and lonely. She glanced at him, hoping he wouldn't notice her uneasiness.

He didn't seem to. He leaned back and crossed his feet on a footstool. "Then when some neighbors moved in, I decided to put a grocery store and a small mechanic shop downstairs.

This area's changin' now. When I was a kid, wasn't anybody around. But now the recreational industry is demandin' new places to go. Part of that mountain's public land, but it's nearly surrounded by private land like mine. New opportunities openin' for people like me."

He stroked his chin. "Along with my flyin' contracts with the wildlife agencies and BLM—that's the federal Bureau of Land Management—now that I have a chopper, I can make a good livin' just ferryin' hunters to the top of the mountain. Trophy-size game up there."

Again Darcy squirmed. She had trouble following Clark's rambling thoughts. Worse though, he was getting off the subject and she wanted to hear about Sarah.

He poured fresh coffee into both of their mugs. "There's an old fellow who owns the ranch next to mine. Has a large family and wanted to live out here. That jeep trail you came down is on the edge of his property, and a couple of his older boys are outfitters and guides for hunters."

He shifted in his chair. "That old fellow owned a huge dairy farm in Colorado and worked his boys on it until the oldest ones left for college. Put themselves through college with their earnin's. Most of the children are married now. Then he sold the dairy and bought this ranch four years ago. Some folks think he's some kind of religious radical because all their children have Bible names. And because he talks in parables." A laugh shook his shoulders. "Also because he looks like Moses. But he's a nice guy. Good man."

Parables! Darcy's memory drifted back to Lydia, her high school friend whose "religious radical" father forced her to wear dowdy clothes and long, stringy hair. Fighting the resentment that welled up against "Moses," she made herself listen, but her thoughts churned. She studied her doubts while he rambled.

"Some of his daughters wanted to open up a little shop and sell homemade doughnuts and handicrafts durin' tourist and huntin' seasons. Only lasts four or five months. So we fixed up one of those small buildin's across the street. They started marketin' their crafts to shops in Flagstaff and Phoenix and Denver, wherever their men go on business trips. Got a little birdhouse factory in that long buildin'. Couple of the men started a consultin' business. People can do their work electronically almost anywhere nowadays, you know. So now I have six of my buildin's rented out. Startin' to look like a real town."

"That's all interesting," she interrupted. "But I'd rather hear more about Sarah and Jim and the mine."

He lowered his head and looked up at her. "Sorry about that—guess I got carried away. Say, I've got some lemon pie." Without asking if she wanted any, he got up and cut two pieces and poured more coffee.

"Well, anyway—yes, you'd like Sarah. Great gal. Took to that cabin like a duck to water. She was so organized. Always had a list of supplies for two months ahead. Not just groceries, but clothes, Christmas stuff, everything. Jamie gets his blue eyes from her. By the way," he added, "I flew Jim and Sarah down to Flagstaff when it came time to birth Jamie."

Caught up in Clark's description of this woman she had never seen, Darcy listened to every word. He bragged like a proud father about Sarah canning fruit and sun-drying tomatoes.

"And besides that, she home-schooled Jamie," he said. "Smart kid. Good manners, too."

Again, Darcy squirmed gently. Her mind began to drift again. She wanted to learn more about the mine.

No need to ask. Clark was talking again, turning a pencil over and over in his hands as he spoke. Long tapered hands, she noticed. Hands that could tame a horse or cut a piece of pie without breaking the crust.

"Jim thought he could work his granddad's mine, maybe get a little ore that he could sell after they came out. Doubt he got much. Said his granddad told him once that the real treasure was bigger than gold." A new grin spread across his face. "And Jim figured the mine was worth a lot to his granddad as a hideaway. His grandmother was the tyrannical type. They lived in a fancy little house near St. George."

It was good to see him smile; his craggy face seemed to light up from inside.

"Well, I didn't see any gold bricks stacked around." she said. "But I did see the cougar."

Clark's eyes widened. "Can you believe that? Besides bein' a crew chief, Jim was a sharpshooter in Desert Storm, and he saved my hide more than once. But just think of him pickin' off that cat in mid-air right over his kid's head. Nerves of steel. They made sure Jamie got over the scare. Had me get that pelt tanned."

She smiled. "And they hung it over his bed. He calls it Cougey." They both laughed. She relaxed, but only for a moment.

"You said that you had *two* bits of good news for them."

He slumped in his chair. "Yeah. I would've told them that their exile was ended."

"What? You don't mean..."

"Yep. Few days ago, I read in the Salt Lake newspaper that the murderers were caught."

Noticing Darcy's puzzled expression, he paused. "Before I tell you what the newspaper said, let me explain a little bit more about why this case went unattended to by the police for all this time. I was baffled. Like I said, I kept searchin' the Salt Lake papers every day for any mention of criminal intent involved in that lady lawyer's accident. Not a trace. Then, right after they got Sarah hidden at the mine, I saw that 'Wanted' poster. The first time Jim and Sarah came here after hidin' out at the mine, I showed it to them. We flew

65

down to Flagstaff and Sarah called that number from a pay phone." His head swayed slowly and his forehead wrinkled. "The voice on the phone was her boss's voice.

"That confirmed Sarah's suspicion. She hung up, of course. If her boss was conductin' his own search, that meant the real police may not even be aware the 'accident' was actually a murder. She figured the detective who took her statement could have been an impostor hired by her boss. And the Missin' poster, of course, was a fake."

He paused for another sip. "She and Jim both were smart enough to keep quiet. They were too skittish to go straight to the law—they didn't dare trust anyone by that time. Besides, she had given the duplicate tape to the detective, along with her signed statement. If the detective *was* in cahoots with her boss, fat chance she'd have—without that tape—convincin' the law that a crime was involved in the lady lawyer's death. Just her word against theirs. 'Hearsay,' they'd call it, and remember—these guys are high-pressure lawyers. They know the ropes. Jim insisted on stayin' at the mine until the law caught the murderers. Since it was uncertain whether the law enforcement people were ever gonna investigate, that could be a long, long time! So he and Sarah and later Jamie hid out there more than six years. I kept watchin' the newspapers all that time. Never a mention of the case."

"Six years?" Darcy exclaimed. "That's a long time. I'd think by this time the crooks would have given up on the hunt for Sarah."

"You'd think so. But those guys were persistent. They've been down this way several times. After all, they knew Jim and Sarah had a cabin in the Arizona Strip. Even came to my door a few weeks ago. Said one of the young ladies in the coffee shop downstairs is almost a dead ringer for Sarah, and they were right—but I didn't let on that I knew Sarah or anything about her whereabouts. Had to keep a straight face, which wasn't easy. They've been keepin' a watch on this place, for sure."

"Then that explains all the secrecy?"

He leaned on his elbows. "Yep. Then about two weeks ago, I saw a story in the Salt Lake newspaper's obituaries, along with a photo of the detective. It said the detective had been killed in a traffic accident. Sound familiar?"

Darcy felt herself stiffen again, but kept her voice calm. "What led you to think the picture was of that detective? Did you ever see him?"

"No, but I was sure it was the same fellow. Let me show you somethin'." He went to the drawer of the hutch again and returned with a sketchbook and two folded newspapers. He first opened the sketchbook to a drawing.

"See? Sarah drew this. Said it was a picture of the 'so-called detective'—her term for him—and that she drew it from memory. Now compare that with this. He opened one of the folded newspapers to the obituary page and pointed to the photo. "Look at his bulgin' eyes. See the resemblance? Oh, Sarah was quite an artist. So was Jim. I've looked at it dozens of times. But there's more."

Darcy bent over the drawings and the photo. "So, you notified the law?"

"No. His wife did. See this?"

He unfolded the second newspaper to the front-page section. "This came out a week or so after the paper ran the obituary. Take a look." A banner headline proclaimed:

SALT LAKE DETECTIVE'S DEATH NO ACCIDENT
Law Firm Duo, Vegas Operative Rigged Auto to Crash

A large photo of the deceased detective took up a good portion of the front page, along with smaller photos of the woman lawyer, the two junior lawyers, what Clark called the "enforcer," and Sarah's boss.

"How about that?" Clark said. "The detective's wife—and by the way, he *was* a real detective, it turns out—found evidence that proved he was murdered the same way the lady lawyer was. A few days after her husband's death, while goin' through his things, she opened his strongbox and found the duplicate tape that Sarah had given him. That, plus a copy of Sarah's statement, her sketch of the 'enforcer' and a two-page note that began, in large capital letters: 'IF SOMETHING HAPPENS TO ME, GIVE THIS TO THE SALT LAKE POLICE.' It described in detail how the two attorneys had the Vegas guy somehow rig the right front wheel of the detective's car to grab at high speed and cause the car to roll over. Police went back to their accident report on the lady's car and found it had crashed the same way. Like Sarah, that detective's wife feared for her own life. But she was brave enough, thank goodness, to give the police the evidence she had found."

He scratched his head. "Know what I think? I think that detective was in cahoots with Sarah's boss and the two attorneys, but was blackmailin' them. Just a guess, but I think it makes sense. Anyway, after all this time, the murderers are in custody. Includin' Sarah's boss."

His jaw twitched. His voice broke. "And Jim and Sarah will never know."

* * * * *

Even as she sat quietly giving Clark time to compose himself, Darcy's mind couldn't stop asking questions. If the mystery was solved, why was he pretending he hadn't been to the mine? For that matter, if he and Jim were such great friends, why didn't he know where Jim's mine was?

She tried a direct approach. "You said you haven't seen the mine?"

Clark took her forgetfulness in stride. "Right. Jim wouldn't tell me where it is, and I didn't want him to. He knew I wouldn't disclose their hidin' place until they were safe, but in case the law located me, I could truthfully say I didn't know where he was and not be guilty of perjury. He was afraid for Sarah's safety if she was named as a witness. And besides, one thing a guy doesn't do, especially a best friend, is to ask a miner the whereabouts of his mine."

He stood and leaned against the refrigerator. "Quite a few old abandoned mines up there. In an emergency I could have located it through the minin' records, I suppose. But first I'd have to find out his granddaddy's name, which, as I said before, I never knew. Maternal grandfather, so the name isn't Granger. I know it's a two-day trip though, because Jamie says his favorite part is campin' out. Must be on the back side of the mountain."

Two days! She said to herself. *It only takes four hours if you don't stop for a swim.*

She looked at her watch. Two a.m. Before either of them could mention bedtime, Jamie wandered into the kitchen, rubbing his eyes.

"Trouble sleepin'?" Clark asked.

Jamie stood next to Darcy. "I had a dream and I took a present to my mom and dad's special place. Darcy, when we go back, can I take a present?"

Her jaw fell. Go back? She hadn't told him they weren't going back. How could she have been so insensitive? Her thoughts spun. She had read somewhere that children need closure, and that a funeral provided that for them. Jamie needed to say good-bye to his parents more than she needed to go to Elko right then.

Go back? Why not? Nobody was expecting her anywhere, except for the high school people and, of course, Carol. If it cost her that job, she'd find another one. Her eyes met

Clark's as she answered Jamie. "That would be very nice. Let's talk about it in the morning."

She helped the boy back to bed and smoothed the light blanket over him, sensing that she was getting in over her head. But there was something about this blue-eyed kid. And something about that mine....

Clark still sat at the table when she returned. "I didn't even *think* about him expecting me to take him back," she stammered. "He wants to say good-bye to his parents. And he needs to. He'll have a hard time getting over these memories. I'm not surprised about his dream."

"And he brought it straight to you."

Quickly she cleared her throat. "You know, I didn't bring anything out—things he should have, like his cougar rug and his mother's coral necklace. Mementos are important. Why didn't I think of that?"

Clark's voice had a soothing effect. "You were in survival mode, lady. Must've been some experience, gettin' lost and findin' that little guy out there alone." His forehead bunched into wide furrows. "Jamie tell you about that coral bead?"

"Oh, yes! He's quite proud of it. He said God gave it to them when his baby sister died. He says she's buried in the bread box."

Clark leaned back with his hands behind his head and his long arms folded into angel wings. "That's right. Not any ordinary bread box, though. Jim carved it by hand for Sarah. It has a scripture from the Bible carved into it. The baby was stillborn, months too soon, right there in the cabin in the middle of winter. Jim had to bury her there, and then he had to bring Sarah and Jamie here. Miracle they made it. Strapped Jamie on his back like a papoose and carried Sarah in his arms all the way to the truck."

He gestured behind him. "She was white as that refrigerator when they got here. We were both afraid to take her to Utah, so we flew her to Flagstaff, same hospital where Jamie was born. Only time I ever flew across the Grand Canyon at night. Got there just at daybreak. Jim thought he was gonna lose her."

He swallowed and the corners of his mouth twitched downward. "Same way I lost Lillian." Her gaze followed his to the photo on the hutch. No need for words. He read her eyes.

Darcy's thoughts went back to that trail from the cave to the truck, watching Jim struggle to carry his wife and child over those rocks.

She yanked her mind back to attention when Clark next spoke. "Somethin' interestin' about that coral bead. It's really old—hand drilled hole and all. Jim told me that when he was lookin' for a place for a grave for the baby, he saw a big anthill. That little bead was right on top of it. So he kept it and Sarah made up that story for Jamie about God givin' it to them." His shoulders lifted into a shrug. "Don't know any better explanation. So we put it on a chain."

"And I didn't even think to bring it," she said. Her mind was not standing still. Clark seemed to know everything about Jim and Sarah, except where they were hiding. There was so much to discuss. Could the bodies be identified? Should they be removed? The authorities would have to be notified.

They discussed and agreed on their agenda for the next few days. Clark had a flying job tomorrow. The following day he would take her and Jamie back to the mine to get Jamie's things. After that, he would notify the coroner. She figured that by driving all day and night, she could possibly get to Elko barely in time to sign her contract.

CHAPTER 5

"Oh, boy! Sourdough pancakes!" Jamie's voice drifted in from the kitchen, and Darcy's eyes popped open. By the time she dressed and sat down at the table, he was having a second helping.

Breakfast was noisy with banter between Jamie and Clark. It was a thoroughly pleasant morning, except she was still weary from the late night talk session.

Clark explained to Darcy that morning's flying job. "This'll be my first trip of this kind since I bought the chopper," he said. "I put ads in the Mesquite and St. George papers, and these three guys responded. They want to scout some of the mountain areas up there for game, so they'll be ready for huntin' season. Should take me about an hour or so."

After Clark was gone, Darcy noticed Jamie looking out the window at the dirt street below, where a group of small boys had gathered for batting practice on a flat park. "That looks like fun," she said. Have you ever played softball? Do you know those boys?"

Jamie grinned. "No. But my dad pitched the ball to me sometimes down on the flat place. I can bat pretty good. Do you think they'd let me play?"

"You can ask them."

His eyes widened in disbelief. He broke into a broad grin and dashed downstairs. Darcy watched from the window as the boys greeted him and handed him a bat. For a kid who was never around people, he made friends easily. He seemed to have no sense of distrust. Jim and Sarah had done a good job.

She heard one of the boys in the outfield call out to him: "What's your name?"

"Jamie," he shouted back.

"We already have a Jamie. You got another name?"

"Sure. You can call me Chad."

Her gaze drifted to the shop Clark had mentioned last night. She had to get out—if she didn't, she'd fall asleep. She grabbed her handbag and hurried downstairs.

Three women—probably wives of the hunters—sat at a table in the tearoom. The room overflowed with handmade gifts and a familiar fragrance, a blend of eucalyptus leaves, soap, and candles. The windows and shelves displayed a variety of the most beautiful birdhouses she had ever seen. She looked closer to study the details: a whole village of birdhouses, some shaped like family dwellings, some like churches and schoolhouses, stores and blacksmith shops, each one with numerous details.

Soft music played in the background. Her ear caught a smattering of lyrics—phrases about awesome wonder, forest glades, and birds. A young girl with soft, wavy hair falling to her waist greeted her, then held the door open for a white-haired lady carrying a tray of homemade cinnamon rolls. A buzz of chatter drifted in from the back room. She noticed the women there had their shiny hair pulled into braids or buns. They were impeccably groomed, and their clothes were exceptionally modest.

Some of the shop's handicrafts didn't tempt her. Cal hated cute things, and somehow that had rubbed off on her. A table by the window gave her a view of the ball field and a chance to soak up the atmosphere. Already stuffed with pancakes, she ordered tea and a cinnamon roll. She overheard the servers' plans for a church supper and sensed a happy dignity that prompted her to wonder about this community.

Did Clark's friend, "Moses," set the standards? Were these people religious radicals? Would Jamie fit in here? Whatever, everything appeared serene.

"This is a beautiful shop," she said as the waitress refilled her tea. "Is there enough tourist traffic to support it year-round, or is it a seasonal business?"

"It's seasonal." the woman answered. "We decided to open this shop just during the tourist and hunting seasons. We call it 'Guilt-trip Souvenirs' because hunters ask for things to take home to the family. Or if the wives are here, *they* usually pick them out. These birdhouses sell like hotcakes.

"This shop is a real going business," she continued. "It's a family project. Three of my sisters and I have a craft business. This tearoom space and the gift shop are just parts of the shop building." She pointed to a door at the rear of the tearoom. "Back there," she said, "we design and manufacture craft kits for sale to distributors. These birdhouses you see on display are trial designs we make before choosing which designs to mass-produce."

Darcy decided to change the subject. "I noticed some boys outside playing softball. Are these hunters' kids, or do they live around here?"

"Mostly the latter, though I did notice one new boy. Visitors' kids are welcome. As for our own boys and girls, we don't have a public school out here, so we home school our children. We also give them recreational opportunities. Older students use this shop for their business class. They learn retailing and bookkeeping from my sisters, who were business majors. It gives the young people something to do. They need that."

She sat in the chair across from Darcy. "We didn't plan to have a tearoom. But when we opened our craft business, we figured the tea and doughnuts would fit right in. Our mother is a wonderful cook, and she loves to teach the grandchildren her secrets."

Darcy wanted to know more about Clark. Maybe she should ask these people about him, but not directly. That would be too obvious. "Can you tell me where to inquire about renting one of these buildings?" she asked on impulse. Not that she needed to ask. Clark had told her he owned the buildings, but she wanted to know what these people knew about him.

"You could ask Clark Tygard. He's such a good man." Without prompting, the waitress expounded on Clark's generosity, the building he had donated for a church, the way he encouraged her husband in his business.

Despite that glowing report, Darcy's mind remained unsettled. *If Clark knew Jim and Sarah lived at the mine, and if he didn't know they were dead, why didn't he try to see them when he flew the old Navajo man over there?* One possible answer came to mind, and she didn't want to believe it: *Maybe he knew they were dead.*

But no, he wouldn't have left Jamie there alone. So, if he was telling the truth about not knowing where they lived, what was the mystery? Did she dare trust him?

She had decided to take pictures at the mine and compile a scrapbook for Jamie. After paying for her pastry and two rolls of film, she went on a leisurely tour through the shop. On impulse she bought a bird schoolhouse and a small plaque. Its message, "The most precious things in life... are *not* things," would be just right for her home in Elko.

Batting practice was still in progress. She hurried back to put her purchases in her truck, then climbed the stairs to Clark's apartment. With luck she would have a few minutes with him before Jamie returned, and she knew exactly what to ask.

The door had barely closed behind her when she heard Clark's steps on the stairs. "Good trip?" she asked.

"Great trip! Those hunters were real impressed. Said they'd be comin' back in huntin' season, and would tell all their buddies about it. Looks like it's gonna be a good business." He went to the kitchen, filled the coffeepot and set it on the stove, then excused himself to wash up.

After they both settled, she started the conversation before he could get her sidetracked. She decided on an oblique approach: "Clark, you know, I was thinking Jamie should learn about the history of this area. In Vegas we took our children on field trips to learn about Native American culture. Do you know of any Native Americans around here?" *If he lies about that old man in his helicopter,* she decided, *I'm out of here.*

His eyebrows lifted. "Your children?"

There he goes again, getting off the subject. Darcy struggled to hide her impatience. "I should have said 'my students.' I tend to think of them as my children—I have none of my own."

"Sorry, my mistake. Native Americans? Sure. One of my oldest and best friends is a Navajo. Name's Bert Two Goats." He gestured toward the living room. "His wife, Clara, made that rug on the wall. I'd like for Jamie and Bert to get together. Maybe I could take the two of them for a ride in my chopper. Bert loves to ride in that thing."

He got up and set two mugs on the table. "Matter of fact, couple days ago he asked me to take him to a special place of his." His hand gestured toward the desert. "He heard about a minor earth tremor somewhere around Kanab, and he wanted to check on that place. Kind of a sacred site for him with a tall rock, and he wondered if the pillar was still standin'. The desert there's too rocky for any ground vehicle, and he can't go on foot or horseback anymore like he used to. I needed to get the feel of the chopper anyway."

He poured coffee and set a box of cookies on the table. "Bert's quite a storyteller and an expert on native rituals.

Taught me all about the peace pipe ceremony when I was a kid. He was my dad's ranch hand, but he's retired now."

Clark's expression softened as he took a drink. "My mother died in '89 and my dad died while I was in the Gulf War. When I got back home with a head full of bad ideas, Bert didn't bat an eye. Just kept me busy, kept me talkin', and went on like everything was gonna be okay." He sighed and slurped his coffee. "And after a while, it was."

Darcy had stopped listening. Her mind was in a whirl again. He wasn't lying about flying to the mine. She could have spared herself this turmoil. All she had to do was ask. This was the best time to set the record straight before Jamie came back.

"Clark," she began, "I have to tell you something. You *have* been at the mine. I saw you there, you and your Navajo friend."

He bolted upright, scattering cookie crumbs down the front of his shirt. As she described the touching scene out by the tall rock, the contortions on his face registered every emotion between disbelief and acceptance.

"Out there on the desert? That close? Heck, if I'd-a known, I could've flown a rescue crew there in fifteen minutes. Jim and Sarah had a radio for emergencies, but we didn't count on anything happenin' to both of them." He shook his head and with a heavy sigh let his shoulders sag. A long silence separated them as they sorted through their emotions.

In disbelief, he waved a cookie toward the southwest. "But they drove up on the mountain. I don't see... well, how'd they get over there on the desert? There's no road."

Darcy couldn't keep her eyes from smiling. "It's like Jamie told me, 'You turn around the red-eyed toad.' That takes you eastward, around a meadow to the edge of the flatland."

Clark lifted one eyebrow and Darcy's smile widened. Something was extraordinary about his eyebrows; they seemed to operate independently of each other. She had never seen anyone who could lift one brow that close to the hairline while the other one stayed in its usual place.

"Red-eyed toad?" His smile deepened the creases around his mouth. "Sounds like somethin' Sarah thought up. She was always playful and funny."

"And you know what?" Darcy said. "Jamie knew the way here like the back of his hand. So why didn't he just come on out here when his parents were killed? For some reason he thought he had to wait until the calendar said he could come."

Clark hesitated before he spoke. "When you're hidin', you live by the rules. It's almost like bein' in the military. You can't make choices. Jamie grew up that way, and he knew the drill. And remember there's still cougars out there. He sure didn't forget *that*. Good thing he *didn't* come out! Besides, I've been gone a lot."

Darcy then described her bewilderment over Jamie thinking God had sent her. When she told about the boy showing her Jim's hidden truck and the cougar rug, they once more found themselves laughing out loud. She felt the tension leave her shoulders. It had been too long since she had laughed with another adult.

"Too bad we don't all have faith like Jamie's," Clark said as they moved into the living room. He glanced toward the bedroom. "Is he takin' a nap?"

"No. He's outside playing ball with those boys."

Nothing could have prepared her for Clark's reaction. Before she finished the sentence, he whirled, wide-eyed, to face her. "Outside!" he yelled. "You let him go outside?"

She backed away, stammering as he glared at her. She had dealt with anger before—many times. But this wasn't anger. It was panic, and it frightened her. Something was very wrong here, and Jamie was right in the middle of it.

Her voice rose to a squeak. "Yes. Should... shouldn't I? It's only a ball game. Anyway, you said the killers were caught. How could there be any danger now?"

Shrinking, she tried to hold back the humiliation that crept up her neck, darkening her face. Her hands pressed against her mouth to quiet her trembling chin. Cal had said so many times that she should not make decisions; she should do exactly as she was told—implying that she always did things wrong.

Clark coughed and cleared his throat a half dozen times, looking out the window while Darcy gathered herself. When he turned to face her, his breath came out in a puff. "I'm sorry, Darcy. I scared you and I'm real sorry." He shook his head. "I started to tell you last night about all this secrecy, but somethin' sidetracked me. Have to get used to the idea that it's no secret anymore. At any rate, that's no excuse for scarin' you."

He sat down and rubbed his chin with his callused hand. "Let me explain. I mentioned my neighbor, the one who owns the ranch over there."

"You mean 'Moses?"

He nodded. "Well, what I didn't finish tellin' you is—his name is Henry Chadwell. He's Sarah's father."

"Her *father?*" Darcy tried and failed to prevent her skepticism from spreading over her face. " 'Moses' is Sarah's father? And you didn't mention it? "

Clark stared at the floor, then looked up sheepishly. "Guess I was still in the secretive mode."

Puzzled, she waited for him to explain.

He could only stare at the floor. Finally he shook his head. "When he finds out I knew where she was and didn't tell him..."

After a long pause, he gathered himself and looked up at her. "Let me explain. Henry and his big family moved here from southwest Colorado about four years ago. Had a big dairy ranch there. First time I met Henry, he pulled out one of those posters and asked me to study the faces and tell him if I knew them, or had any idea of their whereabouts. All I could do was shrug. But that shrug meant different things to us. To me it meant 'How do I answer?' To him it meant I didn't know them or anything about them."

"But why couldn't you just come right out and tell him the truth?" Darcy asked, her suspicion growing.

"Well, I thought about it. But somethin' inside said, 'hold on.' You see, Jim and Sarah were still in hidin' and I had no right to go out on my own on such a matter. Don't know what else I could've done. Next time Jim and Sarah came here, they both agreed I did the right thing.

Jim said if those killers suspected Sarah's family knew where she was, they could trick them into tellin', or put a lot of pressure on them. That's why we've had to be so careful about Jim and Sarah's visits here. They had to come here by night, stay inside durin' the day, and leave by night. Couldn't risk bein' spotted by the crooks *or* family members. "

"Now I understand why Jamie said we had to wait till after dark to come here," Darcy said. "Isn't it a strange coincidence, though, that of all the places they could go, Sarah's family came here? To this desert country?" She wanted to believe him.

"I know... it could stretch the imagination, but not all that much if you knew about Henry. He's highly respected in the cattle industry, and he always kept his eyes on land values. He knew about this place. Their ranch here's huge. So was the one in Colorado, but Henry thought this was a better place to settle. There's good grazin' on this side of the mountain, and some deep wells and septic systems the military left behind, just like I have on my place. I'm glad to have the Chadwells here. When I bought my chopper, I figured Jim and I, when his life got back to normal, could carry on a business that could support both of us. Also figured Sarah would-a been thrilled to be so near her family."

He stood and walked over to the window. "Sarah used to peek out from behind these curtains, tryin' to catch a glimpse of her family. And when she saw them, it was even harder on her than if she'd never looked."

"It's so sad," she said. "And all this time, she had no way of communicating with them."

"Well, yes, as a matter of fact—she did."

"Really? How so?"

"One of the first things we decided when Sarah and Jim came down here was to find a way of lettin' the family know she was safe and alive, without revealin' their whereabouts. That Sarah was a bright woman! One of her concerns was that Henry would contact the FBI and ask for a missin' persons investigation. Either that, or the crooks might do so—not likely, though, because they'd risk bein' implicated. So right away, she got off a letter to her folks tellin' them, without goin' into any detail, that she and Jim were safe but were hidin' out from a dangerous group of crooks bent on silencin' her. She told her folks that if the FBI did inquire, they should tell them the situation in order to stop them from any further investigation."

"But how could she do that without revealing her whereabouts?"

"Easy. That's where I came in. She wrote the letter and I posted it. Not from here, but from Provo, the first time, anyway. Later on, I mailed her letters from Boulder, Denver, Boise, wherever my work took me. Of course, she never left a return address, so her folks had no way of writin' back to her. She also insisted we make sure the letters couldn't be traced to me, so she'd slip the letter into a plastic bag and I would dump the letter from the bag into a mailbox without leavin' any of my DNA. Very thorough, that lady!"

"So if they didn't have her address, how could they communicate with her?"

"They couldn't. At least not directly. But when Jim and Sarah came here, I would bring them up to date on news from the family, what little I could pick up. Of course, she never hinted in her letters that she knew what was goin' on with them. That would give *me* away."

Darcy was impressed, but had a further question. "You say that twice you took Sarah and Jim to the hospital in Flagstaff. One was when Jamie was born, and the other was when you took Sarah and Jim there after the baby died in childbirth and Sarah needed treatment. They would have had to leave a trace there at the hospital in both cases. How did they handle that?"

"Easy. They gave a fictitious address. They did the same with a document notarized in Flagstaff namin' Jamie's guardian, plus a will leavin' the mine and acreage to Jamie in the event they both died." His voice almost broke.

"And now they *have* died. I sure dread havin' to tell Henry and the family."

He wiped his eyes with his sleeve, sat quiet for a while, then looked into her eyes. "Let me give you a little background. You see, Henry didn't approve of her marriage to Jim, because Jim wasn't 'of the faith.' That's how Henry put it."

He paused. "Sarah went away to college and fell in love with Jim. Henry wouldn't let her bring Jim home to meet the family, so she married him without her father's blessin'. The Chadwells lived in Colorado at the time, and Henry was the patriarchal type. He's mellowed since then— called it 'gettin' his faith on straight'—and would welcome them both. Too late, though. By that time Sarah and Jim were in hidin'."

"How did you come to know all this?"

"Well, the first part, Sarah and Jim told me. As for the mellowin', Sarah's brother Dan told me. He's a part-time minister, by the way. Of course, I never let on to Dan that I knew either of them, but I did relay the good news to Jim and Sarah next time they came here."

He stroked his chin. "Of course they were elated, but it was still a sad situation. Ever since the Chadwells moved here, besides hidin' from the killers, Sarah had to hide from her own family right across the road. Been hard, like walkin' a tightrope."

He paced the floor again. "Hate to think how angry and hurt Henry'll be when he finds out I deceived him. Sure hate to lose his friendship. But like I said, I don't know what else I could-a done under the circumstances." He stared out the window. "Wonder what Henry'll do about Jamie."

He turned around and sat down. Darcy remained quiet. There was no need to say anything more. He was reading her eyes again. She wondered what he saw.

The lines in his face softened. His hands reached out to grasp her shoulders, sliding down to rest lightly on her arms. "It's okay, Darcy. Just need some time to think it over. We'll take Jamie back to the mine tomorrow to get his clothes and toys and as many of Jim's and Sarah's important things as we can bring back. We'll have time to, uh, think of somethin'."

At his touch, every muscle in her shoulders relaxed in a flood of relief. Clark was in charge now. Her eyes squeezed tight to hold back her tears. Her lips tightened to stifle her bobbing chin. No man had ever touched her with such gentleness, such kindness—after he yelled at her.

She walked over to the window where Clark had stood before, and looked down at the ball field. Clark was now seated on the sofa. Batting practice had ended and a white-bearded man herded the boys into the back of a pick-up truck. *Could this be 'Moses'?* she wondered. *Or more properly, Henry Chadwell?*

"Bye, Chad," one of the boys called out. She heard it only faintly. Jamie turned and waved back.

The old man stiffened and turned around. His eyes followed Jamie intently as the boy walked up the staircase to Clark's apartment.

Darcy froze. *Oh no! What have I done? Will Clark ever really forgive me?*

* * * * *

During dinner that evening Darcy and Clark tried to listen as Jamie talked about the ball practice, but their minds were on other things. Darcy's was on what she had seen downstairs, and whether or not she should tell Clark. Clark's was on tomorrow's trip to the mine.

"Jamie, you know what you want to take as a present for your mom and dad?" Clark asked.

Jamie swallowed quickly. "I think my mom would like a cup and saucer. She always looked at yours. And, well, I guess my dad might want a horse like yours."

"Okay, I'll tell you what," Clark answered. "You go pick out the cup your mom would like from the hutch. And I have a horse in the bedroom."

A pang of sadness shot through Darcy's chest. How difficult it must be for this man to part with his wife's things—keepsakes that plainly meant so much to him.

Jamie chose a cup and saucer with a spray of tiny blue flowers painted on the side of the cup. "Darcy, what kind of flowers are these?"

"I think they're called forget-me-nots."

His face brightened as it always did when he came up with one of his good ideas. "Then she'll know I didn't forget, won't she?" Darcy's eyes filled. She wanted to cry.

She was glad for the diversion when Clark came in carrying an expensive porcelain horse. "Oh boy!" Jamie said. "My dad will like this a lot!" *Cal would never have given that away, especially to a child.*

By the time the boy had finished his ice cream and was ready for bed, they had agreed on a plan. Early tomorrow morning Clark would fly them to the desert and help Darcy camouflage the mine entrance. Her truck would stay in his garage. Jamie could put a present on his parents' special place, and they would pack all the mementos. She and Jamie would stay overnight while Clark kept his appointments. He would return the following afternoon to bring them back before he called the coroner. He'd offer to ferry the coroner's team to the site, in hope that as few people as possible would learn its location. He'd deal with the legal aspects later.

Darcy's brow furrowed. "When do you tell the Chadwells about Sarah and Jim?"

"I've thought it over. If I were squeamish about legalities, I'd wait'll the crew brings the bodies out and the coroner positively identifies them. But I don't really need to wait that long. I'll tell 'em soon as we get back."

He raised his left eyebrow. "After all, Jamie's a reliable witness. He knows what he saw. I'd take his word any day."

* * * * *

Darcy wasn't sure at what moment she lost her distrust of Clark. It seemed to be pushed aside by Jamie's needs. A burden lifted from her shoulders. She lay in bed letting her mind drift over the events of the last few days. Jamie would be happy here. Funny little guy; she'd miss him. She'd be starting her own life in Elko. Independent at last!

And alone.

CHAPTER 6

Morning dawned clear and bright. As the helicopter lifted into the sunny sky, Clark gave them a quick tour over the tiny village. Beyond the hangar ran a row of empty buildings like those he had rented out. "If things go well," he shouted over the engine noise, "I'll turn a couple of those old barracks into a motel for hunters. In the summer off-season the Chadwells will use them as a wilderness experience camp for city church youth groups."

He pointed to the old ranch house at the foot of the mountain. "That's where I grew up. Bert Two Goats and his wife Clara live there now, with their grandson and his wife. They keep an eye on my horses."

"You grew up here?"

"Yeah. My great-grandparents settled it. Old-time pioneers. Eventually, my dad inherited it. When the military leased it and put in the improvements durin' the second world war, livin' here got a lot easier. When they left, we inherited the buildin's and improvements."

In the distance stood the big Chadwell house, surrounded by several manufactured homes. A narrow gravel road connected the ranch site to the village and wound up into the new recreation area on the mountain.

"What's that?" She pointed to a knoll where a steep-roofed building stood, flanked by two rows of tall trees. A cross gleamed on its roof. *It must be the building Clark had donated for a church.* She wondered if he would take credit for his gift, or if he was too modest.

"It's a barn, but it'll be a church when it's fixed up. Henry's boys are workin' on it. Nice place for a church and a park. My dad planted the trees—intended to build a house there someday. Henry and I put the road in. That's how we control access to the huntin' grounds this side of the mountain. But the road's too slow for some sportsmen. That's why this chopper's gonna pay off—that and the contract flyin' I'll be doin' for the BLM and the wildlife agencies."

"But how do these folks make a living out here?"

She noticed the admiration in his voice when he answered. "One of the guys, Dave, is a writer for a church college. Also sells free-lance articles and teaches the writin' classes for the home school." His eyes twinkled. "Funny thing. His wife, Dawn, writes for huntin' and fishin' magazines. They have big generators to run computers and radios. Built a tower to operate cell phones, too. Hey, these folks are educated and capable. Dan's business is science-based, and along with pastorin', he teaches those classes. So the kids out here get a superior education."

He went on to explain. "These folks are not a weirdo clan. Nothin' like that. Just a big happy family. Live close to each other because most of 'em travel quite a lot in their work. Also do a fair amount of volunteer missionary work. They have built-in child care, and they're able to help their parents. Esther and her husband live in Denver. Jake lives in Phoenix. Both have big mobile homes for vacations here. Donate the use of their homes for the schools when they're not up here. Sam's the cattleman. He also has a white-water raftin' concession on the Colorado River in the summer. Employs several of the teen-age boys. They work it out pretty well."

He pointed the chopper toward the desert. Below, Darcy could make out a faint trace of the jeep road she and Jamie had come down two nights ago. As if retracing their route, Clark swung the chopper to the right and she looked down at the meadow.

So did Jamie. "Look Darcy! There's the meadow with the lilies. And one of those boulders down there is the red-eyed toad!"

Beyond the meadow the terrain turned into rocky desert through which a path of boulders wound through the brush like an ancient river of stone. "Used to be water out here," Clark said, still shouting above the engine's roar. "Now it's all dried up. Nothin' for cattle anymore, but plenty of browse for game animals. Dad's old maps show this area belongin' to a French family."

He shook his head. "Lady, you sure picked a dandy place to get lost. Can't figure how you got here from Mesquite in that truck. How'd you maneuver around those big washes and cliffs? How'd you get around Black Rock Mountain?"

Darcy could only shrug. "It was dark, so I couldn't see it."

Jamie seemed not at all annoyed at the need for explaining it again. "It was 'cause God knew I wanted someone to come." A silent smile passed between Darcy and Clark.

Soon Clark spotted the mesa where he had taken his friend Bert. The tall rock pillar stood out like a milepost, but Darcy had to point out the tiny canyon, which was concealed from overhead view by a dense canopy of cottonwood and juniper. Tall brush distorted the lines of the spring and the cave's doorway. The shadowy edges blurred against the darkness of the canyon floor, confusing the eye of anyone standing on the mesa or flying overhead.

Clark was amazed. "Flew this close and didn't even see that canyon! If I'd-a done that in Iraq, I wouldn't be here today. Jim's granddad must've followed a deer in there. How else would he have found it under all that brush? The ancient ones must've needed a landmark like the tall rock. Same goes for Jim and his granddad. Of course with today's high-tech devices...." He broke off. "Well, let's see what we've got out here."

The chopper sat down in a whirlwind of red dust and a queasy sensation came over Darcy. This was not a good time for nausea. She kept her head down and jumped out, noticing again the circular pattern left in the dust by the rotor wash when Clark had landed here before. This open place, surrounded by tall brush, was the only landing spot she saw. They would have to carry Jamie's things over the mesa and down here before Clark returned.

They grabbed the flattened cardboard boxes and climbed over the mesa, down into the little canyon and back up to the cave-house. Clark's reaction when he saw the cave didn't surprise her. "Never would've looked for them in a cave. Nice place, though. I can see why they didn't mind stayin' here."

Darcy was always curious about early pioneers. "How did Jim's grandfather get all these things in here? Especially that heavy stove? Did he drive over the mountain?"

Clark shrugged. "Could be he drove a Model T Ford truck, but more likely he packed everything in on donkey-back and assembled it when he got here." He laughed. "Probably wished a dozen times he'd-a been content with a campfire."

While Jamie climbed the cliff to check on his "mine," she took Clark to the landslide and pointed out the area where, according to Jamie, Jim and Sarah were walking when the slide occurred. She didn't stay—he needed to be alone. Meanwhile, she knew exactly what she needed to do: find something to hang over the entrance to Jim's mine. The cellar door, well hidden, wouldn't need a camouflage. She remembered a piece of old tan canvas covering the back wall of the cellar. It would be just right.

She tugged at the heavy cellar door and propped it open to let the light penetrate to the back. A tinkling sound made her turn and look back. A small stone rolled down from the brushy slope and plopped into the scattered gravel in front of the cellar door. She pushed the stone aside with her foot and jammed a heavy box against the open door.

In the cellar she again admired Sarah's knack for organization. Everyday items were stored near the door. Others, less often used, sat on rickety shelves that stood at right angles like room dividers. Here Darcy saw old oil lamps, mining gear and a copper wash boiler. In the dark space behind the divider, against the back wall, lay a jumble of barrels and galvanized tubs.

Old wooden crates had been stacked on their sides along the back wall to form a wall of shelves. She hoped they weren't nailed together. She would have to move some of those shelves in order to reach the canvas behind. A flashlight placed on one of the shelves lit the space as she bent to move the boxes out of the way. After clearing a path to the wall, she stood and stretched.

Again a sensation of dizziness swept over her. It reminded her of an old inner ear problem. She felt herself falling. Reaching for the wall to balance herself, she grabbed the canvas and heard a ripping sound as the rotted fabric tore away from the metal grommets along its edges. Her hand, grasping for something solid, touched nothing but emptiness. She found herself sprawled on the stony floor, enveloped by the rotten canvas.

Thick dust filled her mouth. Coughing and sputtering, she unwound herself from the filthy tarp. A draft of cool air flowing from a jagged crack in the wall touched her skin. She grabbed the flashlight from the shelf and turned its beam into the dark crevice. Nothing there to see except a rough opening in the cellar wall. Judging from the age of the canvas, Jim's granddad, not Jim, must have hung it there to cover the crevice.

She shoved and yanked the boxes and baskets aside and pulled the canvas tarp toward the cellar door. She was still tugging it out into the sunlight when Clark came along the path, his jaw locked tight and his mouth set in a straight line.

He saw her pulling the dust-filled tarp and grinned. "That mine doesn't look very prosperous, does it? Hard, dirty work." He took a second look at Darcy's filthy hair dangling in front of her muddy mouth and eyes. He bowed gallantly. "Been doin' some minin' of your own, Little Lady?" His sense of humor still seemed to be intact, despite his sadness from viewing the rockslide. His eyes twinkled for a moment. He saw her holding her arm. "Are you OK?"

Darcy rubbed her skinned elbow gently. "I'm okay. We have a shower down by the spring. Wait'll you see our deluxe accommodations."

She grabbed a towel and a bar of soap from the cellar and led him to the spring, where she dipped cold water into the wash-pan, scrubbed her face and lightly washed her elbow. After toweling her face she noticed the freshness of her skin. She had worn no makeup since she left Vegas. She looked back at Clark. It was worth a little dirt just to see that grim expression leave his face.

She called Jamie for lunch and noticed Clark's amazement as the sure-footed boy zigzagged from his "mine" down the steep cliff wall. After lunch they stowed all of the mining equipment inside Jim's mine and nailed the tarp over the entrance. Clark wrestled large limbs of brush and fastened them to the tarp. "I'm not as good at this as Jim was. Clever guy, very resourceful." Nothing could camouflage the pain in his eyes.

Jamie was still going strong. "Clark, wanna see my mine?"

"Sure. Let's go."

Darcy stayed in the cave-house to pack a few boxes that Clark would take today. She rolled the cougar rug inside a sheet, then packed the books inside the copper boiler. On the floor near the bookcase, she noticed a flat metal box on the bottom shelf. It was neither hidden nor locked. Curious, she opened it and unfolded the paper on the top. Though usually intimidated by legal jargon, she could understand this document quite easily. In the event of Jim's and Sarah's death, it stated, Jamie would have a legal guardian, a friend named Clark Tygard. It had been signed by Jim and Sarah and notarized in Flagstaff.

The second paper was a photocopy of the mine's patent, registered to Jim's maternal grandfather, Harley Willis. Attached to the original patent was a deed for two adjoining sections of land, purchased many years later from someone named Raineau. Underneath were copies of Jim's and Sarah's legal papers. A handwritten note stated that the originals were stored in a safety deposit box, and gave a Utah address. The key to the box lay in the bottom of the metal box, with a note stating that Clark had a duplicate key, since it was registered in both Jim's and Clark's names.

Clark now, for all practical purposes, had a son—though his guardianship was not as legally binding as an adoption. Darcy felt a new emotion: envy.

Other thoughts insinuated themselves into her mind. Thoughts of Aunt Belle—a distant cousin, actually—who became Darcy's guardian after Grandmother's death. Thoughts of the sale of Grandmother's big house and the money spent remodeling Belle's house. She wondered about Arizona law: *Who guards the guardian?*

Clark returned, puffing, from Jamie's "mine." "Wow, that's some path. I felt weird up there." He threw himself into the rocking chair.

She handed him the box and pointed to the deed. "How much land is in a section?"

"Six hundred forty acres. One square mile."

Clark studied the papers. "Harley Willis! I should've guessed that. Jim's middle name was Willis! Looks like his granddad bought those sections from that Frenchman just before he died. Bet this legal description will show the new sections are called the Raineau place, which joins mine. So now, Jim's—that is, Jamie's—place joins mine."

She wondered if Clark and Jim had grown up close together. "Were you school friends?"

"No, I didn't go to school—Mom taught me at home. Jim lived in St. George and went through high school there. Never heard of each other till we joined the National Guard with an Arizona outfit."

He read the guardianship paper, and after a long pause, spoke. "Yes, I knew about this. We agreed on it when Sarah was in the hospital in Flagstaff. Never expected it to happen. How could I ever be a dad like Jim?"

"You'll be a wonderful dad," she whispered. "Jamie loves you."

Darcy's thoughts didn't stand still. "Will the Chadwells challenge it in court?"

Clark straightened. "Could be. They might want to name one of Sarah's brothers as guardian. They'd want Jamie to have some religious trainin' and I don't know much about that."

He caught the question in her eyes. "Oh, I don't have any quarrel with religion. I go to the Christmas programs and a church supper or two. The Chadwells always invite me. When Lillian was alive, we belonged to a little church. But it's different when you're alone. Just not the same. Doesn't feel right." His shoulders lifted into a shrug. So did hers.

* * * * *

An hour later, Darcy and Jamie stood on the mesa and waved as the helicopter lifted out of sight. Jamie's funeral service had been touching. Clark had helped him scrape a place beside his tiny sister's grave, and the boy had placed his parents' gifts there. Holding the service on the rock pile was out of the question. Too rugged, and anyway the coroner's crew would be excavating the site.

When she realized they had brought no present for "Baby Sister," Darcy had felt in the pocket of her safari vest and found on her key chain a small pewter figure of a rag doll. She removed it and gave it to Jamie. Thrilled with it, he placed it on the shallow grave. She smiled now, recalling how Clark had coughed and shuffled his feet when he heard Jamie's closing prayer. She'd forgotten to prepare him for "Now I lay me down to sleep."

"It makes me feel lonesome to see him go," Jamie said as the aircraft disappeared.

"Sure does." But Darcy didn't intend to stand around thinking about how she felt. "He'll be back tomorrow, and we have lots of work to do."

She turned back toward the cliff, thinking of how she would dismantle the shower stall before they left. She decided they would leave it there and cover everything with brush, then drag sagebrush across their footprints to erase all evidence that anyone had lived here. After all, this was now Jamie's property. Better not to attract squatters or anyone else who might want to get into that gold mine. Maybe Jamie would want to vacation here someday.

Another sound caught her ear. She watched as a fist-sized rock tumbled from the high cliff to the depths of the canyon. The vibration from the chopper must have loosened it.

"Okay, kid. Let's get some more boxes and you can pack your things while I pack some things in the cellar. Then we can have hot dogs for supper." His eyes lit up and he ran to the cave-house.

While Jamie occupied himself by packing his clothes and toys, Darcy set to work in the cellar filling the cardboard boxes they had brought, hoping to have them hauled to the landing site when Clark returned. She would pack everything, even the groceries, though he couldn't take them all out on one flight.

Before long she needed more containers. With flashlight in hand, she began to explore the space behind the shelves for something lighter than wooden boxes, stumbling over wash tubs to reach some lightweight fruit baskets with wire handles. The light's beam fell on the rough wall and the crevice she had uncovered, illuminating a passage leading to her left. Hoping to find more boxes back there, she crept gingerly into the crevice and aimed the flashlight ahead.

Once again she felt her breath suck in and catch in her throat. "Oh," she gasped before her voice failed. Her senses left her and she could do nothing but stand and stare—and shiver.

She tried to make sense of what she saw. Her gaze, following the flashlight's beam, swept over the walls of a huge cavern. Pottery lined the walls. Large pots and bowls sat on folded burlap sacks. Others had been carefully stacked into old wooden crates. The uneven floor held vessels of all sizes and shapes.

She recognized various kinds of baskets—burden baskets and food baskets woven of willow yucca. Some appeared to be in very good condition. Near enough to reach, a shallow basket held bits of broken pottery. Among the jumble of plain shards she noticed a few colored in black and red, or black and white. Something about those decorations, those jagged and curved lines, teased her memory.

Her mind started its usual list of questions. Had Jim and Sarah been making pottery? No, these things looked old. Very old! This place looked like some kind of ancient warehouse. She struggled to recall Clark's words. What was it Jim had said? Something his grandfather said, too, something like "Gold is not the real treasure." Her mind raced: *This cache of ancient artifacts is the real treasure!*

Carefully she picked up a pottery shard and turned it over in her hand. The back of the shard had a small label with the number 226 in shaky handwriting. Every shard she examined was numbered, as was the basket itself. Darcy felt sure this was not Jim's or Sarah's handwriting. This was done with an old-fashioned ink pen.

"I wish I had my books here," she whispered to herself. Her books on Anasazi artifacts were in her truck in Clark's garage. *Big help!* She could recall only a smattering of what she had learned. Maybe if she looked closely she could remember something. Her flashlight shone only halfway into the chamber. Its beam came to rest on a primitive woven yucca sandal and several stone tools. A tattered basket held large chunks of turquoise and some curved white shells. A large basket out of her reach held a piece of rough fabric woven in a striped pattern. One thing Darcy did remember was that artifacts are very fragile and should not be handled, except by experts. Fighting the urge to walk into the chamber and examine the objects, she stood in the passageway and observed only what her flashlight revealed.

The light fell on a black-on-red seed jar—a flat jar with a small opening, the only intact piece she had seen so far. Behind it she saw a small black and white pot she could not resist lifting. It was numbered 287. As she turned it over in her hands, her mind went back to Clark's house, to that pot on top of his hutch. Her hands flew to her mouth. Sarah had one too, in the cave-house—the chipped pot that held Sarah's supply list. *Did she know what it was?*

Darcy reminded herself that she hadn't known, either, when she saw them. She had supposed them to be some kind of child's handicrafts, so rough and irregular. So *primitive*, to be precise. Did Sarah arrange those shelves across the middle of the cellar as a convenience? Or did Jim's granddad? If it was Sarah she must have thought, as Darcy had, that the canvas covered the back wall, and she had probably never looked behind the wall of stacked boxes. Evidently, neither Sarah nor Jim had ever discovered the narrow opening to the chamber or the fortune it held.

She turned the light to her left side. There, resting on a wooden box, lay a dusty ledger. She stretched to reach it. Unable to open it while she held the flashlight, she tucked it under her arm and returned to the front of the cellar. Sitting in the doorway there, she opened the fragile book and sat spellbound as a fascinating story unfolded.

The handwriting on the first pages was smooth and executed with something of a flourish. It told the story of Harley Willis, a rancher and old time prospector who discovered gold in this mountain. As a young man, he worked the mine for many years. He made a modest living, but never found the riches he anticipated. In his middle years he discovered a small cache of artifacts in an old campsite. He had sold none of them. They were worth only a pittance in those days. This ledger, though, revealed Mr. Willis to be a man of vision.

"I have a sense of certainty about the primitives I have found on my property" the ledger read. "Collectors are willing to pay a few dollars for these unbroken pieces. As I see it, folks will someday recognize their value. That value can only increase in the future, when the pieces become scarce. Some government leaders want to outlaw the sale of artifacts altogether. There will be a day when no more will be sold. I am convinced that my fortune does not lie in the gold mine, but in the surrounding land. My plan is to purchase as much land as I am able. I shall continue to present myself as a rancher and a gold miner, as my dear wife looks with disfavor on pot-hunters."

The story, beautifully expressed, flowed through the pages in separate chapters. Between the chapters Darcy saw meticulous bookkeeping: a catalog of his discoveries, the location of each dig and an opinion of the age of each piece.

His evaluations impressed her. Not guesswork; they were based on textbooks of that time, and on numerous archaeological papers from prestigious museums.

What a heritage Jamie had—not only these artifacts, but this ledger written by his great grandfather's hand. She could hardly wait to show them to Clark. As Jamie's guardian, he would control all of this wealth.

Though she still had much to do, Darcy read on through the ledger, sensing in those pages the intelligence, the resourcefulness, the humor of Jamie's ancestor; sensing as well his admiration for those ancient people. She wished she could have known Harley Willis.

From between the pages she lifted a yellowed packet and dumped the contents into her hand. Here were old snapshots, sharply clear black-and-white images on heavy paper with decorative borders. She had seen pictures like this in her grandmother's old photo album. Taken with a simple box camera in the 1920's or 30's, these were better preserved than most modern photos. They had no people; they were landscapes of desert country. Each photo was numbered to correspond with a map folded inside the envelope. She leafed through them, and at last found a picture of the place where she now sat. The cliff, clearly shown, looked different. At its base it had more foliage with larger growth. The photo had been taken from the mesa. The tall rock stood out like a signpost. From that viewpoint she peered closer. Something about the cliff itself was different.

Carrying the photo, she walked out away from the cellar and studied the face of the cliff. Its lower half lay covered by rubble, an old landslide, sprouting gnarled shrubs. The picture though, revealed the cliffs' appearance in the 1920's or 30's. At the level where she stood, about halfway up the cliff wall, ran a deep layer of sedimentary rock. The same layer formed the roof of the cellar and the cave-house. In the picture, that rock was exposed all the way across the cliff.

Beneath it lay a series of dark areas, cave openings arranged like a row of motel doors.

Suddenly her memory flashed a view of a similar cliff she had visited on a field trip. A national park somewhere. *Walnut Canyon!*

These were cliff dwellings! Ancient cliff dwellings! Darcy stood once again with her mouth agape. Beneath that old rockslide was a piece of history, a place where people had lived centuries before. She tried to imagine how those prehistoric people survived in such a barren place. Her gaze went back to the stain on the canyon wall. Jim had told Jamie there had once been a waterfall. She tried to remember what little she knew of primitive civilizations. Her thoughts turned inward, her memory keyed into clues, and the pieces began to come together.

She began to recognize what she had seen all around her. As always, she made a mental list of clues, beginning with the cave-house. Did ancient people live in that very same space? The artifacts they had left behind were possibly the first ones Mr. Willis had found. What else had she seen? Those stone steps and foot holes on the cliff. She'd assumed that Jim had built them for Jamie. But did ancient people dig them? The steps definitely needed scrutiny. What about the mine? Was it one of the old cave openings?

Darcy was now more interested in exploring the cliff than in packing to move away. She looked up at the mesa and the tall rock. That must have been a landmark for people centuries ago. Clark had said that his friend Bert considered it a sacred site.

What about the coral bead and the turquoise pendant God gave Jamie? Clark said they were old, and handmade. Were they ancient, too? A new thought jolted her. *The mesa! How sacred is it? Sometimes, places sacred to some are dangerous to others.*

It was getting late. Jamie came around to the ledge, interrupting her thought. "Darcy, are we going to eat our hot dogs?"

"Sure. I'm about starved. Let's stop working and have supper." She took the ledger along to the cave; it would be good bedtime reading. First though, she wanted to pay more attention to Jamie, to hear him read his lessons and say his prayers. So little time remained.

Soon the wieners were sizzling. Potato salad was in the ice chest that Clark had brought, and she knew that Clark had slipped some ice cream bars in for dessert.

Again she jumped, startled by a sound that was becoming too familiar. Sounds of scurrying desert creatures didn't bother her anymore. But that tinkling sound didn't seem natural. They turned to watch the gravel roll down the slope.

"That sounds like the day Cougey tried to eat me." Jamie said.

Darcy felt her spine prickle. "Are you sure? Do you remember that?"

"That sound makes me think about it."

"Sounds do help us remember things." She squinted out the window at the cliff. But how could she expect to see a cougar crouching with its ears laid back against its head when she could barely see a full-sized truck hidden in the brush? She turned back to the grill. If only Harley Willis were here. Or Jim. Or Clark.

Supper was delightful nevertheless, filled with laughter and stories. As she cleaned the table, Darcy asked. "Do you know where your mom got that pot with the pencils in it?"

"My dad found it when we were playin' ball one day."

"Clark has one just like it. Is that where he found Clark's?"

Jamie pondered a minute. "Yeah. Dad found 'em both at the same place. He gave Clark the better one, 'cause it doesn't have any busted places in it like ours does." He added: "Clark does lots of stuff for us. That's why he got the good one."

"Did your dad dig them up?"

Jamie shrugged. "He just saw 'em stickin' out of the dirt where a badger lived."

She decided against questioning him further. It was too intensive for a child. They played games and read stories instead, and finally, after he finished a cup of cocoa, she tucked him in bed. Only one more day left with him in this funny little house—her desert retreat.

Darcy sank into the bed with the lantern at the bedside. Reading far into the night, she became acquainted with Harley Willis and again decided she would have liked him immensely. Page-by-page, she shared his excitement at each new discovery. She tried to recall the names he used for the artifacts. Some, like Keyenta, Pueblo and Tusayan, were familiar names of southwestern towns, but most of them she had never heard of, or had forgotten. Still, she enjoyed speculating along with him about the age of each piece.

"The way I have it reasoned out," he wrote, "is that in the distant past, this area was a stop-over on a trade route from the Pacific coast to the Midwest. I have listened at length to many old Indian storytellers, and these historians related to me that the old ones had an active trade business. I believe that is why I find items from the seashores of California and Mexico, as well as one item from the far northwest country."

The account continued. "I believe this site to be a small trading settlement. I have also found squash seeds, pinion nuts, and other foodstuffs, which lead me to believe these folks were perhaps farmers as well as foragers. The caves were not enclosed at the time I discovered the site. I learned from other sites and built the front wall of my house. The window came later. But my guess is that this site could have been as highly developed as those at Mesa Verde."

On the following pages he had cataloged a wide variety of items he had discovered: abalone shells, tubular white shells, chunks of turquoise, feathers, copper disks and weapons made of flint and bone. He described one item that Darcy yearned to see—a child's doll. The list included primitive utensils for cooking and tools for sewing hides into clothing. He seemed especially touched at the way the household items were so beautifully decorated. Simple sketches of pottery bowls and pitchers, as well as dippers and effigies, adorned the pages. He mentioned a number of covered jars used for storage and for ceremonies. It was as though a town had thrived here for centuries, then vanished, leaving behind the evidence of its inhabitants' skills, intelligence, and love of beauty.

"I do not expect to realize much gain from these arti-facts in my lifetime," he wrote. "My daughter died young. Someday I will reveal them to my grandson Jimmy. I hope he will share my interest." A later entry, barely legible, said, "I have but one regret. I have learned that artifacts are of greater research value when they remain in their place of origin. I now wish I had merely mapped my discoveries, as each of them was obtained on my own property. From now on, I will map the sites not yet excavated and pray they are not trampled by animals." His words were followed by an extensive list of sites.

There was no other entry. She held the ledger against her chest, wondering what happened to this man she had known only by his handwriting and his words. She wondered if he had been able to reveal this treasure personally to his grandson.

She wished she could learn more about it, then caught herself in mid-sigh. She *could!* She could take photographs. Universities in Arizona and Utah and the Heard museum in Phoenix would be much interested in them.

She blew the lamp out and settled in bed. As the wind howled and whistled through the cave openings, her imagination heard the sound of wind instruments—the high notes could be Kokopelli's legendary flute, the low ones a fore-runner of the bass clarinet... or the moaning of a ghost. Gentle breathing sounds filled the cave as sleep overcame her. She didn't hear the tinkle of pebbles rolling across the flagstones. A shadow darkened the doorway as a cloud moved over the face of the moon.

CHAPTER 7

Darcy had known Jamie for only a few days, and she already had come to enjoy his noisy mornings. This one was no different. He excitedly rattled off his version of the day's agenda.

"Today we have to finish packing your things," she reminded him. "Then we have to carry them over to the mesa. This afternoon Clark will come and get us and you'll go to live with him."

He stopped eating and raised his eyebrows. "And you'll live there too, huh?"

His question didn't surprise her. Even so, Darcy didn't feel prepared for telling him that she planned to move to Elko, but she had to. "I have to go to Nevada. I might have a job there."

His face clouded. "Can you come and see us sometimes?"

"Sure." She had to get off this subject. "But today I want to see your mine."

That seemed to satisfy him, and soon they were busy carrying heavy boxes and stacking them near the landing place. Darcy stood to rest her back as the boy scampered around the mesa.

"See, this is where my dad pitched the ball to me." He kicked the dirt. "Here's where we found one of those little pots."

Darcy took a closer look at the circular pattern left by the helicopter. Near the edge of the circle she noticed flat stone slabs barely protruding from the sand, arranged to form a low curved wall. Bending and searching, she followed the wall, sometimes losing sight of the stones, then finding them where the circle resumed until it disappeared under a tall dense shrub. Something was familiar about this. Delving into her memory, she came up with a term. A *kiva.* A ceremonial place.

Was this an ancient *kiva?* No. It seemed too large.

Nevertheless, she stepped outside the circle. Whatever it was, it had been important to someone long ago. It was not meant to satisfy a modern woman's curiosity. Too large for a burial cist; maybe it was a ball court. She could imagine that centuries ago a copper-skinned man played ball here with his son, just as Jim had played with Jamie.

"Did your dad tell you anything about these stones?"

The boy shrugged. "I guess we didn't see 'em."

Of course. The stones had been buried until the helicopter landed and blew the dirt away. The site begged her to investigate more, but there was too much to do. She made a mental note to point it out to Clark that evening.

By mid-morning Darcy had photographed all the items in Harley Willis's secret vault, as well as several shots of Jamie's cliff-side home. She had packed the handmade quilt, the photo albums, the coral necklace, the sketchbook, the ledger, and the chipped pot in the stoutest box. They would be Jamie's most precious mementos. *That ridiculous picture of the hen and the chicks can stay here,* she decided.

Her last discovery was a small metal footlocker pushed far under the bed. Inside were five broken pots, a pottery dipper and a tin can filled with buttons whittled from antlers. Jim and Sarah must have found them. These artifacts must have been all over the place. If they had lived, they would surely have found his grandfather's collection. Now, as

Jamie's guardian, Clark would have to find a way to protect them.

She called to Jamie. "Did you get all your toys ready to go?"

He shook his head slowly. "Not my back-hoe. I lost it the day the rocks came down." He pointed to the top of the cliff. "It's up there in my mine. My mom and dad got it for me for Christmas. It's my favorite toy."

An indelible memory crept back into her mind: a picture of a small rag doll with button eyes. Kids should get to keep their favorite toy. "Shall we go get it?"

She followed breathlessly as Jamie scampered like a mountain goat up the steep cliff to the play area he called his mine. At the top Jamie went into the mine while she stood to rest on the wide ledge in front of the cave. Its outer wall, edged with stacked stones, concealed the entrance from sight of anyone standing below, yet commanded a sweeping view. Situated high on the cliff, it seemed safe enough for a child as nimble as Jamie. The entire face of the curved cliff was visible from this ledge: Jim's mine, the wash bench, and the door to the house. From here, Jamie could always have seen where his parents were.

She looked beyond the rock pillar toward the distant mountains. The tawny desert, with blended shades of earth, sand and sage, strewn with boulders and savagely carved into deep arroyos, stretched toward the mountains. She noticed everything around her, even the acrid smell of sage and choking dust. How strange, she thought, that the desert that once had seemed menacing now felt so comforting.

She tried to imagine what ancient eyes would have seen from this watchtower. Her mind conjured images of brown-skinned women carrying water from the spring and cooking over an open fire. She saw old men making stone weapons and scrapers for cleaning the animal hides after the hunt. Children playing on the cliff and mothers warning them to be careful. Groups of women laughing and singing as they wove their baskets and fired their clay pots in this sheltered canyon home.

In those civilizations, she wondered, did the men have all the power? Did those people fall in love? Were they happy?

Twittering birdcalls interrupted her thoughts. She understood why Jim and Sarah enjoyed living in this serene place. Yet a strange feeling clung to her, a sense that she had stumbled onto a forbidden secret, a sense that she was being watched by unseen eyes.

She hurried into Jamie's mine and found Jamie waiting for her. A narrow cave with rough walls, it afforded a sheltered play area in sunshine or shade. Tracks of toy trucks wove around the rocks protruding from the dusty floor. The cave looked shallow, but along a sidewall lay a jumble of stones below a wide vertical crack that opened into blackness. Here the tiny tracks wound between the rocks and disappeared into that jagged opening.

"Did you go back in there?" Darcy asked.

Jamie nodded. "Uh huh. I had this flashlight. My backhoe is still in there."

That dark shaft didn't look like a place Darcy wanted to go into with nothing but a flashlight. "Maybe we should take the kerosene lantern in there," she said. "Wouldn't that be better?"

Without prompting, he scampered down the cliff to bring the lantern. "Not the reading lamp," she called after him from the ledge. "Bring the one on the kitchen table. And the matches." She had not used that lantern, but it had a handle and would be easier to carry.

Darcy sat on the ledge, hugging her knees and reflecting on the past few days. Her wilderness experience would provide memories enough to last all winter. No—a lifetime. The pictures she had taken of the artifacts would keep her entertained. She would do her own research on Anasazi artifacts. The subject had interested her for a long time, but Cal....

An unexpected wave of dizziness swept over her. As she stood to clear her head, a covey of quail burst from the brush on the mesa. A coyote yipped.

"Here it is." Jamie, puffing from his down-and-back trip, handed her the lantern that had provided light for the cave-house. It was an old-style lantern with a wobbly glass chimney inside. When lit, its mantles gave off a bright light. She let Jamie lead the way into the dark recesses of the cave, following the tiny wheel tracks around the exposed rocks. Holding the lantern high, she could see the sides of the narrow cavern. She smiled at the boy's footprints and knee prints in the dirt floor, ignoring the waves of nausea that engulfed her with the feeling of descending on a fast elevator.

The passageway turned sharply to the right; then, just beyond a pile of rocks, it zigzagged deep through an opening into a high chamber. Darcy grew wary. "Are you sure you know where your back-hoe is?"

"Uh huh." Jamie's blue eyes smiled from his grimy face. "It's over there."

The cavern was wide and high, its floor strewn with sharp rocks. Its ceiling was not sheathed with canvas as the house and cellar were, and she felt the dust filter down into her hair. Turning to look where Jamie pointed, she lifted the lantern. The dark shadows grew smaller, revealing a depression in the floor, an oval, slab-lined pit. Inside the pit lay a pile of litter, with curved sticks and pieces of coarse rope.

"Did you bring this rope in here?"

"No, it was already here. I didn't ever come in here till the day the rocks came down. That's the day I brought my back-hoe in here."

Her mind did a quick flashback to the pile of stones that lay in front of the opening to this chamber. She felt a chill slither up her spine.

"Those rocks back there—did they come down that day, too?"

"I guess so. But they weren't there when I was in here. "They must've fell down after I was outside." He paused, then spoke with a tremor in his voice. "That's when I saw the rocks fall down on Mom and Dad. They were comin' home to supper."

She scanned the chamber. How could this little kid come in here with nothing but a flashlight? She wasn't that brave. Her gaze now fell on a yellow object lying in the depression, near the edge. It was Jamie's backhoe, surrounded by footprints in the soft dirt. They just had to grab it and get out of there.

As she set the lantern down and stretched to reach the backhoe, something in the toy's scoop caught her eye. It looked like a stone, or maybe a small toy. Always curious, she picked at the embedded dirt, then turned the object over in her hand. She caught her breath and felt her face go pale with a horrified recognition: This was no stone or carved fetish. *In her hand lay a bone. A human finger bone!* Not daring to move, she looked sideways at the pile of litter in the shallow pit. Those smooth curved objects—were they sticks or ribs? Peering closely, she could make out the shape of long bones of the arms and legs and a flat pelvis. Then she saw, half-buried under a pile of faded feathers, the unmistakable shape of a skull.

Slowly her understanding began to take shape. They were standing in an ancient burial site. Jamie must have been mining human bones from a sacred chamber on the day of the rockslide. Though she didn't consider herself a superstitious person, Darcy's memory rushed full throttle with scenes from old books and movies. In those scenes, the spirits and witches so prominent in Native American lore cursed the desecraters of ancient graves.

She had to keep her voice calm as she gently and delicately placed the finger bone in the pit. "Jamie, I don't think we should stay in here. This is somebody's private place."

"What does private mean?" he asked.

"Private places are special places where people don't want other people to go."

As she turned to hand him the toy a new wave of dizziness overwhelmed her. A clump of dirt thumped to the floor, followed by a string of dust that sifted against her face. Fighting to keep her balance, she staggered and fell. A scream escaped her throat as the lantern flew from her grip and landed against a rock, stretching the shadows into looming obstacles.

Darcy scrambled on her knees, tumbling over the rocks and straining to reach the lantern. She had to grab it before.... Her hand grasped its handle. In the same instant, the glass chimney shattered against the fragile mantles. The light flared for a mini-second and vanished. A curtain of deep velvet blackness shrouded the chamber.

This wasn't the first time sudden darkness had paralyzed Darcy into immobility. Strangely, the night of that awful faculty party flashed into her memory. Yet the cause of her torment then wasn't the darkness itself; it was her humiliation when the spotlights sought her out. There she stood in that horrid sequined gown and "Marie Antoinette" hairstyle that Cal had demanded she wear. And there stood the other faculty wives wearing tasteful dinner dresses and condescending smiles.

She couldn't think about that now. She dared not panic and lose control. No time to worry over her skinned wrists and ankles; no time to feel guilty for bringing the boy here when nobody knew where they were. She had to keep her wits about her, had to protect Jamie from any more fright.

Darcy knew they were in the center of the chamber with sharp rocks blocking their pathway to the outside. But she was disoriented. Which direction was the passageway? Where was that burial pit? She didn't want to fall into that. She had to get her bearings. If she could just touch the wall, maybe she could feel her way to the opening. Most of all, she had to keep calm for Jamie's sake.

"Jamie, where are you?" She struggled to steady her voice. "Give me your hand."

A weak, tiny voice seemed to come from miles away. "Darcy, I don't like the dark. My stomach feels funny. And somethin' keeps ticklin' my face."

She had to think of a positive response, anything to keep the fear down. "I think we both have the flu. There's some flu medicine we can take when we get back to the house. And that's just some dust tickling you. Let's hold hands and then we'll find our way to the outside. Just keep talking to me and I'll feel for your hand."

Even as she followed the sound of his voice, she knew she was getting farther from the wall of the chamber. Her panic rose—no light penetrated the chamber, so how could she find the passageway in the dark? It was already nearly noon. What if it got dark outside before they found their way out? *What if they never found it?*

They were inside a mountain, in an unknown vault. Maybe Clark would find their tracks, but he wouldn't be here until later that afternoon. Her knees began to wobble. Her arms trembled. She couldn't breathe, and waves of nausea overwhelmed her. She had to get hold of Jamie's hand, to feel his touch.

A new revelation burst through her confusion. She needed him as much as he needed her. Even more, perhaps.

"Jamie, are you holding your hand out to me?"

"Uh huh. But I can't feel you. Can you make the light come on again?"

"No, but we can feel our way along the wall till we come to that opening to the outside." His voice was closer now. A rush of relief and joy washed over her when his small warm hand found hers. Like a silent benediction, his touch told her she wasn't alone.

Time was immeasurable; they searched through the darkness with no idea if minutes or hours had passed. She finally shrieked with relief as her hand brushed the rough stone.

"Here's the wall! Now you just hang onto my vest. We'll find the way out."

With the boy in tow, she inched along the wall, feeling ahead with her foot, hoping to find an empty place that would be the passageway. She had to keep him talking. She asked questions about backhoes she had never wondered about, and listened to his informative answers—anything to keep their fear in check. Luckily, he was a good conversationalist.

"Darcy?" Jamie's voice had a different ring; it sounded tight and strained. "Is that why the rocks came down? Is it because I got in somebody's private place?"

She knelt to hug him. "No, Jamie. It wasn't your fault. Sometimes things just happen."

She wondered how Sarah would have explained it. *If only someone had explained it to me when Grandmother died, instead of letting me think I should have squeezed my eyes tighter and prayed harder!* Jamie seemed relieved, and that's what mattered right now.

She still hadn't located the opening and her disorientation grew by the minute. This was worse than her mindless wandering in the desert that brought her from Mesquite to Jamie's door. And that wasn't brought about by her navigational skills. Maybe Jamie had the right idea after all. He told God what he needed.

"Darcy, you know what? Maybe we could tell God that we don't know where the door is. We could ask Him to show us. You know, like when I needed to go to Clark's."

Strange. He must have read her mind. Could that be?

"That's a good idea, Jamie. Do you want to ask God to help us get out?" She could probably frame a proper prayer, full of thee's and thou's, if she had plenty of time—but not now, not off the top of her head. Her mouth was so dry her lips seemed stuck to her teeth. Besides, her idea of God's help would have kept them from being trapped here in the first place.

In the darkness, she sensed that Jamie had bowed his head, though he still clung to her vest. "God." His voice was stronger now. "See, we got lost in my mine and our light went out and we don't know how to get out. So, do you think you could show us where the door is? Thank you. Amen."

For a moment Darcy was glad for the darkness that hid the tears on her cheeks. Funny little kid—thought he could talk to God in everyday language!

"While we're waiting, we should keep feeling the wall," she suggested.

Jamie interrupted her, his voice full of hope. "Darcy, you know what? You got a flashlight."

What was he talking about? She didn't have a flashlight. His fear must have been making him hallucinate. Better to keep him talking. "What do you mean? Where do I have a flashlight?"

"On that chain with your keys. I saw it when we were at baby sister's special place."

Her memory flashed like a lightning bolt. Yes, she had a tiny light on her key chain. Hardly ever used it—did she have it with her? Scarcely daring to hope, she felt in the pocket of her vest for her key chain. Her fingers found the keys, then curled around the flat light. Now, if it still worked. *Please, God! Let it work.*

"You're right! Here it is!" She pressed the middle of the soft pouch and a narrow beam lit her hand. The faint glow revealed the boy's expression as well. He looked so relieved, so happy. No, it was more than that. This was the look of love, as if he loved her as much as she loved him.

"Now," she said, "all we have to do is follow our footprints to the passageway."

The glow was too dim to illuminate the chamber. She must preserve the light, just flicker it from time to time. With Jamie holding on, she flashed along, straining her eyes in the dimness, scratching and bruising her elbows until the footprints led them to a dark empty place. When at last they stepped into the narrow vault she let out a yell. A faint light gleamed around the corner. She smiled down at the blue eyes and the grubby arms cradling the beloved toy. Her throat tightened. She couldn't speak, but instead knelt and hugged this warm little kid who had known all along that all they had to do was ask God.

Emerging into daylight, Darcy checked her watch. A brief time in the cave had seemed like a lifetime. "You got us out, Jamie. You and your prayers." More than anything right now, Darcy wished she had his kind of faith.

They stood on the ledge and pulled the fresh air into their lungs. For a moment they lingered, letting their gaze flow over the desert. Then, hand-in-hand, they walked down the cliff.

Back in the cave-house, Darcy found the flu medicine. "Let's drink this. It'll settle our stomachs," she said. She poured the thick concoction into two small glasses, then drank hers in one long gulp. Jamie took longer.

"We'll feel better if we walk around on the flat place," she said. "I saw some birds fly up out there. We'll carry the last of the sacks along."

Clark wouldn't be here for hours, but she was ready to leave this place right now. She looked out the door of the cave, her gaze scanning the silent cliff. A general uneasiness lay on her mind. Not a superstition exactly; maybe a primal signal for caution. She resisted that idea. On the other hand, those ancient folks must have had *some* reason to believe in ghosts and evil spirits.

Jamie finally finished his medicine and was ready to go. Once again his chatter lifted her spirits. Half listening to his voice behind her, she climbed the mesa and paused at the top to catch her breath. The boy was only halfway up the mesa when she caught sight of two deer bolting from the brush. Just as she called out at him to look, a flock of birds burst from the other side of the mesa. *So much wildlife today,* she thought. *And the air is so dusty.*

The dizziness and nausea hit again. Turning to look back at Jamie, Darcy felt her gaze drawn to the cliff, where a wave of motion rippled downward. The trees were swaying. Her vision blurred. No! She couldn't let herself faint. It would scare Jamie. Obeying her first impulse, she sat down and lowered her head between her knees. Her mind couldn't make sense of this. What was that rumbling sound? Why were the trees shaking when there was no wind? And all that choking dust. No! It couldn't be! No!

Her brain began quickly to itemize clues as though she were reading a mystery novel: the pebbles rolling down the slope, the trees swaying, the dust sifting down from the ceiling of the cave, the birds blasting off the ground, the deer leaving their daytime cover. Even their nausea. This wasn't the flu. It was an earth tremor! Aftershock! The mountain had been trying to warn her. Against her will, her eyes lifted up to the face of the cliff. High on the stony wall, a dark horizontal crack was forming. *A landslide!* Like the one that killed Jim and Sarah!

"Hurry, Jamie! Hurry!" She didn't realize she was screaming. They had to get down the other side of the mesa and out onto the flat desert. Her eyes were fixed on the sinister line that widened straight above the cave and cellar. She gasped in horror as a thick veneer of dirt loosened from the bedrock, and in the slow-motion style of suspense movies, began to nudge its way down the steep slope. Dust billowed forward as the mountain, like a prehistoric reptile, shed its skin. Rocks tumbled, crashing onto the canyon floor. Gnarled oaks cracked and splintered as they fell, lifting their tangled roots to the sky. Why couldn't she move faster? Her feet were rooted to the soft dirt, like in a bad dream.

She had to grasp Jamie's hand. She looked behind her. "Jamie! Where are you?" she screamed. He had been right behind her. She screamed again before she saw him running toward the cave-house. Toward the landslide!

Before she could scream again, he turned and shouted something back at her. She understood only three words. *"... get God out!"*

Stumbling and falling over the roots and rocks, Darcy skidded down the steep bank of the mesa. What was Jamie thinking? He must not have heard her yelling. He had reached the cave-house and dashed inside, leaving the door ajar. Didn't he know the dirt threatened to cover it?

As she started up the foot of the cliff toward the cave, a ringing crack, sharp and clear as a rifle shot, stopped her. High on the cliff, a gray boulder snapped loose and tumbled, gaining speed as it fell directly toward the cave. Panic over-shadowed her reason. Blind to the danger, she rushed toward Jamie's door as the falling boulder slammed against the cellar's roof and careened over her head. The canyon roared like an enraged animal as the boulder struck its floor. The mountain's voice, that evil grating of stone against stone, assaulted her senses. Daylight failed as billows of gritty dust cloaked the sun.

Screaming through a raw throat, she clamored over the loose rock. Though not loud enough for Jamie to hear, she yelled as she looked at the menacing mass inching down the slope. "Jamie!" she screamed again and again, until at last she reached the open door. Horrified blue eyes looked out at her as the boy crammed something under his shirt.

"Jamie, hurry!" She reached toward the doorway only a moment before a heavy clump of dirt knocked her off-balance and sent her sprawling down the slope. Springing to her feet, she saw the horror of the scene. The landslide had completely covered the door, and was still sliding. A layer of unstoppable earth nudged and sifted its way down the mountain, entombing a terrified child in blackness.

Darcy didn't feel herself rise from the debris. Like a dreamwalker, she charged the force of the mountain. She didn't feel the skin of her hands shred away as she clawed through the mass of stony earth. She didn't hear herself screaming. She didn't feel the grit in her throat or the tears that turned her face to mud. No sense of passing time, as though her spirit had stepped aside and now watched her body's desperate struggle. She had only one thought. A child she had known long enough to love was trapped inside a mountain and she would get him out or die right there at his side.

Rocks thudded around her as she knelt in front of the rubble where the door should be. She had to get to him. She needed a shovel, but Jim's tools were buried inside the cellar. Was there anything she could use to move the dirt away? She looked at the sky. Her voice choked. "Please, God, show me what to do!"

Something overhead caught her eye. The stovepipe! No, it was that thing Jim had wired to the top of the pipe. The old rusty hubcap now barely protruded above the debris. In desperation she scrambled up the dirt pile until her hand connected to the metal. Powered by adrenaline, she ripped it from its moorings with one yank. She could dig better now, but the dirt sifted in almost faster than she could move it out. She dared not stop her rhythm of digging to call for help. Besides, there was nobody to help her. Nobody but God. *God!* This was no time to bow her head or try any fancy language. She could only dig and scream, *"GOD, YOU'VE GOT TO GET JAMIE OUT! HE BELIEVES IN YOU!"*

Almost mockingly, the earth shuddered. The landslide loosened and shifted like the hide of a wet retriever. Dirt and rock moved in as fast as Darcy plowed against it. Fueled by white-hot anger at the mountain for turning on an innocent child, she refused to stop digging. No power on earth could force her to abandon Jamie, even if she could only claw and scream to let him know she was here.

Every cell of her being focused on that spot of earth. She didn't pause to wonder why God had not stopped the earth from moving. Her ears no longer heard the din of rocks bouncing from high up the cliff. They didn't pick up the familiar sound, that hollow chopping sound of rotor blades. She didn't look up as, directly overhead, a blue helicopter twirled in a circle above the rolling dust. With no sense of the passing time, she scraped and plunged the hubcap into the devilish earth. She neither heard the deep voice screaming alongside nor felt Clark's hands shoving her back as he attacked the rubble with a shovel from the chopper. With no thought of personal danger, Darcy threw herself at the opening that appeared behind the dirt pile and crawled on her stomach into the cave.

"Jamie." Her voice failed in the choking dust as she pulled the terrified child to her. Her first instinct was to sit and hold him, but Clark's strength yanked her legs out of the cave. She and Jamie clung together and skidded on their stomachs free of the doorway. Strong arms pushed them away from the sliding earth and shoved them down the canyon. Dumbly, she scrambled in the direction Clark pointed—not toward the mesa where she would have gone, but out the end of the canyon under the thicket Jamie had pointed out to Clark only yesterday.

CHAPTER 8

They didn't stop running. Clark wouldn't let them, until they reached the landing place. When at last they sprawled, coughing and gagging on the ground, Darcy couldn't tell if she was sobbing or gasping for air.

It didn't matter. She had to get her mind back in focus, had to check Jamie for injuries; but she could scarcely remember how to do that. He was alert and his pupils were equal. He was scratched and scraped just as she was, but had no broken bones. Undoubtedly he would be covered with bruises before long. Completely exhausted, she curled her body around his on stony ground and held him close until their trembling stopped.

Clark climbed the mesa for the remaining boxes Darcy had left there, then handed them each a can of cold root beer from the chopper. After a soothing swallow, she turned to Jamie.

"Why did you go back to the cave? Didn't you see the dirt falling down?"

His blue eyes widened. "I had to get him. We forgot to get him out."

Darcy tried to respond. "Who? I got Cougey out. Who did we forget?"

"God." Jamie reached under his filthy tee shirt and pulled out a rumpled paper.

Thunderstruck, Darcy could think of nothing else to say. Both her hands and Clark's hands were bleeding. Her fingers, nails broken off past the quick, throbbed with pain. They had barely escaped being buried alive—all because he had to save a piece of paper.

She took the crumpled paper from his hand. "Okay, let's have a look at God." From far back in her memory came a description of God: the phrase "high and lifted up" and something... something about a temple. If this were God, as Jamie said, it would be a heavenly scene. Maybe a throne surrounded by angels.

Clark sat down beside her as she smoothed the thin paper. Together they stared. She was glad he was there, but at the same time wished he weren't. She wanted to laugh and cry at the same time. No—she didn't dare laugh. She might become hysterical. She couldn't embarrass Jamie. He had risked his life to rescue this thing in her hand, this stupid magazine picture of a red hen and her chicks.

A wave of remorse and guilt swept through her. She had deliberately left that picture in the cave. Jamie's picture of God. What right did she have to do that?

While she tried to think of an appropriate comment, Clark stood and began loading the boxes into the helicopter. Her mind, still in a state of sensory overload, had not questioned why he was there so early. But Jamie did.

"Clark, we're sure glad you came now instead of waitin' till supper time."

As they hobbled to the chopper, Clark answered the question her eyes were signaling. "Henry Chadwell's in the hospital," he whispered. "Had a heart attack yesterday in St. George. One of his boys left me a message. Said Henry is askin' to see me. And..." Here Clark's voice changed from softness to something that sounded like an accusation. "He wants me to bring Jamie." His eyes bored into hers.

"What?" Darcy's breath escaped with force. "Jamie? But how did he know?" She felt herself turn cold. *"The ball field!* Mr. Chadwell saw him there. Is that what brought on his heart attack?" She felt a deep surge of guilt. How many more mistakes could she make?

"Not likely. Henry's had a heart problem for years. If seein' Jamie had shocked him that bad, this probably would've happened on the spot."

Relieved, Darcy nodded. At least Clark didn't blame her.

He had Jamie buckled in his seat before Darcy's mind cleared. Like a lead weight, her body eased into the front passenger seat. As the craft lifted, she looked back at the cliff. Through a billow of dust she saw the mass of dirt that buried the cave and the mine. She sank low in the seat and avoided Clark's eyes. Neither of them noticed the little nose pressed against the window, or the grubby little hand that waved good-bye to a china cup, a porcelain horse and a pewter doll now buried in the settling dust.

"We'll stop at my place and get cleaned up," Clark shouted over the noise of the engine. "While we're in town, you two better get checked over for injuries."

Minutes later, they touched down behind the hangar on his ranch.

Darcy closed her eyes so Clark wouldn't see her fear. She didn't want to go to another hospital. She just wanted to get away from here. Clark didn't need her to be there.

But Jamie did. She slumped in the seat. So far, nothing about her life had been under her control since she left Vegas. Independence wasn't working as well as she had dreamed.

Jamie clutched his magazine picture and chattered all the way as they limped to the apartment. "I didn't like the dark in there. But it wasn't my fault, was it, Darcy?"

"No, Jamie. None of that was your fault."

* * * * *

While she filled the tub for Jamie's bath, Clark helped him undress, checking him over for deep cuts. "First, we'll soak the dirt off, then I'll put some salve on these scratched places. After that, we'll ask the doctor to look you over." Darcy was glad for his soothing voice. Even if he was angry at her, she was calmed by his tenderness.

While the boy soaked, they sat again in the kitchen. Clark wouldn't let her apologize. "Not your fault. Sorry if I gave that impression, but I was tryin' to tell you somethin' without actually sayin' it. Didn't want Jamie to hear too much."

He went on to explain. "Yes, Henry Chadwell saw Jamie on the ball field and somehow put the facts together. Seems he still carried one of those posters. He never dreamed that bearded man was me. He went to St. George yesterday and was tryin' to get some information when the attack hit him. No way of tellin' if the shock of findin' out about Jamie brought it on, but it wasn't his first attack."

Clark paused to clear his throat again and again. "This mornin' the doctor told his family that the damage to his heart is severe. He can't survive. But he's alert and says he's ready to meet his Maker. Refuses to be transferred to another hospital. No more heart surgery, none of that.

"His oldest son Dan called me on my cell phone and told me about Henry's heart attack. Also about Henry's suspicions about Jamie. I told him the whole story, includin' the rockslide that killed Jim and Sarah. Also about you. Explained why Jim and Sarah had to hide out; why it'd be risky if anyone, myself included, knew their whereabouts. A few minutes later, Henry called me and said he now understands why I kept all this from him."

Clark sat with his head lowered. "Henry forgave me for keepin' my secret. He's quite a man. Wants me to bring Jamie to the hospital. All the family members—the ones there now with Henry, anyway—know the story. The rest are on their way there. Wants to say good-bye to *all* his family. Includin' Jamie."

Darcy's mind stopped registering at the moment she heard, "Wants to say good-bye...." Cal hadn't said good-bye. Neither had Grandmother, who denied her impending death. She told Darcy that everything was fine, resisting the truth through her last breath and leaving Darcy to face reality alone.

Darcy sat quietly until Clark looked at her. "Do you want me to tell Jamie about his grandfather?" she asked. "Or do you think you should?"

"I... I'll tell him, but he'll need you to help him know what to say to Henry. You go ahead with your bath while I tell him. Then you'll have some time with him while I get cleaned up."

Jamie left the bathroom wrapped in a towel. While the tub filled again, she pulled her slim jeans over her feet and unfastened her bra hooks. Her hands throbbed with pain. Unable to manage ordinary clothes, she would have to wear her loose fitting jumper and pullover bra. Braiding her hair was out of the question.

As she soaked in the soothing bath, she heard Clark's deep voice. She leaned back and listened to the boy's questions and the gentle answers. Mud seeped from the corners of her eyes. *I couldn't have said it better. Nobody could.* She finished her bath, combed her hair straight and hurried to the kitchen, where lunch was waiting.

Between bites, Clark said. "I just phoned Dan. We'll drive my truck to St. George. The chopper's most likely clogged with dirt, and I shouldn't fly it with these hands, anyway. We'll bring some supplies back. They'll need extra groceries."

Darcy nodded, amazed at this man's capacity to look out for other people. He stared at her straight hair. "Lillian wore her hair that way." As he turned quickly from the kitchen for his turn in the tub, she looked again at the smiling photo on the shelf. And looked again.

She marveled at Jamie's calm reaction. "Clark says I have a grandfather. He's that man with white whiskers I saw at the baseball field." Jamie's only question came later as they drove along the bumpy dirt road. "Should I take my grandfather a present?" As Darcy and Clark cast about in their minds for an idea (maybe the hospital had a gift shop?) the boy answered his own question. "I know what. I'll give him my picture of God." The disheveled magazine picture he had risked his life for lay in his lap.

*   *   *   *   *

Darcy cringed at the thought of going to another hospital. The bland walls and the smell of disinfectant brought back too many memories. To her, hospitals were places of pain and death. But then, babies are born and sick people are healed there, and hospitals conduct needed research. She found it difficult to balance the equation. She only knew that according to her experiences so far, a hospital would always be a symbol of hopelessness.

Dan Chadwell met them at the hospital entrance. Clark introduced them and Darcy liked Dan immediately. A handsome man with a ready smile, he offered his hand, then pulled it back in amazement as he saw their wounds. To explain the wounds, Clark gave him a condensed version of the landslide.

"Dad's sleeping right now." Dan said. "You should go to the clinic next door and get those hands fixed up." He touched Jamie's shoulder. "Jamie, I'm your Uncle Dan."

Darcy handed him the sketchbook she had brought from the helicopter. "I think the family might like to see these drawings Jim and Sarah made. And Jamie has a special gift for his grandfather."

After the clinic nurse treated their hands and sutured a deep gash on Darcy's knee, she asked if anyone in the family could change their dressings daily. "Rebekah's a nurse," Clark said. "She takes care of everyone." They received pain medication and a young nurse-aide braided Darcy's hair. Feeling much better, she entered the hospital waiting room with Clark and Jamie.

Jamie's family welcomed him with wide smiles. "Hi Chad!" said one of the boys from the ball field. Though the group spoke in hushed tones, this was not the somber room Darcy had expected. Each person had said a private good-bye. And they honestly expected to see him in Heaven someday. It was so different from Cal's deathbed.

Dan introduced them to Esther and her husband, the couple who had flown in from Denver. "This is Jamie, Sarah and Jim's son. And Clark Tygard, Dad's friend who protected them. And this is Darcy Callahan, who saved Jamie's life." Darcy detected none of the undertones of blame she had anticipated.

Someone served cookies and punch. The soft voices, combined with the effect of mild pain medication, were comforting. Jamie's head rested in Darcy's lap while they waited for his grandfather to awake.

One by one, Sarah's sisters and brothers sat beside them for a brief visit, each one expressing thanks to her and Clark for bringing Jamie to them. Along with Dan were four other men: Dave, Joe, Jake and Sam. Darcy was confused. Bible names? *Oh, sure! Daniel, David, Joseph, Jacob and Samuel.* The women were Rebekah, Rachel, Esther, and the twins, Ruth and Naomi. "And this is our little sister, Debbie. We all have Old Testament names," Dan explained.

Debbie? A Bible name? For a moment Darcy searched her memory of Bible characters, hoping the question wasn't written on her face. Then she remembered: *Of course! Deborah!*

They thumbed through the sketchbook, feeling, one of them said, as if Sarah had returned to them; and they thanked Darcy for bringing it to them. They were treating Darcy like a heroine, but she didn't feel the least bit heroic. She was only a survivor. Jamie was the one who knew the way to Clark's house, and Clark had rescued them both from the landslide. She glanced toward Clark.

"Let them say it," he whispered. "It's important to them." More than the strength of his voice, his sensitivity prompted her to respond with a grace that Grandmother would have admired.

Taking stock of the women's clothes, Darcy's old perceptions took a complete turn. From Clark's description she had visualized the Chadwell men as being like her friend Lydia's father; men who, in the name of religion, require their women to dress like pioneers but allow themselves to dress like other businessmen. Though these women dressed modestly, Rebekah's plain style contrasted sharply with Esther's. A prominent architect from Denver, Esther seemed to exude a sense of confidence without being brassy. In her silk shirt and mid-calf skirt, she balanced fashion with modesty. Grandmother would have approved. Cal would have sneered.

"Here's Mother now." Dan said. Every eye turned as the white-haired lady entered the room. When Clark introduced her to Eunice Chadwell, Darcy immediately recognized her as the lady with the cinnamon rolls at the tearoom. It was easy to see where Jamie got his bottle blue eyes. Her shiny white hair lay in loose waves over her ears, ending in a loose bun on her neck. Soft wrinkles formed a network on her face. Not the down-turned worry lines or frown lines Darcy had always associated with wrinkles, but up-turned lines near her eyes and mouth.

Smile lines, Darcy said to herself. *But how can her face keep smiling, when her heart is breaking? This family seems so emotionally sturdy.*

"Dad's awake and wants to meet his new grandson." Eunice told the group. "And Clark, he would like to speak to you, too, and meet your friend who brought Jamie to us."

Panic grabbed at Darcy's throat. She was so out-of-place here. These people were religious. They knew the right things to say, but she couldn't pray as well as a six-year-old. She wanted to protest, to get out of there. She could claim it was too soon after her husband's death. But Clark's hand was on her elbow. Like an obedient zombie, she approached the room where "Moses" lay dying.

The moment they entered the room her panic dissolved. In his loose hospital gown, this white-bearded man truly did look like Moses. His plastic oxygen tube couldn't hide his smile. He extended his hand to Clark and spoke in a weak voice. "Good to see you, my friend."

He turned to Darcy as Clark introduced her. "Mrs. Callahan, I want to thank you for bringing our grandson to us." He then reached toward the wide-eyed boy. "Hello, Jamie. I saw you at the ball field. I didn't know you were my grandson, but I thought you might be. You sure look like a Chadwell. I'm your grandfather."

Jamie moved close to the bed. "I brought you a present. It's a picture of God."

Darcy's shoulders tightened as Mr. Chadwell's pale hand took the crumpled picture and smoothed it on the bedspread. What would he think when he saw that ridiculous chicken? Was it her imagination, or did the wavy green line on the heart monitor increase in tempo as he studied the picture?

"Oh, yes indeed, Jamie," he said. "This is God all right." Chuckling, he reached out to pat his grandson's head. "Yes, son, this is about the finest picture of God I've ever seen."

Darcy did not miss the look of joy that passed between the man and his wife.

Joy! Darcy's breath eased out as a smile lit the boy's face. This must be the nicest grandfather a child could have.

Without hesitation, and against Darcy's better judgment, Jamie climbed onto the bed with the sketches. "See, this is my mom and me in the rockin' chair, and this is my dad and me doin' piggyback, and this is when we sang on Sunday."

Now his face lit up as it always did when he had a good idea. "I know what! Clark said you're goin' to Heaven." Darcy felt her heart turn instantly to ice, then just as quickly melt as his words tumbled out. "Do you think you can see my Mom and Dad? And Baby Sister? And can you tell them I'm okay, and Darcy took me to Clark's house and they're takin' good care of me? Can you tell them that?"

Darcy didn't hear a reply. Unnerved, she swayed on her feet. Her mind was in another hospital room, standing beside her dying husband. How different it was. Not only did this family say their good-byes; they also knew what to say. If Cal had wakened from his coma, what would she have said? Certainly nothing about going to Heaven. Cal wouldn't listen to that nonsense. Nothing about dying. Some phony denial, some pretense. Anything but the truth—like everything else in their marriage.

Darcy couldn't have talked about Heaven anyway. In her youthful rebellion, comparing Grandmother's religion with Aunt Belle's, she had abandoned it all. Not that she hated God or denied He existed. It was more as if her soul had shrugged and turned aside.

She had to get out of that room or she'd faint. Before she could look at Clark, his hand gripped her elbow. Softly he said his final farewell to his good friend and guided her from the room. Someone brought her a cup of tea and asked about her hands. "A recent widow," said a soft voice in the background.

These people were so kind, and so strong. From all appearances, she was the only person here who felt the impact of Henry Chadwell's passing. She wanted to run as far from this room as she could, but they had to wait for Jamie. Time felt endless, something like the time she and Jamie had spent while they were lost in the dark cave. Her hand shook too much to hold her cup. She took another pain pill and felt like a fool.

Determined not to embarrass Clark any further, she sat back and listened as the others reminisced about their father. A picture of Henry Chadwell emerged from their stories.

Then there was the day Dad resigned," Dan was saying. "He was quite stern in our early years. But one day he attended a management seminar at a dairyman's conference, and the next Sunday he told us he was resigning some of his jobs. He said the seminar taught him that supervisors who micromanage don't allow their employees to develop their own business skills.

"He realized the same thing was true with families. He wasn't giving us a chance to make the right decisions; he'd been doing it *for* us. As he put it, he had to 'get his faith on straight.' So he tendered his resignation from what he called his 'self-appointed position as our wardrobe chairman, activity chairman, and conscience.' "

"Yeah," Jake said, "Dad never got over the fact that he found spiritual wisdom in a business meeting. He said he used to speak about 'old fashioned virtues' as though they were one word." Soft laughter filled the room. Darcy cringed. Didn't these people know there are times when laughter is out-of-place? Behind her forced smile, she felt herself strangling.

Esther spoke up. "The change nearly scared us to death till each of us figured out who we are, and learned to make our own decisions."

"Yeah!" Debbie added, "It sure felt good, especially the day I got my long hair cut and had it set in a bouffant style!"

Who they are? Did they have the same struggles as I did with Cal? Does she mean that the way they dress is now their choice? Darcy noticed that Rebekah's denim jumper was identical to her own. *Look, Cal. I'm dressed like Moses' daughter.* There must be some irony here.

At last, Jamie's grandmother brought the boy out and they hurried off to the discount store. Darcy barely noticed the pair of boys' dark slacks, the white shirt and a clip-on tie Clark tossed into his shopping cart. She wondered what Clark would wear to the funeral. Probably one of those slim suits ranchers wear, the kind with arrowheads at the corners of the pockets. She watched him load his cart with groceries, including hams and turkeys, for the Chadwells.

As they drove south from St. George, Darcy admired the yucca and cactus blossoms tucked among the brush. "The desert has it's own kind of beauty," she said. This ruggedness fascinated her as cliffs of pale, chalky green competed with the terra-cotta hills nearer the town. Nearing the state line, where the pavement gave way to a dirt road, she saw ahead the large BLM sign that proclaimed, "The Arizona Strip, Where the West Stays Wild." She asked Clark to stop so she could read it. It admonished travelers to be adequately prepared in case they became lost or stranded, and described what to do to prevent that.

"When I came by here, I was too much in a hurry to stop and read this," she confessed. "I suppose I thought it was just a bunch of hype advertising the Strip. Looks like I broke every rule in the book—I didn't stay on a designated road, didn't have a supply of food or water, or extra fuel or a decent map. And I didn't tell anyone where I was going for certain. What would I have done if Jamie hadn't found me?"

Clark's only response was a lingering sidewise look, his head moving from side to side.

* * * * *

The sky had turned blood red when they reached Clark's place. Clark carried the sleeping boy to his own bed. Exhausted, he and Darcy dozed on living room chairs until a sound awakened them.

Clark moved to the window as a string of car lights announced the family's return. "Henry's gone," he said, and turned away.

A short time later he answered a rap on the door. Ruth and Naomi came in with a hot dinner and asked Darcy how she felt. "You and Clark can't cook with your bandages on," Ruth said, "so we'll bring meals over and take care of the dishes. And Mrs. Callahan, Rebekah will be glad to braid your hair for you when she comes to change your dressings."

"Thank you so much. And please call me Darcy." The lump in her throat had barely eased, and now here it was again. Despite their loss, this family was concerned about Clark and about her, a woman they had just met. How much more they must have cared about Jamie. Accustomed to doing for herself, she wanted to refuse their help. Then, remembering Clark's admonition, she accepted the offer gracefully.

The "quick meal" was welcome. While they ate their supper, she told Clark about the artifacts in the cellar.

His forehead puckered. "Artifacts?" He pointed to the squat black and white pot on the hutch. "Like this one? Used to find some of these around here when I was young. My dad found some big ones when he plowed a garden spot, and of course lots of 'em showed up when the base was built. Nobody paid 'em much attention in those days. I never unpacked 'em since I moved here. Still, one turns up sometimes when we dig foundations or post holes."

Darcy continued: "Mr. Willis thought they might be from the Anasazi period. I have his journal in the box you got from the mesa. I've forgotten most of what I learned about artifacts, but I have some books in my truck."

Noticing that his guarded expression seemed to melt, she went on to explain Harley Willis's educated guesses about his discoveries. It felt so good to visit with someone like Clark, who had an interest outside of himself. She could have sat in his kitchen all night; her only dread was telling about her and Jamie's ordeal in the darkness of the burial chamber. She wanted this man's respect, but he needed to know what the boy had been through. She'd better tell him before Jamie did. Taking a deep breath, she plunged in, dreading his reaction. Clark sat slacked-jawed as her tale unfolded.

"Lady, you must have nine lives like a cat," was his only comment. No lecture, no anger.

He changed the subject. "I've notified the coroner about Jim and Sarah, and he's arranged for a crew to go in tomorrow. Better call him right now about this latest slide. The site might be too unstable."

Darcy overheard his conversation with the coroner. The recovery project would go as scheduled. She stiffened, thinking of the danger to the crew—and to Clark. Jamie needed Clark, she quickly reminded herself.

Holding the coffeepot in both hands, he refilled their cups. "I'd like for you to stay with Jamie while I'm out there."

Darcy's jaw tightened. He paused, and when she didn't respond he continued. Once again, he had accurately read her mind: "Lady, you can't even consider drivin' all the way to Elko till those bandages come off your hands. It's a hard two-day drive, at best."

He leaned back in his chair. "Besides, I think it'd be good for Jamie if you're here till after the funeral. Dan says Henry wanted them to include memorial services for Jim and Sarah and the baby along with his, so Jamie wouldn't have to go through another funeral later on. And after their bodies are identified, they'll be buried beside him."

Darcy's head quarreled with her heart. Why borrow other folk's problems? What about her own life? Her job? Would she ever play piano again, or would her hands be too scarred? She was tempted to stay, for Jamie's sake. *But Henry Chadwell's funeral?* She didn't want to listen to all that depressing religious music and those long-winded prayers. Maybe she could beg off on the pretext that she was still mourning the loss of her own husband.

One look at Clark's face told her that wouldn't work. He needed her. And Jamie needed her to be there. Unsure if she felt reluctant or relieved, she nodded in agreement. "I suppose I could call the school tomorrow morning and rearrange the appointment."

As if to establish the decision in her mind, Jamie woke up and came in sobbing. "Darcy, I didn't like that dark place." He leaned against her. "Is it dark where my mom and dad are?"

Darcy tried to think of an appropriate answer. "No, Sweetie. Heaven is filled with light." She wished she could quote scripture the way her friend, Carol, could. It seemed to help people in hard times. Other people, anyway.

Her answer appeared to satisfy him. After he ate his supper and was ready for bed, she tried to sing a lullaby her school choir had sung. "Sleep, my child, and peace attend thee, all through the night." She wasn't comfortable singing without accompaniment. Minutes later another voice joined hers, as Clark began humming along. He then started to pick up the words. She changed to harmonizing notes and liked the way their voices blended. To her, no choir had ever sounded better.

Jamie grinned and looked up at Clark. "You know the one about the buckaroo? My dad sang it to me."

"Yeah. My mom used to sing that one to me." Clark poked around in his mind and finally found some words. "Go to sleep, my little buckaroo." He sang several verses, each one interspersed with phrases of "da da da-da da-sumpin'-sumpin'— my little buckaroo."

Darcy swallowed hard. This was no lilting Irish tenor like Cal's; no perfect pitch, and certainly not a voice for the concert hall. Yet, from that narrow chest, from beneath that protruding Adam's apple came a soothing tone—a tad off-key, perhaps, but a sound gentle enough to quiet a child's fear. And totally unselfconscious. She had never known anyone so completely at home in his own skin. Nothing was missing.

For a moment she felt transported back to her childhood. Not that anyone had ever sung a lullaby to her. No; according to Grandmother, little ladies put themselves to bed exactly on time. Not that anyone ever laughed or cried, or expressed their true feelings. No; evening in that house followed proper forms of etiquette. She remembered the manners Grandmother taught around the big dining room table, so beautifully set with fine sterling silver, English china and Irish crystal. She thought again of Ramon, the caretaker with the only warm heart, the only sense of fun she knew in those days. It all came back: the days when she and Ramon ate lunch in the kitchen, and the day he whittled her a wooden bird. She hid that treasure under her pillow, because Grandmother disapproved of makeshift toys. She remembered the two blissful days she stayed with Ramon and Rosa in their little house. This house—Clark's house—had that same glow of love she had felt there.

While Clark went downstairs to the store, Darcy sang Jamie to sleep. Soon Clark returned and plugged a night light beside Jamie's bed. "Wonder what the child psychologists would say about this," he said, arching his left eyebrow.

"Well..." she replied, "I doubt that a manual has ever been written for a six-year old who saw his parents killed, stayed alone in a cave for eight days, got stuck in a burial chamber with a demented woman, and then got buried in a landslide."

His eyes twinkled. "Guess we won't trouble ourselves over it, then."

* * * * *

Late the following day Clark returned from the mine. Again his face was gray and grim. His mouth clenched into a straight line when he conveyed the news to Dan. The recovery had been successful. The coroner was certain that death had been instantaneous and thought the bodies could be identified quickly through dental records. After Rebekah changed the dressings on his hands and she and Dan left, Clark sank into his chair. A heavy silence filled the room—not the withdrawn sulk of anger that Darcy knew so well from her life with Cal, but a silence of bone-deep weariness, a companionable silence to be respected and shared.

"Too much like Desert Storm?" Her question was soft enough to be ignored if need be.

He nodded. Moments passed before he answered. "Exactly. Jim and I went through so much together, flyin' troops in and body bags out. Never expected to bring *him* out that way."

Then, as though his memory bank had been unlocked, he talked through the late evening. With a faraway gaze—that thousand-yard stare she had heard of—came anguished words that flushed his soul of memories held back too long.

Later, as she lay sleepless, Darcy's thoughts wandered. She thought of the Chadwell family, such considerate and happy people. Of how lonely Clark must have been before they moved here. She thought of Clark's loyalty to Jim, how it had changed his life. How his life would have been diminished without Henry Chadwell's forgiveness. Thoughts of Clark who loved Jamie, and who needed a wife. Of Rebekah, so capable and attentive—and single. The thought struck her: If Clark married Rebekah, the Chadwells wouldn't take Jamie from him. A happy outcome? Maybe, but something inside her rebelled against the thought.

CHAPTER 9

"Darcy, what's a funeral like?" Jamie tugged at the neck of his new white shirt. His bruises were fading from purple to a greenish tinge.

Her bandaged hands struggled to clip a tie to the boy's collar. Every muscle in her body ached. "It's a time when people play music and sing and read the Bible and tell stories."

"Like my mom and dad did in our house?"

"Something like that, except it's a good-bye time." *And not a happy time,* she started to say, but caught herself. She tucked a handkerchief in his pocket. "All we have to do is listen."

She checked her reflection in the mirror, hoping she was dressed appropriately. No black suit today; she still couldn't manage buttons and zippers. She hoped the short sleeves on her loose-fitting beige linen wouldn't offend the Chadwells, who kept their arms covered.

She would be glad when this day ended. Her tongue had developed a permanent cramp from holding her emotions in check. With luck, the extra dose of medication would keep everything under control.

When Clark stepped out of his bedroom in a gray pinstripe suit, Darcy's mouth dropped open in surprise. His hair was combed back, no longer falling loosely over his forehead. His hands, nearly healed, were no longer bandaged.

"Gracious! You look sharp!"

He grinned. "Mother always said I'd clean up just fine someday."

They drove to the church in Clark's truck. Darcy was surprised to see the throng of people who had traveled here to pay their respects to Henry Chadwell.

Against her will, her thoughts flew back to her girlhood, to Grandmother's funeral. Once again she was twelve-year-old Drucilla O'Rourk, listening to the solemn organ music. She rode in the big dark car behind the hearse, wondering how those people on the street could go about their business now that Grandmother was dead. She heard again the mean-spirited whispers. "Stella shouldn't have worked so hard to impress the judge." And, "Belle, it's a shame you'll be burdened with the child." She could hear those voices behind her back—voices that spoke *about* her but never *to* her, as though she were invisible. She couldn't argue or protest, because they weren't talking to her. She despised those ladies. Growing up in fear of being just like them, she had hidden all that loathing inside. It was still there.

Darcy jerked to attention as Jamie's young cousins greeted him with wide smiles. When she walked into the church with Clark, she stopped to look around. This building was nothing but a barn in the process of being converted into a church, but its starkness was striking. White painted walls reflected in the polished floors. No pews yet; the chairs were ordinary plastic deck chairs. At Henry Chadwell's request, the plain gray casket was covered with a simple cross of wildflowers the grandchildren had picked for him.

Darcy studied the room in amazement. No stained glass windows, no ornate altar or velvet carpets. What would Grandmother have said?

The service followed the usual formula of hymns and prayers. One of the hymns had a line, "I once was lost, but now am found."

Jamie smiled at Darcy. "That's like us when we got lost in my mine," he whispered. Her lips smiled back, but her eyes began to fill. She clenched her lips and tried to disengage her thoughts, tried to keep from listening to the words.

One by one, the Chadwells rose to share an anecdote about their father or Sarah.

Esther spoke about Sarah and Jim. "Dad used to say that each person's life leaves tracks the same way an animal leaves tracks at the river's edge. We seldom see the animal, but if we see its tracks, we know what kind of animal was there, and what it was doing. Dad believed that the tracks of a father and mother are often seen in the child. He was thrilled when he met Jamie, because he knew that Sarah had not turned away from the teaching of her childhood. She had brought Jim into it."

That must be one of Mr. Chadwell's parables, Darcy thought. She listened carefully as other people stood to speak of the way Henry's life had affected their own.

Dan didn't speak until the crowd walked to the grave site behind the church. He began by quoting Ecclesiates 3:4: "God's word tells us, 'there is a time to mourn.' You see, grief is not a bad thing, but a good and healing thing." He then quoted 1 Thessalonians 4: 13. " 'But I do not want you to be ignorant, brethren, concerning those who have fallen asleep, lest you sorrow as others who have no hope.' We don't sorrow that way, because we know we'll join Dad someday." He smiled and continued. "Dad was a happy man, filled with hope and joy. Psalms 144:15 says, 'Happy are the people whose God is the Lord!' "

In all her life Darcy had never heard of such a concept. In her mind, religion was repressive—a list of shalt-nots, allowing people no control over their own lives.

Dan continued, "On the evening he died, Dad requested something special to be included in his funeral service. He read the passage in Psalm 91 that speaks of abiding in the presence of God. 'He shall cover you with His feathers, and under His wings you shall take refuge.' Dad wanted us to sing his favorite song together."

Dan's wife, Cindy, joined him and handed him a guitar.

Darcy was aghast. *Sing together? How could these two sing? Weren't their throats tight, too? What was Henry Chadwell expecting from his family?* She squirmed uneasily and tried to hide her reaction.

Dan strummed the guitar and he and Cindy began to sing:

"Under His wings, I am safely abiding;
Though the night deepens and tempests are wild,
Still I can trust Him, I know He will keep me.
He has redeemed me, and I am his child."

Their voices blended beautifully. Darcy could never resist listening to beautiful harmony. She looked around the crowd. Everyone looked so calm, so relaxed. *How could they?*

Feeling Jamie's hand slide into hers, Darcy looked down. His blue eyes were wide open. "That sounds just like my mom and dad singin'. That's our song about the wings."

Her jaw clenched. The song about the wings! In her mind she saw Jamie's picture, that rumpled photo of a red hen with little chickens tucked safely under her wings. *So that's why Sarah told Jamie that God was like that hen. Baby Sister must be one of those chickens. That's what Henry Chadwell meant when he said it was the best picture of God he had ever seen.*

She also saw in her mind that drawing of Jim and Sarah singing on a Sunday evening in the cave. She imagined these voices as those of Sarah and Jim, and felt swamped by another emotion. How she envied that couple whose love and faith were all they needed. Suddenly she felt so... so... left out.

It was time to sing the chorus. Dan nodded to the crowd to join in and their voices rang out together. Darcy was glad she didn't know the words. Her throat wasn't working. She listened to hear if Clark was singing. He was humming along. But someone else was singing, in a child's clear voice. Jamie knew the song! Her mind was in turmoil as she listened to the words:

"Under His wings. Under His wings.
Who from His love can sever?
Under His wings my soul shall abide,
Safely abide forever."

She tried to think about something else, but her mind refused to cooperate.

After that song, Dan delivered his own eulogy to his father and followed it with a short sermon. Now Darcy was able to force her thoughts away from the music. She wanted to slip away, back to Clark's apartment. She couldn't breathe and she could feel her face getting dark. Her chest heaved with sobs that threatened to break loose. She had to keep herself under control. She had to be strong for Jamie. Clark needed her to be strong. She didn't even know the people being memorialized here, yet she was the only one whose emotions were out of control. As a sob escaped her throat, Clark's hand touched her elbow. Her hand pressed against her mouth.

The service ended and the crowd began to mingle. The Chadwells had prepared an enormous lunch for their guests. The smell of baked ham and turkey and gallons of coffee nearly made her sick. Beautiful salads and homemade hot rolls appeared from the families' homes. Jamie was invited to sit with the boys at the children's table.

Darcy wanted to escape, but saw Mrs. Chadwell coming toward her. Darcy stepped back. She couldn't possibly make conversation now, much less eat. Frantically, she looked for Clark. His back was turned as he spoke to Bert and Clara Two Goats.

When Mrs. Chadwell appeared at her side, she could do nothing but nod and force a smile behind her handkerchief. She should be expressing her condolences, but she couldn't speak. If she tried, her tears would come in a flood.

"My dear," Mrs. Chadwell whispered, "You've been through so much. Maybe you'd feel better if you could lie down for a while and join us later."

Darcy nodded, then turned away. She would suffocate if she didn't get away from this place. Her thoughts sped ahead of her. If she hurried back to Clark's apartment, she could toss her things into the truck and be on the road to Elko before Clark and Jamie left the service. No—she couldn't leave without saying good-bye to Jamie. And to Clark, of course. She had to wait for them to get home.

Home. The thought stung her eyes. Clark and Jamie had a home. She didn't have—never did have—a home of her own. Oh, she had shared a home with her grandmother and later with Cal, but neither of those homes had been hers.

Blinded by unshed tears, she stumbled across the grass. Fortunately, Grandmother couldn't see her now. Where was the composure that Grandmother had tried to cultivate in her? Grandmother, the star pupil of Miss Stafford's Academy in England, claimed that Americans wore their hearts on their sleeves. Young Drucilla hadn't understood those words, but she knew by the way Grandmother sniffed that it was "bad taste" to let your emotions be seen. At an early age she had developed a detachment that masked her emptiness. She had shut her feelings away in a silent place in her heart, in a world more real than the one around her. Now those pieces of her past would not be held back. The shell around her soul threatened to crack and expose the rottenness inside.

"Darcy." Clark's hand was once again on her elbow guiding her toward the truck. She couldn't see his face. Her bandaged hands covered her eyes.

"Let it go, Lady. Let it go." He helped her into the truck. She shook her head furiously. "Can't... talk... about it."

"No need to." Sitting beside her in the truck, he leaned close—the way she did when she comforted a distressed student. "Just let yourself think it." He started the truck and gently drove away.

That soft command summoned images from her memory. Strange. She wasn't mourning the Chadwells' loss; it was her own loss. She felt like Jamie's landslide. Her veneer was sloughing off, revealing the concealed bedrock. She found no words to define her feelings, but one thing was clear: This wasn't self-pity for what she had lost, but anger for what she had never had. She had never belonged to a family whose members, like the Chadwells, showed love to one another. She had never known anyone who loved God and felt comfortable talking about Him the way the Chadwells did.

As scenes of her past came into view, scenes she had so carefully filed away, her last shred of composure disappeared like smoke. She didn't know she could cry so loud. As a child, she wasn't allowed to make noise. Tears must be subdued and ladylike. With Cal, tears always invited ridicule. Now, here she was, sniffing and bawling like a cow. And this quiet man sitting quietly at her side no doubt thought she was mourning her beloved husband.

Grandmother's God was stern. He lived behind stained glass and demanded perfection. Until today, Darcy had never heard about Jamie's God, that red hen sheltering those little chicks. It was a new concept, a God who loved His children.

145

Her thoughts tumbled. Love? Loving parents don't go off to Europe and leave their little daughter with Grandmother. And loving husbands don't control everything their wives think and do... and wear. They believe in sharing, and respecting each other's individuality. They admit their mistakes the way Henry Chadwell did when he resigned his role as a controlling father. They talk all night in the kitchen. They sit beside you and hold your elbow while you cry.

Clark guided her up the stairs to the kitchen table. He clanked around at the stove and in no time two mugs of coffee were ready.

Darcy stared into the dark brew, mentally picturing the contrast between the last two funerals she had attended. Henry Chadwell had been laid to rest by his family, who sang of a loving God. The only song at Cal's service was an over-dramatized rendition of *The Impossible Dream*, sung by one of his students. Mr. Chadwell's eulogy portrayed a man who loved his family and his God. Cal's emphasized his quest for excellence. What a sham. Everyone knew his quest was for nothing but fame. Quickly she edited her thoughts. At least Cal hadn't been caught up in the lust for wealth that Grandmother disdained in "people of low breeding." Mystique was what he craved, a distinctive aura to match his physical elegance.

As for God, His name wasn't mentioned at Cal's service. Darcy vaguely recalled Matt's allusion—dictated by Cal—to "the cosmic omniscience that men attribute to a Supreme Being." She supposed this was the kindest way to signify that Cal had outgrown God along with Santa and the Easter bunny. Cal wouldn't bother with religion unless he could be either the Pope or the Archbishop of Canterbury.

Her throat strained to keep her sour thoughts from pouring out in regrettable words. Clark, still in love with his dead wife, would never understand it if those flood-gates opened and she disclosed things she didn't know she had remembered. Things that still haunted her. No point in burdening him.

But her best efforts couldn't erase the list of her own failures that paraded through her mind. One was her failure to fulfill Cal's desire for the most and the best of everything. She couldn't forget his prized collection of European porcelains or his contempt for her interest in folk art. Nor would she forget the way *her* things were 'accidentally' broken. She could still hear his sarcasm: "Those things are too primitive for a house like this."

"But my roots are in Appalachia," she had tried to explain. "I've always loved folk art."

"So, get over it!" Cal had shouted. "Did you spend years earning your degrees just so you could brag about your roots in poverty? Don't start singing about how proud you are to be a coal-miner's daughter."

She had to bite her tongue to keep from shouting back, "I'd be proud to be anybody's daughter." She soon grew to despise the home that reflected his interests, but never hers.

Her mind would not let go of Cal's demand that she share his string of obsessions and his personality changes. She had struggled to be a dutiful wife, trotting alongside through each new persona, each new vocabulary and wardrobe he adopted. Unpleasant memories flitted through her mind; like the time they sang a series of vocal duets in a music competition where Cal dreamed of breaking into show business. They won second place, and he went into a protracted sulk.

She remembered her uneasiness when he bought a steel guitar. Cal, who had always considered the guitar a low class instrument, plunged headlong into country and western music—with outrageously priced boots, a Stetson hat, a phony drawl and a four-wheel-drive truck he never drove off the highway.

That phase quickly gave way to his last hobby, Renaissance music. She cringed, reliving the day he bought an expensive twenty-eight-string lute, an instrument so rare in this area he was certain he could win the competition. Her uneasiness turned to alarm when, without warning, Cal sold their furniture and redecorated their home in Old English style. As Lord of the Manor, he dressed like a troubadour and peppered his conversation with words like 'methinks and 'perchance.' Not only did he confuse image with substance; he seemed no longer able to distinguish reality from fantasy. On the day of the competition, when another musician received top honors for his mastery of the instrument, Cal listed his lute for sale. One student joked, "Callahan doesn't play second fiddle."

Regret hardened to bitterness as she recalled his opposition to her career plans, in his belief that a paycheck should give her enough satisfaction. Cal considered himself a modern husband because he "allowed his wife to work;" and though her earnings had put him through graduate school, he considered her education very much beneath his. Uninterested in her writing as well, his only concern for her career was how well it complemented his own.

Some of his friends' wives were executives. Their expensive business suits impressed Cal. He expected Darcy to dress like them, yet her hair must be loose and flowing, even in the summer heat. A load of resentment weighed her down; resentment for her own deceptiveness, for those mornings she dressed in career clothes until Cal left the house, then changed into her school teacher clothes, braided her hair and washed off her makeup.

Deception, she reminded herself, was part of her history, learned at Grandmother's knee. She felt transported back in time to the day Grandmother was delighted and surprised to receive a lovely Mother's Day corsage. "From my son in Europe," she crooned to her club ladies. Darcy, still young and impressionable, detested those ladies for smirking behind Grandmother's back. *How did they know?* They hadn't overheard Grandmother ordering the flowers from the florist, as Darcy had.

Though she hated it, Darcy learned to accept Grandmother's posturing, calling her house "The Young Ladies' Academy" when it was nothing but a boarding house for girls. Darcy dutifully referred to the girls as dinner guests, knowing full well that their monthly checks were Grandmother's only income. Her way of casting a golden glow on a plain life had oddly prepared Darcy for marriage to Cal.

She admitted to herself that her personality as Cal's wife was put on like a change of clothes. Relaxed and confident at work, she fit in well; her colleagues never suspected the change that transpired when she went home. She couldn't count the times she had considered walking away from that demanding marriage. But what would happen to Cal, that earnest student she had married, and who, she hoped, still existed inside this human chameleon? So she had stayed and gradually became Mrs. Chameleon—until that tragic day in April.

Still fresh in her memory was Matt's phone call to her at work. "Todd's car hit a truck out on Boulder highway. Cal and Todd are injured." And Matt meeting her at the hospital lobby and leading her to the room where Cal lay comatose in that hospital bed, his head swathed in bandages.

"Cal was conscious when I got here," Matt had explained. "But just long enough to tell me his last request. He said, 'If don't make it, Matt, I want to be cremated. No one is going to see me like this.' "

Cal, ever the stage director, gave Matt specific instructions for his memorial service, in case he didn't make it. He didn't make it. Handsome Peter Callahan did not regain consciousness.

She felt her chest tighten again at the memory of Matt's downcast eyes when she asked if Cal had left a message for her. Cal, still so absorbed by his precious image, had left Darcy—his wife for nine years—with nothing but anger to crowd out the pain.

Now, as Clark set a box of tissues on the table, her mind found unspoken words to define Cal's view of marriage: A wife's purpose was to decorate her husband's arm, to support his every whim, and to enhance his image. He didn't want a soul mate. He wanted a glamorous sidekick, a trophy wife. For the first time she could acknowledge it. *I couldn't make him happy, because I didn't really love him. He changed so often I didn't know who he was anymore. I wasn't the kind of wife he needed.*

Clark had finished his coffee by the time she quieted and wiped her eyes. She had to get control. By habit, she wrapped her anger and stowed it in her heart where Clark would never see its ugliness. "Sorry. I shouldn't have let myself go to pieces."

He spoke for the first time, with uncharacteristic precision. "That's exactly what you *should* do, Lady. Just look at what you've been through in the past few weeks. You lost your husband. Then you lost yourself. You've gone through shock and fear and injury. Your spirit is bruised, and you're tryin' to carry on like it was a normal day."

He paused, then added. "I shouldn't have asked you to stay for the funeral. I was thinkin' of Jamie. I apologize, Darcy." He paused again, his brow furrowed and his fingers stroking his chin. "Look. I don't know much about psychology, but I can tell you somethin' Bert told me when I got home from Desert Storm after Dad died."

Every muscle ached as she straightened in her chair. "Bert, your Navajo friend?"

Clark nodded. "He told me a story about myself, a vision kind-a thing like one of Henry's parables. He said I was lyin' in the water at the edge of a deep pool. Every time a pebble fell into the pool, the water rippled toward the shore.

And as the ripples moved, they swamped me until I nearly drowned." He shifted on his chair.

Something told Darcy to pay attention to what he was saying. He spoke so carefully, putting the first word on each sentence. She thought, *He knows exactly how I feel! He knows this is self-pity and self-condemnation more than grief, and he isn't mad at me.*

Clark paused for a long sip of coffee. "And then Bert asked me a question. 'Who's tossin' the pebbles?' "

Bewildered, she stammered. "Pebbles? That's all? What did he mean?"

"He meant somethin' was drownin' me. I had to look and see what it was, and more importantly, where it came from. And when I looked, I knew. You see, Bert showed me somethin' about myself. It wasn't that the whole world was untrustworthy, like I thought it was. I'd just forgotten how to trust. I didn't trust anyone except Bert until I met Lillian. Guess I was tossin' pebbles at myself.

The ticking clock measured their silence until, finally, she recognized her own smothering guilt. Guilt for not challenging Cal's ridiculous whims, fearing his disapproval. Guilt for maneuvering to avoid his tantrums, and for losing herself as surely as she had by driving around the gullies in the desert. For behaving like an intimidated child, stomping off to bed instead of talking with him in the kitchen. For choosing unhappiness over loneliness, criticism over indifference. Endless pebbles plunking into the pool of her soul. Relentless ripples engulfing her in a past that could not be changed.

Slowly, painfully, the realization worked its way through her mind: Cal was no longer her accuser. Cal was dead. At last she could admit that many of her failures came from her own expectations. The source of her despair glared like a Vegas neon. Unable to meet her own standard as a wife, she had swamped herself in self-condemnation.

After a long pause, she looked up. "Time to stop tossing pebbles?"

A suggestion of a smile deepened the seams of his weathered face as he leaned forward. The richness of his voice emphasized each word. "Time to get out of the pool."

Her voice wavered with uncertainty. "You mean I should change. But how?"

Clark leaned back and crossed his feet on a chair. "Nope. I'm sayin' you should look at all the things about yourself that don't need changin'. Look, you're a successful teacher and writer. You saved Jamie's life more than once, and helped him through a major crisis. I see a lot here to be proud of." His voice seemed to lighten. "Give yourself credit, Lady. Cut yourself some slack."

A comfortable new silence settled in the kitchen. Her feelings for Jamie and Clark had changed from pity and distrust to love and trust. Maybe she could alter her feelings about herself.

* * * * *

By the time Dan brought Jamie home, Darcy had shed a lifetime of tears. The lump in her throat had dissolved. Her desert retreat—though she had found it in an unexpected place—had done its work. Still not sure who she was, Darcy knew who she wanted to become. Tomorrow she would move to Elko. Never again would she relinquish control of her life to anyone. Never again would she be measured by someone else's standard.

Jamie ran through the door bubbling with excitement. "Aunt Naomi says I can go to school with Pete and Martha."

At midnight Darcy fell exhausted into bed, her door slightly ajar in case Jamie woke up. She had tried to avoid it, but she had fallen in love with him. And now he had a family who accepted him and loved him. She felt sad to leave him and this quiet nurturing settlement... and Clark, of course. She had never had such a heart-to-heart talk as they had today in the kitchen, not even with Carol. It was so intimate. Her eyes popped open. Intimacy! I've discovered what intimacy really is. Her face flushed in the dark. At last she slept.

CHAPTER 10

Sunshine streamed through the window as Darcy finished packing and closed her suitcase. Jamie had been trying to whistle the way Clark did. Now his voice drifted in from the kitchen. "Clark, you know what? We could just ask God to tell Darcy to stay here with us. Couldn't we?"

A stab of anticipation went through her in the long silence before she overheard Clark's voice. "Well, now that might not be fair to Darcy. Maybe we should just ask God to help her do what she wants to do."

There was no mistaking Jamie's disappointment. "Will she come back someday?"

"Maybe someday," came Clark's soft reply. Darcy hurried to get to the kitchen before this conversation went too far.

Clark had checked her truck and had repaired the minimal damage he found. Today, after a stop at the clinic in St. George, she would be on her way to Elko. She had called Carol and arranged to stay with her for two weeks while Carol's husband was away on business. Carol had found a rental place and would help her get settled. Then Darcy would be on her own.

Clark interrupted her thoughts. "Which road do you plan to take?"

She pointed to the map of the western states on the kitchen wall. "I'll go from St. George to Cedar City, swing over to Nevada and take that highway north to Wells, then west to Elko. It's shorter than going up through Utah."

"Yep, it's shorter, all right, but still a two-day drive. Those roads out there are known as the loneliest roads in America. I'd feel a whole lot better if you'd stay on Interstate 15 all the way to Salt Lake, then take 80 across the Bonneville Salt Flat to Elko. Hardly any other travelers on that road you're lookin' at, and you sure couldn't change a flat tire with those hands." His left eyebrow arched and a teasing grin curved up behind his toast. "Besides, you might get lost."

An amused contentment washed over Darcy. "I suppose I could. Wouldn't be the first time! I'll take the route you suggest."

"Give us a call when you get there." He handed her his business card.

"Sure." Compared to those marathon kitchen table talks, this nonverbal conversation spoke volumes. Jamie slumped in his chair studying their faces.

She hurried to gather her bags. No sense prolonging his pain. Or hers.

Clark loaded her truck. Then, after a clinging hug from Jamie, a soft pat on the shoulder from Clark and the usual parting remarks, she drove away. Her vision blurred as she waved through the rearview mirror at the child who wanted her to stay—and the man who cared which road she took.

Trying to keep her mind occupied as she drove, Darcy noticed the steeples in the small towns along the Interstate, and was reminded of the numerous churches in Vegas she had passed with a blind eye. She wondered about the people who worshipped there. Did they know about Jamie's God?

Her hands throbbed painfully by the time she checked into a motel in Provo. A good dinner and a strong pain pill took care of that, but she'd had to learn to get along with those bandages. As usual, when she fell into bed her mind tabulated tomorrow's difficulties. *God, please show me how to cope.* She couldn't braid her hair. No problem. The desk clerk had told her about a nearby beauty shop that accepted walk-ins. In Elko, Carol would do it until her hands healed. If they did heal. Would they be too scarred to play the piano and violin? If so, she would teach choir. She turned over and slept.

*　*　*　*　*

The humid salon smelled of chemicals when she arrived the next morning. While waiting, she leafed through a magazine, half-listening to the hum of voices. When someone asked about a woman who made dolls for children undergoing chemotherapy, Darcy's ears perked up.

"She has the doll finished, but she needs some long blond hair," the stylist said. "She'll make the doll look like the child did before her hair came out. The kids usually take their dolls with them when they go for their treatment at the cancer clinic. It's amazing how much it helps them. Reminds them how they'll look when their hair grows back."

Old images of long hair swirled along the edges of Darcy's memory. She thought again of Lydia, whose father considered short hair sinful, and of Cal, who thought it lacked glamour. She smiled inside, remembering Debbie Chadwell's haircut when Henry got his faith on straight. Turning the pages idly, she thought about what the stylist had said, something about a doll making a little girl happy. Her thoughts flew back to the happiest Christmas she had ever known, yet one that still gave her a tinge of guilt. Of course it wasn't her fault that Grandmother was suddenly hospitalized, or that Aunt Belle was gone and there was no one to look out for little Drucilla. Or that Ramon had taken her to the tiny, spotless cottage—a shack really—where he lived with Rosa and three smiling brown-faced boys.

Darcy had never forgotten the welcome she received–
–like a member of the family, not a pitiful waif whose
Grandmother was ill. So many memories stayed with her:
the scrawny Christmas tree with homemade ornaments, the
spicy smell of cumin wafting from the steaming platter of
tamales, the wooden trucks Ramon had built for his boys.
Most of all she remembered the small rag doll stitched up on
short notice and tucked under the tree for her. With button
eyes and yellow yarn hair, it had immediately become her
most treasured possession, one she had kept over the years
and still had, packed among the memorabilia in the trunk.

Darcy smiled to herself. The warm glow of love and
happiness in Ramon and Rosa's house reminded her of
Clark and Jamie's home. And Jim's and Sarah's cave. And
the Chadwells' big house. Not Grandmother's. Not hers and
Cal's.

She took a chair when her name was called, explaining
to the stylist about her injured hands. "So I want it cut to
shoulder length." Unrehearsed, those words felt as strange to
her ears as her spontaneous decision felt in her mind.

"Are you sure?"

The stylist and several customers spoke in the same
breath. "Your hair is so beautiful! It must have taken years
to grow it so long."

"If that was my hair, I'd never cut it off," declared a
young woman with a stringy bleached mane.

"I'm sure." Darcy took a deep breath and continued.
"I heard you mention someone who needed hair for a doll.
Could she use mine?"

The stylist's eyes widened. "Yes. My mother-in-law."
She explained again about the dolls. "If you're sure, I can
call her and she'll come over and see if it's the right color."

When the mother-in-law arrived and saw Darcy's luxu-
riant hair, now freshly shampooed and dried into soft waves,
her hands flew to her mouth and her eyes glistened. "It's

perfect! It's an answer to prayer!" Tears spilled down her cheeks. She searched her handbag for a photo of the child who would receive the doll.

Gazing at the beautiful child, Darcy couldn't prevent one sad thought from creeping into her mind. *Will I ever have a pretty little girl like this?* She held the picture a long time.

Sensing Darcy's hesitation, the doll maker said softly, "You want to be very sure about this before you give up your lovely hair. Cutting our hair is an emotional thing. That's why the wig and dolls are so helpful when little children lose their hair to chemo. But be fair to yourself."

"Oh, I'm sure." This was something Darcy could do to help someone. She could learn to be helpful, like the Chadwells. And like Clark.

The woman smiled. "When I get the doll finished, I'll send you a picture of it."

Darcy refused her offer of payment, insisting that it was a donation. When the scissors bit into the silky strands of Darcy's hair, the women in the salon cringed as though they were witnessing an amputation. To Darcy, it was something else. She thought of how her hair, her identity for most of her life, could now make a child happy. She couldn't recall a single day it had brought her happiness.

To forestall any regrets, she mentally listed the benefits of shoulder-length hair. No braiding, no curling iron; this was hair she could manage herself. When the stylist finished, Darcy fluffed the ends under to frame her face and studied her reflection. She liked the way this new style enhanced her eyes. She was no longer Cal's trophy wife. This was the new and authentic Darcy Callahan.

She gave the doll maker Carol's address and hurried to the one-hour photo shop where she had left the film of the artifacts. Though outwardly her stride was unchanged, her spirit strutted like a drum majorette. She felt pounds lighter and years younger. Her indecisive inner child had grown up.

Now she would find her own path; she would no longer be a backdrop for someone else's life.

Still, a few pesky questions tugged at her conscience. She wondered: What part of her decision had given her the most satisfaction? Helping a sick child? Making her own decision? Or defying Cal and Grandmother? It didn't matter. With a shrug, she tossed her hair and started the truck. At last she was on her own. Merging onto the Interstate, she sang a phrase from a familiar song: "I once was lost, but now am found; was blind, but now I see!"

CHAPTER 11

Darcy turned from her window view of the Ruby mountains that thrust upward so abruptly from the low undulating terrain. Soon they would be capped with snow, but now autumn's golden haze shadowed the deep vertical ridges that lay like the claw marks of a giant bear. That glow now seeped into the room.

She had been here for sixteen months now. She felt contented here in Spring Creek, a large subdivision over the hill from Elko. This small manufactured home, though lacking the uniqueness of the Vegas house, suited her needs exactly. The bedroom facing the cul-de-sac made a perfect writing office. Above a corner desk hung two small Navajo rugs and a wedding basket. In the living room, a second-hand spinet nestled among a leather sofa, a chair with arms wide enough for a notebook, a tall bookcase, and a few tables.

She smiled with satisfaction at the sparse accessories surrounding her. She had seen no need to rush into decorating. On the kitchen windowsill sat the motto she had bought in the Chadwells' shop. A quilted wall-hanging purchased from Melinda, a new friend, hung above the sofa. A photo of a little blond girl and a replica of her doll sent by the doll maker smiled from the bookcase alongside the birdhouse. A small, framed snapshot of a beaming Ramon and Rosa. Not a single piece from a decorator shop, nothing trendy, nothing chosen to impress anyone but herself. Every item in her home earned its place by reflecting her own interests and memories. Like road signs, they charted where she had been, emotionally as well as physically. She alone decided which memories to keep. None of Cal's decorating. The Vegas house was his. This was hers.

Behind the china closet's low wooden doors were old photos of Grandmother. Two large boxes held her cherished silver tea service. Darcy smiled, remembering the story of its journey from England, hearing once again Grandmother's pride when she told Judge Collins's wife about it. "I snagged it in a jumble, for a paltry sum."

According to Grandmother, her Auntie Louise had been a day worker for one of the finest families in Manchester. Darcy could recite the story by heart—how, along with the skills Grandmother had acquired from Auntie, the silver service had launched her status in America as the town's social paragon. So many times, as she instructed Darcy in the proper care of silver, Grandmother had suggested that "a young lady, when selecting a husband, would be well advised to master the refinement of serving tea." In her estimation, tea was almost as important as the British accent she had so carefully steeped into Darcy's speech and shielded from "common language." Just as the silver, the china and the crystal concealed their poverty, the austere elegance of Grandmother's house set Darcy above the neighborhood "ragamuffins."

A familiar heaviness settled in Darcy's chest. The ornate silver service with its heavy-footed tray—the centerpiece of Grandmother's life—was all that remained of her lovely things. Having promised it to Darcy, Grandmother had left it with Judge Collins for safekeeping, and he had passed it on to Darcy.

Unhappily as it turned out, Grandmother was right. The silver had played a larger part than Darcy wanted to admit in her romance with Cal. Too late, she learned that it was only her cultured image that attracted the impressionable student. The tea set held a prominent place in their first home until Cal's interests changed. It was then shoved aside, tarnished and forgotten.

Again her gaze played over the sagebrush-covered equestrian trail that ran along the acreage across from her home. She enjoyed this high desert country more than she had expected. For the first time, she'd actually noticed the rabbit brush in bloom and the soft orange blossoms and silver-green foliage of Globe Mallow. She'd seen pictures of them in wildlife books, but here she could smell and touch them, and savor their unique beauty. Those glittery neon years in Vegas had made her feel impoverished, but the desert brought fulfillment. It was alive. She was alive!

She thought about that morning when Clark flew Jamie to Elko on a return business flight from Boise and Jamie had enjoyed watching the horseback riders. Clark explained that Esther was designing a bell tower for a church. "There's a beautiful one out in Lamoille, right at the foot of the Ruby Mountains. Thought I'd get a few pictures for her."

As they drove along, Darcy sensed, by the way Jamie snuggled against her, that the trip was more than a photo session.

While Clark snapped photos and Jamie explored the terrain, she asked, "How is he handling the changes in his life?"

"Slow, but sure. Seems like everybody's grief doesn't run on the same timetable."

"Or need to." A sense of peace settled over her. Jamie would get through it. Clark would see to it.

At lunch, Clark made nice comments about her home and her cooking. How well she would remember his grin when Jamie said that the porcelain doll's hair looked like hers. She could almost hear the wheels turning in Clark's head. Or his heart.

He was surprised by the piano, and pleased that her hands had healed well enough that she could give private lessons. "My mother used to play a song called 'Lisa,' I think. Da da da da da da da da da." Off-key though it was, Darcy recognized the melody, and after lunch she played Beethoven's *Fur Elise*. Then they all sang "Home On the Range." She had never sounded worse—or felt better.

That day she gave Clark a set of the pictures of the artifacts in Jamie's cellar. She had studied them enough to know they were valuable. His eyebrows flew up when he saw her maiden name, Drucilla O'Rourk, on the envelope. She explained that the wrong person might see the photos and be too interested in the pots. Clark called her "Miz Drucilla" the rest of the day. When he and Jamie drove away, the sun seemed to go behind a cloud.

It was a day she wanted to remember. Now she tried not to think about Clark and Jamie in their cozy apartment.

She had phoned as promised when she first arrived in Elko. "Clark says I can call you once a week," Jamie said. With each call Jamie's voice had brought tears to her eyes. Once he said, "Clark's teaching me to ride a horse. And our school gets to have a Christmas program. Can you come?" That was in November, a year ago. When Clark came on the line, Darcy made a noncommittal response about the bad driving weather. She shouldn't hang on to Jamie. He had friends and family down there. Yet she thought of him so often. And now, almost a year later, she longed to see him again. Maybe this Christmas.

Jamie had sent her a color drawing of his horse, Bucky, and one of Clark astride his big palomino. Jamie had his parents' talent for art. In his childish way he had captured Clark: his unruly red hair, his weathered face...and his loneliness. The drawings, now matted and framed, hung in her dining nook.

Her writing projects filled her evenings. Cal had belittled the idea of ghostwriting because it brought no acclaim. It paid the bills though, and his lifestyle was expensive.

She grinned now, recalling Clark's mischievous response when she mentioned her ghostwriting. "Ghostwritin'! How do you do that? With smoke and mirrors?"

As hoped, she had landed a position with the high school choir. It gave her enough hours to provide the income she needed and some social contact as well. She soon learned that in northern Nevada, towns are few and widely spaced. School teams travel for hours to extracurricular events. So, along with her new friend Melinda, she helped chaperone the buses that carried the marching band to the games and competitions.

Elko's vibrancy and friendliness delighted Darcy. It had a different sort of Western spirit from other towns she had seen. The hotels were booked for months in advance of the Cowboy Poetry Festival. She and Carol often met after class at Cowboy Joe's for iced mocha, or at the museum and the Western Folklore Center. She loved being part of it.

Like herself, many families were recent arrivals lured by the promise of jobs and new lives. The enormous open-pit gold mines far out in the desert employed hundreds. Now learning to make her own choices, Darcy fit in here. Self-assurance. She liked the feel of it.

The jangle of the phone disrupted her thoughts. It was Carol inviting her to a church meeting. The formerly cynical Carol from Vegas! As though she could read the question in Darcy's mind, Carol explained. "It's a joint service among several churches in the area. They call it a 'Singspiration.' They meet in the convention center to sing. I like it because I can see different people's ideas about church music, and about worship." She paused. "Even about God."

She waited, giving Darcy time to decide.

Darcy had noticed a change in Carol and Bob since they moved here and joined a church. Their attitudes were more positive than before. They were happier. But she had squirmed inside a few days ago at Carol's definition of salvation: "God has already chosen us. It's like He has given us a check for our salvation, but we have to endorse it. It's our choice." Though Darcy had considered herself a nominal Christian during her childhood, it wasn't something she talked about. Grandmother said debates over religion ended in quarrels.

She tried not to sound too eager now. She had told Carol about the Chadwells' faith only because it seemed so special. They not only looked forward to eternal life; they enjoyed *this* life. She had mentioned Clark, but only in a detached way. Some things must be pondered in the heart before they are shared, she reasoned. But she was curious. If Christians all believed in the same Christ, why wasn't their faith more alike? More like Jamie's?

"Sure," she said, "I'd love to go. Church music can provide an interesting study of an area and its culture." Her pompous statement shocked her. It sounded like Cal. Hastily she agreed to meet Carol and Bob for dinner. It might turn out to be an enlightening evening, and she had nothing else to do tonight.

Darcy was not prepared for what she saw and heard when she entered the large room. Nothing here resembled the traditional church she had known. No anthems, no subdued organ music. Nothing was subdued here. These people mingled about the room, chatting in normal voices. They wore wide-open smiles, not the pursed lips she remembered from Grandmother's church. Grandmother, who always insisted on appropriate attire, would have been shocked to see their casual clothing.

"Hi, Ms. Callahan." She recognized Melinda's teenage daughter. Melinda was playing the piano. Others were tuning up guitars or keyboards. Several of her fellow teachers greeted her, and surprisingly, she felt right at home.

After an opening prayer—a simple one in everyday language—the minister said, "Let's worship the Lord in song." Then the singing began, singing like she had never heard. Loud, exuberant singing. No downcast eyes glued to a hymnal; the words were printed on a screen by an overhead projector. Not the somber words she expected. Joyful ones! Darcy, who had always focused on the notes, now began to hear the songs' messages.

She looked around at the varied manner of worship going on all at once. Some people sat with folded hands the way Darcy had been taught. Many sang softly and reverently; others sang loudly. Some even clapped their hands, or raised them, along with the music. *Clapped their hands in church!* Darcy's first reaction was a knee-jerk reflex. That would never have happened in Grandmother's church, where any display of emotion was considered distasteful, if not irreverent.

But this wasn't irreverence. It was joy! Grandmother would never have understood or accepted this type of worship. Poor Grandmother!

Worship, the minister said, was God beaming His love down on us. "We are like mirrors, reflecting it back," he said. Curious, Darcy looked around. Here were real people, tough people who worked at the mines, drove huge earth movers, built roads, and operated the powerhouse. Here were ranch families, rodeo cowboys, casino employees, merchants, and office workers. The idea was that everyone was free to worship in his or her own way. Darcy couldn't miss the truth here. However they chose to express their worship, these folks knew God the way Jamie and the Chadwells did. God was right here in Elko, Nevada. And He was real, not that abstract entity she heard about during her college days.

An incident from long ago in West Virginia flashed through her mind. How could she have forgotten that day when Mrs. Greer, her Sunday School teacher, had told her that Jesus wanted to come into her heart? And when Darcy asked Him to come in, she'd really believed He did. When had she stopped believing?

All her adult life she had insisted on having a choice. In her mind, that meant not allowing anyone to manipulate her. In fact, most of her anger toward Cal centered on his habit of choosing for her. But in matters of faith she had neglected to choose. Her studies, her career and her marriage were more important. Her child-like love for God, like her early love for Cal, had withered and died.

Now she wanted that love restored—by her own decision. That burning desire would gradually blossom into a quest for a church home. If she had to visit every church in town, she would find a cozy, homey one like the Chadwells'. Elko couldn't be mistaken for a formal town. There wasn't a lot of stained glass here and the churches varied in their degree of pomp and ceremony.

As the days and weeks went by, she noticed changes in herself. Not only was she more content, but the Bible was more interesting and easier to understand. Somehow the plan of salvation became clear, too. Forgiveness of sin was what it boiled down to. But it was more than that. For Carol and Bob, Jesus was no longer someone they talked *about* but someone they talked *to,* and it showed in their lives.

Darcy wanted to know God that way herself, not only by observing Him in other peoples' lives. She wanted faith that was real. Like Henry Chadwell's faith that let him meet death without fear, faith that freed him to stop controlling his family and to entrust their care to God. She began to question one of her old perceptions: *Was that what Grandmother meant when, on her deathbed, she said that everything was okay? Did I misunderstand?*

Something still troubled Darcy. Where was the fruit of her new-found faith? She had heard others tell how their lives had changed when they became Christians. After she renewed her commitment to Christ, she began attending a study group. She became less wary and more positive. Maybe she was simply mellowing with age. Maybe it was because she had gotten away from Vegas—away from unhappy memories. But she still had some unsettled issues. She hadn't exactly grown a sweet spirit like the Chadwells.

It was later, on a school bus trip to Reno, that she learned what the problem was. Ignoring it didn't work. More than a year had passed; yet something held her back—something in the bottom of her entry closet.

CHAPTER 12

"Darcy." Carol's voice was excited when she phoned from Salt Lake just before Christmas. "I'm stuck here for three more days with that dental surgery. Why don't you drive over when school ends for the holiday? We'll finish our Christmas shopping together."

"That'll work out fine," Darcy replied. "I'll be on my way back to the Arizona strip for Christmas. Maybe you can help me pick out something for Jamie and Clark. I'll be staying with the Chadwells."

Their friendship was special. Carol had a degree in mental health, but sometimes Darcy felt that she was clairvoyant as well. She could see through Darcy's words and read her thoughts. Wisely though, she hadn't pushed Darcy to admit her feelings. Darcy did it on her own. When she first arrived in Elko, she had told Carol how she "blubbered like an Oprah show" at Mr. Chadwell's funeral, and Carol cheered, "Good for you! The strongest person is the one who isn't ashamed to cry." Somehow her little sermons always had a ring of truth.

Darcy jumped at the chance to spend a few days with her. They would share room expenses. Besides, she hated shopping alone. She needed some new clothes. When she left Vegas, she had kept only her schoolteacher clothes. She discarded the stark beige and black outfits that Cal considered chic, no matter that they turned her skin sallow. Carol had once joked that Cal's sense of fashion came from the list of "What's hot and what's not." Gone were the garish evening bags, the glittery jewelry and slinky spike heels Cal favored. No more perfumes chosen for their trendy names.

She would buy gifts for Jamie and Clark and a hostess gift for Mrs. Chadwell. Darcy had accepted Clark's invitation to visit Jamie for the holidays, but only if she could stay with one of the Chadwell families. It was magnanimous of them, she explained, to overlook the presence of a young widow in Clark's home a year and a half ago during an emergency. But an extended visit there now would be unseemly. The trip would be long, but better than spending the holidays alone.

She was ready to leave by mid-afternoon. The drive would take her back through the Bonneville Salt Flat, a stark place so flat and solid that race cars were tested there. Pausing at the door, she turned and grabbed the brown shopping bag she had been keeping in the bottom of the entry closet since moving here. If she hurried, she would reach the Salt Flat by sunset.

The air was icy when she stopped at a turnoff area. Here hundreds of people had memorialized themselves by forming their names with small rocks on the white salt. Darcy faced the western sky, the handles of the shopping bag clenched in her hand. Sunset felt appropriate, but something wasn't right. Her eyes stung from the cold as the horizon turned to deep red, and a dull pink and blue cast rendered the desert floor a dismal gray. Overhead, the sky deepened to a bruised gray-purple.

No. Not in this forbidding place. Not under this hostile sky. Hurriedly, she stashed the shopping bag back in the truck. Some other time. Some other place. The truck lurched onto the highway, leaving behind that ancient bed of dry brine—eons of salty tears.

*   *   *   *   *

Taking a break from their shopping marathon, Carol and Darcy dropped into soft chairs in an old-fashioned tearoom they had discovered. She told Carol, "I'm treating you to High Tea. We'll pretend to be my grandmother and her Auntie Louise."

Carol's eyes gleamed with mock dismay. "You've told me so much about your grandmother's tea parties, and all her strict rules. I wonder why you're doing this. Are you trying to impress me, or is there something you think I should know?"

Darcy smiled. "I'm trying to relax you enough to help me with a decision."

"Help with a decision? Is the independent Ms. Callahan asking for advice?"

"Yes, she is," Darcy answered. "I need some suggestions about what to take to Clark. It shouldn't be too personal." They discussed the options and decided on a book.

When their tea was served, Carol teased. "Okay, it's time for culture and refinement. So, in one easy lesson, teach me everything your grandmother taught you, in case I have to entertain Queen Elizabeth someday."

Darcy laughed. "Grandmother didn't entertain the queen." Then, sipping from paper-thin china cups, they crooked their little fingers and felt like little girls playing house. Between spasms of laughter at Carol's antics, Darcy let her mind steep in the beauty around her, in a room Grandmother would have loved.

"How can you drink from these cups?" Carol complained. "I'm afraid I'll bite a hole in mine."

Darcy's voice softened. "Grandmother taught me. She rated table manners just below religion."

Carol, apparently sensing Darcy's mood, probed. "What was she like? Was she beautiful?"

Darcy looked out the window. "She wouldn't admit to being beautiful if her life depended on it. She distrusted beauty. Said it was transitory." She imitated her grandmother:

" 'A lady must acquire the skills necessary to support herself, just in case.' "

"In case what?"

"She didn't say, and I didn't ask. I knew better. She didn't have time for my questions. She was young when my grandfather died, and I suppose she had a hard time making a living. Apparently, she didn't have a lot of confidence in love, either."

Carol's eyebrows peaked. "Speaking of love, my dear, your dimples are fetching, but you can't catch a man with furrows between your eyebrows, you know."

Darcy's cup clattered against her saucer. "Who says I'm trying to catch a man? As for dimples, they're natural. They're common. I couldn't put them on or take them off. Even if I could, it's just as Grandmother said, and I quote: 'Proper young ladies have no need of cheap tricks.' "

She shifted uneasily and avoided Carol's eyes. Whenever Darcy thought of love and marriage, warning bells went off in her mind.

"I'd rather be lonely. Besides, I enjoy my freedom."

"Well then," Carol drawled. "Let's talk about freedom, and cheap tricks." Clowning, she strummed an imaginary guitar and sang in a nasal voice, "Freedom is o-o-only-STRUM-another word for lo-o-onely."

Darcy nearly choked on her tea. "Girl, you're weird!"

Carol would not be put off. "It's worth demeaning myself in public, just to see your eyes shine. Which they do, you know, since you came to Elko."

Darcy took a deep breath. "That's because my life has changed. Personal independence is worth being alone. Who needs a man?"

Carol's clowning ended. "What does independence mean to you?" she asked, softly.

Darcy's answer came quickly. "To be left alone to make my own life decisions."

Her friend's expression clouded. "Left alone? Why must you be alone to make a decision?"

Darcy searched for an answer. To her, the only sure way of being independent was to stay single. "Marriage and independence can be mutually exclusive," she replied. "Think of all the miserable couples we know."

Carol's retort came swiftly. "Why not think of the happy ones? Darcy, aren't you demanding too much? I can understand that you don't want to feel vulnerable again, but do you have to be invincible?" Her eyes twinkled. "And if that's the case, why did your grandmother teach you all those feminine wiles?"

Instantly Darcy's crystal tongue honed to a knife-sharp edge. "She didn't! She detested feminine wiles, or 'coquetry,' as she called it. She taught domestic skills, poise, and etiquette, but not glamour."

She drew a deep breath. "Besides, I need to get over my old life before I begin a new one."

Sensing that her remarks had struck a nerve, Carol backpedaled. "I'm sorry, Darcy. I should have known better. I didn't mean to badmouth your grandmother, and I realize you still have issues regarding Cal."

Darcy nodded, signaling that the discussion had gone far enough. A nod was all their friendship required.

Nevertheless, she found herself discussing the men she had met recently, but not anyone Carol knew. She described the Chadwell men, how goodhearted they were, and how they obviously loved their wives and children. "And they're all handsome."

"As handsome as Cal? Do they have gorgeous physiques like his? Is that the kind of perfection you demand in a man?

You've turned down several dates so far. Whose approval do you need? Cal's?"

"No!" Darcy swallowed hard. "The Chadwell men are every bit as handsome as Cal, but in a different way. When you're around them, their appearance isn't what you notice. It's something else—something more substantial. Their physiques come from working, not from hanging out at the health club. And they keep their shirts on."

Their silence lengthened before Darcy added: "Besides, I'll never marry any man if I'm not sure I can trust him. And, since it's impossible to know that ahead of time, you see the problem. I'm not about to marry the first man I met since Cal...." Her thoughts drifted: *How do I tell her about Clark?*

Carol must have read her mind. "It's been a year and a half since you met Clark, and in case you haven't noticed, he isn't flying up here just for Jamie's benefit. Are you sure you aren't being too loyal to Cal?"

Darcy stiffened against Carol's probing. Though her natural reticence rose like a wall, she couldn't keep from asking, "Too loyal? How can anyone be too loyal?"

"I don't mean being too loyal, but being loyal for too long—if loyalty is what this is about. You've got to be fair to yourself, too. Life is good, and love is worth your heart and soul. It's worth a risk."

Darcy's mind had grasped onto something else. "What do you mean, 'if loyalty is what this is about?' "

Carol paused, then spoke cautiously, "Maybe loyalty isn't the problem. Maybe it *is* a question of trust. As I see it, the problem is one of two things. Either no man is trustworthy, or you distrust all men, no matter how much or how little you know about them. Have you ever really trusted a man in all your life?"

"I trusted Judge Collins and Mrs. Collins."

"And did they let you down?"

"No! But they died. And I'm not desperate enough to marry a dead man."

Somehow they found a way to laugh at that remark and change the subject. Anything to ease the tension. Their friendship had boundaries, and preserving their rapport was more important than winning an argument. Talking about men and trust in the same breath made Darcy edgy.

"Besides, I don't need a man in my life. Not yet, anyway."

"Of course you don't *need* a man. You can support yourself very well. But you must want a husband and a family. After all, you stayed with Cal." Carol blushed and looked at her lap. "Darcy, you shouldn't be suspicious of all men, just because you couldn't trust Cal."

Darcy's old habit of defending Cal surfaced. She blurted, "Couldn't trust him? That's not it. I was *concerned* about him! So was our friend Matt! He joked that Cal wouldn't be satisfied till he could be Garth Brooks and Pavarotti combined, with a little Bernstein and Perlman thrown in for good measure." She paused. "I think Cal just wanted to be anyone except who he was."

Darcy stared out the window at the Christmas lights twinkling in the trees along the street. She had met more than a few potential husbands in college. She remembered how star-struck she was when Cal first noticed her, and the glorious hours they spent in the campus cafeteria discussing the music they both loved. Cal, so handsome and gallant, was the knight in shining armor every girl dreams of. He would whisk her away to a world of happiness. But her dream had another facet, too. She needed to feel important to her hero. Other men she dated were self-sufficient. Cal needed her.

Eventually her dream became too demanding. Cal had needed more than encouragement from her. His work toward a PhD. was faltering. She tutored him and edited his work, but refused to write his dissertation. Then the pouting began.

He wasn't allowing her to help him through "tough love." He was using her. Her golden boy was tarnished.

It was time for Carol the friend, to back off, but Carol the professional counselor kept probing. "You said you were just concerned at first. When did you stop trusting Cal?"

Darcy couldn't hold back the truth any longer. "When he stole my work," she blurted. "I was thrilled when he said he wanted to conduct a concerto I'd composed before we met. But the program listed 'Professor Callahan, composer and conductor,' and Cal made no attempt to correct the mistake. That's when Matt's jokes stopped, too. He tried to persuade Cal to keep his appointments with a counselor, but...." She shrugged and her voice softened. "Cal was insecure, and I... well, I let him down."

Carol leaned forward, speaking softly. "Darcy, you don't have to protect him anymore. Go ahead and let yourself be angry with him! It doesn't mean you hate him. He was obviously a very troubled man, and he hurt you. Your memories of him are so full of anger and guilt, there's no room for grief. It's time to let it go."

Darcy dabbed her eyes. That's what Clark had said: "Time to get out of the pool."

Finally a crack appeared in the numbing denial that had insulated Darcy's feelings during those years with Cal. The two women fell silent as the impact of Darcy's pain filled the space between them.

During the silence, her memory replayed her own voice reassuring Jamie. "I told Jamie the rock slide wasn't his fault" she finally said to Carol. "I said that sometimes, bad things just happen. Was that the right thing to say?"

Carol nodded her head and smiled, and did not mention the subject again.

* * * * *

The days with Carol passed like a dream before Darcy turned the truck toward St. George. Her suitcase held her new clothes, comfortable knits in soft plums, blues, and deep greens, the colors she had always loved. She had chosen this coordinated wardrobe herself, and she loved it.

She felt good, too, about her gift shopping. She had found a Native American puzzle and books about dinosaurs for Jamie. Careful to avoid anything too personal, she had selected a beautifully illustrated volume of Anasazi artifacts for Clark.

On the long drive she hummed along with the radio. But one of Carol's comments played over and over in her mind. "You don't have to be left alone to be independent. But you'll be alone as long as you compare every man you meet to Cal."

Her thoughts ran rampant. *Is Carol right? Do I judge all men by Cal? Why do I think of him so often? Do I distrust all men? Not trusting Cal was one thing, but why can't I trust Clark? Maybe I have no reason. Maybe it's nothing but a bad habit.*

The truth hovered around the edges of her mind, replaying her friend's teatime lecture. "You're more than interested in Clark," Carol had said, and maybe she was right. After all, every time he and Jamie stopped by on a flight to Boise she had enjoyed their company and stared out the window for days afterward. Was it just Jamie, or was it Clark, too, for whom she was longing?

By the time she reached St. George, Darcy had made herself a promise. She would take a second look at trust. She would let herself see Clark with new eyes.

CHAPTER 13

A light snow was falling in late afternoon when the aircraft hangar came into view. Soft lights gleamed from the Chadwells' homes. A few children skated on an improvised ice rink near the church. With the dark mountain looming in the background, the scene resembled a cozy Christmas card.

A small hand waved from the upstairs window of the store. By the time she got out of the truck and stretched, Jamie came bounding down the steps.

"Hi, Darcy. Clark's cookin' roast beef for supper. And Grandma brought us some hot rolls and pie!" Jamie was never at a loss for words.

She hugged him close. The sight of those vivid blue eyes made her heart jump again, just like it had the day they found each other. It seemed impossible that more than a year-and-a-half had passed since she met him and Clark.

His eyes danced with anticipation and his voice became a loud whisper. "And you know what? I know a secret." He backed up a step. "But I can't tell it yet. It's about Rebekah. I heard Grandma and Rebekah talkin' about it, and they made me promise to keep it a secret."

"Well," she said, "You'll just have to keep that secret. Secrets are made to be kept, and so are promises."

She looked up and saw Clark coming down the steps. Before he reached the bottom step, she noticed a pale band on his ring finger. He wasn't wearing his wedding ring.

"Darcy." His voice was deep and rich, much richer in person than on the phone. Her knees shook when he spoke her name. Their eyes locked and she felt as if she had never been away. *Carol was right,* she admitted to herself. *She's so perceptive! She knew I was in love with Clark before I did. Before I admitted it, anyway.*

Gratefully, Jamie kept a steady stream of chatter as they climbed the stairs, giving her a chance to sort out her thoughts, to think before she spoke. She would have to control any sign of tremor in her voice.

Clark took her coat and she shook the scarf from around her neck. Her hair fell into place around her face. She wore only a little makeup, just a hint of mascara and lipstick she had dabbed on a few miles back. But she knew her deep pink sweater brought out the color in her cheeks.

Jamie grinned as Clark turned from the coat rack. "You sure look pretty, Darcy. Clark, doesn't she look pretty?" She smiled and wondered about her dimples.

"Very pretty." *If Clark was uncomfortable with that, he didn't show it. His compliments were always easy and sincere—a good influence on Jamie, she reminded herself.*

"Do you want to see my room?" Jamie asked. "Clark put all my stuff in there."

She followed him into the room where she had slept the summer before last. His cowboy bedspread covered the narrow bed. There was the usual assortment of toys.

"Hello there, Cougey. You look right at home here," she remarked, nodding to the pelt above the bed. On the opposite wall hung Jim's and Sarah's drawings, and Jamie's picture of God, each of them beautifully matted and framed.

She stood looking at them. "They're beautiful!"

"Rebekah framed them," Jamie explained.

Returning to the kitchen, she commented to Clark, "It's all there. Everything a boy could want."

"Everything except a mother." Clark didn't turn from the stove.

Her heart jumped into her throat. *A mother! Does that mean...?* Before her mind could form its question, she knew her answer. There was nothing she wanted more than to be Clark's wife and Jamie's mother. Carol was right, again. She had seen straight through Darcy's protective armor of denial. It was time to start being loyal to herself. Her feigned loyalty to Cal had been nothing but cowardice, fear of making another mistake.

She blushed inside, recalling Carol's challenge to describe the perfect man. Carol, bless her heart, had squelched a laugh when Darcy listed those attributes without realizing until later that she had described Clark in fine detail.

Yet, instinctively, Darcy stiffened. She'd better not jump to conclusions. Clark might be planning to marry someone else.

Maybe Rebekah? Her mind flashed back to the days when Rebekah had changed their bandages. *She isn't a mother,* Darcy reflected, *but at least she grew up with one.*

Trying to be nonchalant, Darcy asked, "Is Rebekah home for Christmas?"

Clark nodded. "Comin' tomorrow, with Esther and Bill. Whole family'll be here."

She had to change the subject quickly. She turned away from his gaze and walked into the living room—anything to lift the heaviness that suddenly and without warning had settled in her chest. Clark had mentioned Rebekah and "the whole family" in the same breath, as though he were part of the Chadwell family.

She looked around the room. A thick area rug indicated that Jamie, like other small boys, liked to sprawl on the floor. A new bookcase held an impressive collection of books and a few children's videos. On the wide arm of Clark's recliner lay a leather-bound Bible with yellow notes protruding from its edges, just like hers.

As Clark joined her in the living room, she commented at length on the changes. "I like what you've done here, and also in Jamie's room."

"Jamie's room is fine, but it needs a mother's touch," he replied. "Workin' on another room back there. Family needs more space than a bachelor does. Lots of room to expand up here."

A family! She hurried to comment on the Christmas tree decorated with Sarah's folded paper stars and delicate snowflakes. Anything to keep her from getting her hopes too high.

"The tree is beautiful," she said.

Clark grinned. "Has a woman's touch. Sarah's. Interestin' what a woman can do. We found these stars and snowflakes folded in a box we brought back from the cave. Also those folded green paper trees.

"One time our tree was a tumbleweed," Jamie said. "And my mom made it look pretty. We put red berries and popcorn on my dad's fishing line."

Clark's left eyebrow flew up in that way she had not forgotten. "Yep, a tree needs a woman's touch. Like this house."

This time, Darcy noticed, he didn't say a *mother's* touch.

"Sarah was a very special woman." As she spoke, Darcy's thoughts spun. *Rebekah is a special woman, too.* She kept her eyes on the tree, feeling Clark's steady gaze on her face.

While the potatoes cooked, Clark set a mug in front of Darcy and tipped the coffeepot. She had dreaded this moment, remembering all the coffee she had consumed in this kitchen before. "None for me, thanks. Coffee and I don't get along." She smiled apologetically. "I've changed my drinking habits."

His craggy eyebrows seemed to ratchet up like a tire jack. As understanding dawned, it turned his face into a smile and his voice into a twangy John Wayne imitation, the worst she had ever heard: "Well, you've come a long way, Little Lady. Learnin' to speak up." He set the coffeepot down. "How about tea?"

"I love it."

"Then we shall have some tea," he said in a mocking half-falsetto English accent. She laughed. This time, he sounded like Grandmother. Whether intended or not, it was a good imitation.

From behind the lower door of the hutch, he lifted a large teapot. As he set it on the counter, Darcy noticed how the muscles in his arms bulged against his shirtsleeves.

"Lillian liked tea," he said. "Better get some fresh stuff from the store."

While he hurried downstairs, Darcy heated the water and washed the teapot. The cream-colored pot was shaped like Aladdin's lamp, with a flame-shaped knob on its lid and a big swirl of a handle. Decorated in brown and orange, it was identical to one Grandmother had bought from a grocery peddler. That memory would account for the lump in her throat.

Supper was delicious and noisy. Responding to Clark's appeal for help with the gravy, Darcy had demonstrated Grandmother's way of caramelizing the pan drippings and thickening it with cornstarch, plus seasoning it with garlic.

"Nothin' like a woman's touch," Clark said. "Looks pretty, too," he added, admiring the way Darcy had arranged the sliced meat on the platter.

"It's something Grandmother taught me. She said food should not only be cooked properly, but should be presented attractively."

As she spoke, Darcy wondered why it was so much easier to talk about Grandmother now. Was it because she had, in Henry Chadwell's terms, "got her faith on straight?"

Maybe. But deep down, resentment toward Grandmother still weighed on her.

She managed a smile as her eyes met Clark's, then relaxed as Jamie outlined their plans for the next day. Tomorrow they would show her the ranch, on horseback if she felt brave. She did. The day after that was Christmas Eve, then came Christmas Day. Clark had a flying job the day after Christmas. That would allow her some time alone with Jamie before she had to leave.

* * * * *

After dinner, she drove to Mrs. Chadwell's house, where she received a warm greeting.

"My dear Mrs. Callahan. I'm so happy you were able to spend the holidays with us." Her voice lowered. "Jamie would have been terribly disappointed if you hadn't. He mentions you often."

Darcy felt like a long lost relative. "I'm happy, too. I've missed him more than I realized. Thank you so much for letting me stay here. And please call me Darcy."

"I surely will. And you will call me Eunice—we don't stand on formality here."

"Do you have a son named Timothy?"

A cheery laugh spilled from Eunice's throat. "Like Eunice's son in the New Testament? No, I don't. Henry and I gave all of our children Old Testament names. I do have a *grandson* named Timothy, though. In fact all of our grandchildren have New Testament names. Informally, they're called Pete, Andy, Tim, Matt, Tom, and so forth. And of course there's Jamie—two of them, actually. Some of the grandchildren go by their formal names: John, Paul, Mark, Mary, Martha, and Lydia, for example."

She chuckled again and winked. "If my childbearing years had lasted longer, I'm sure we would have covered the

New Testament as well!" Then, more seriously, she reminisced: "God blessed me that way. Child-bearing was easy for me, as long as it lasted; and though we had many mouths to feed, Henry was an excellent provider. A large family can manage quite well on a farm, you know." She seemed to go dreamy-eyed when she spoke about her husband and their years together.

The two recent widows talked until late into the night, and when Darcy fell into bed her thoughts formed their usual bedtime list. She had gleaned much from her visit with this delightful woman. The Chadwells' marriage had not been the straight-laced, tight-lipped union one might have imagined. It was a true love story, warm and passionate. And Eunice was handling her husband's death with far greater aplomb than Darcy was handling hers.

Where did Eunice get that strength? Until she resumed going to church, Darcy had thought she could count on one hand the happy marriages she knew of. Bob and Carol immediately came to mind. They were happy, and they were Christians, too. Maybe there was a connection between faith and happiness.

* * * * *

Their early morning horseback ride was delightful. "Are you a good rider?" Clark asked. "If you are, you can ride Midnight."

"Who else do you have?"

"We have Muffin." Jamie answered. "Clark taught Rebekah how to ride, and now she can ride Midnight."

A wave of competitiveness swept through her, but she decided on the safer choice. She laughed. "I think Muffin will suit me for now."

Plodding along on the small brown mare, Darcy watched closely and followed Clark's instructions to Jamie on how to hold the reins and how to sit up straight in the saddle. Somehow this reminded her of the way Grandmother had coached the girls to hold silverware properly and to sit without touching their backs to the chair. How strange that this man could remind her of Grandmother!

She enjoyed the easy chatter and the jibes between them. Her own tinkly laughter lifted her spirits. She sensed that Clark's spirits had lightened as well. Humor and playfulness had not been a part of Darcy's upbringing. In Grandmother's house anything frivolous was deemed suspect. With Cal, well....

At the end of the ride Clark lifted Muffin's saddle and grinned. "Wanta ride Midnight next time?"

Darcy tried to conceal her doubt. "Sure, if you think I can handle him."

"You can. Muffin's too easy. Makes you lazy."

Her smile came easily. "Did I look lazy on Muffin?"

"Like a cat in a sunbeam." Their laughter couldn't disconnect their gaze.

* * * * *

Christmas Eve at the Chadwell house was a joyous event. The whole Chadwell family was there, along with Bert and Clara Two Goats. Rebekah had arrived early the previous morning with Esther and Bill. Darcy noticed that Rebekah had adopted Esther's fashion sense. Rebekah's raven black hair, smoothed back and twisted into a chignon, emphasized her flawless complexion. She wore a deep red velvet dress. Darcy watched Rebeka's reflection in the mirror as she lit the candles on the mantle. *She's beautiful,* Darcy admitted to herself.

The house seemed to burst with happiness and warmth, as if Henry Chadwell and Sarah and Jim were still among them. The women chattered over tomorrow's dinner preparations. While the teenagers trimmed the huge tree, the men moved the furniture and set up extra tables.

To Darcy's surprise, this family was not austere when it came to holiday decorations. The tables were set with lovely centerpieces, linens, and tableware. With Naomi's help, the youngest children had made place cards for "Jesus' Birthday Party" in art class. They all sang "Happy Birthday, Dear Jesus" at dessert time.

After the evening meal, Dan read the Christmas story from his father's Bible and the children performed music and skits they had learned for their church programs. Jamie was a shepherd boy. Bert's and Clara's eyes squinched into crinkled smiles when their old border collie Duke, wearing a sheepskin vest, appeared playing the part of the sheep.

Solos and duets filled the air. Jamie had informed Eunice that Darcy was a "song teacher." Asked to sing a solo, Darcy was surprised at how easily she agreed. This was not a competition or a performance; not something for Cal to criticize. It was participation, as though she belonged. The minute she took her place on the piano bench, her throat relaxed and her voice regained its lilt. She sang *There's a Song in the Air*, the first song she had taught her girls' chorus at Elko. When she finished, Clark's and Jamie's faces beamed.

Next came the part Darcy loved the most. Rebekah played the piano and everyone sang carols like she had never heard them sung. Voices blended into beautiful harmonies, singing words she knew by heart but had never really listened to before. She had not had such a wonderful Christmas since that night at Ramon's and Rosa's house, when she had cuddled her rag doll close and wished she could live there forever.

* * * * *

Warm feelings remained as she snuggled deep into the soft flannel sheets. Clark and Jamie would come for her in the morning. After breakfast they would exchange gifts. She decided to give Clark the sofa pillows she had bought for her own home, tapestry pillows with pheasants and quail—*a woman's touch*. Did she dare hope for a real home with Clark and Jamie, or was she reading too much into Clark's words? Either way, she would keep this Christmas in her heart.

CHAPTER 14

Christmas morning was more than magical. Darcy dressed carefully in her new deep rose dress that, according to Carol, emphasized her creamy "English" skin. She added just a touch of make-up and plain silver earrings and did not miss the approval in their eyes when Clark and Jamie greeted her at the upstairs door.

When it came time to open the gifts, Darcy felt more eager than she had during her childhood, when her gift from Grandmother was always a new recital dress. Holiday week then was dreary. While the other girls were gone for two weeks, she and Grandmother rattled around in that big house. Grandmother used the time to catch up on her sewing and Darcy practiced for the January music recital. Plenty of kindness, but no fun.

Jamie's face glowed when Clark gave him cowboy boots and a small saddle. He yelped with delight over the book and games she gave him, then impulsively hugged them both and helped them unwrap his gifts to them. Darcy knew exactly where she would hang the bird feeder he had made in art class.

Clark was sincerely pleased with the book of Anasazi artifacts and the pillows. Then, while Jamie sat on his saddle and looked through his dinosaur book, Clark handed Darcy a long slender box. Her eyes brimmed when she pulled out a lovely necklace made by Navajo hands. Multi-strands of shimmering silver tubes poured like water over her wrist.

"They call this 'Liquid Silver,' " he said, fastening it on her neck. "Hope you like it."

"I do, Clark. I love it. It's perfect." Her memory flashed to another Christmas, to a glimpse of Ramon kissing Rosa's black hair. For an awkward moment Darcy wanted to be as impulsive as Jamie and give Clark a big hug.

Clark handed her another box. "Somethin' I made myself...." His words trailed off.

Darcy's heart fell as she lifted the lid. *This again?* The distinctive smell of leather yanked her senses back to moments with Cal, when she would open yet another of those awful handbags while smiling through her teeth and struggling to avoid another of his sulks. If this was one of those horrid tooled leather bags with rustic designs like the ones Cal bought during his cowboy phase... well, she would just have to smile through her teeth again.

She lifted the bag and exclaimed, "It's beautiful."

This was hand-tooled leather, but it was elegant—worked in a simple pattern that resembled fine beading. It could easily be mistaken for one of those in the designer shops in Sedona. But it was more than the perfection of his work that impressed her.

"It's lovely! Thank you, Clark." She absolutely loved the silver necklace he had bought for her, but the bag he'd made himself was the sort of gift a man gives a woman he plans to marry. Even more astonishing was his knack for knowing what she liked. He'd seen her home in Elko only a few times, yet he knew intuitively what would please her. *He made it himself! For me!* Her eyes glistened.

"Been a long time since I looked at pretty things. Used to bring things like that home to Lillian. I enjoyed it."

Something was different in the way Clark spoke of his memories now. The sadness was gone, or at least behind him. He was ready to live in the present. Darcy's thoughts slipped back to Cal's extravagant gifts—gifts she returned for a refund after he had shown them to their friends. She gave him the nicest things they could afford, such as the handsome leather briefcase that he quickly exchanged for alligator.

When Darcy didn't answer, Clark went on. "When I lost her, I thought I'd never love another woman. Figured no one could replace her. It took me a long time, but I've learned that it's possible to love again. Lillian is gone, but I'm still here and alive. Rebekah taught me that. Said I should quit squelchin' my feelings and give myself a chance."

Darcy held her breath. *So that's Jamie's secret! It's Clark and Rebekah! It seems so natural.* Darcy tried to think of an appropriate response, but her mind was an empty slate. What was a woman supposed to say when the man she loved told her he planned to marry someone else? Grandmother's etiquette standards might tell her, but she couldn't bring herself to say it.

Mercifully, the phone jangled. It was time to go to the Chadwells' for dinner.

Her knees wobbled as she walked into the Chadwell house. She offered to help in the kitchen and was soon caught up in the chatter, with teasing references to women catching husbands with their cooking, and other hints about a pending marriage. Her chest tightened when someone asked about honeymoon plans.

"Mexico. In the chopper," she heard Rebekah whisper.

Darcy's spine stiffened with such a jerk she feared everyone saw it. She squeezed her eyes tight. Her breath caught in her throat. But why didn't they act engaged? Why a secret? Her pulse raced and perspiration dampened her forehead.

Darcy wanted nothing more than to run from this place and find a spot somewhere— anywhere—as long as she could be alone. Even Jamie's cave sounded inviting, if it weren't buried under the landslide. But, as Grandmother had always taught, she couldn't make a scene. Cultured people hide their disappointment and pretend it doesn't exist. During the hours she spent with the Chadwells, she held her emotions in check, careful not to react to any of the snatches of conversation going on around her. Determined not to disappoint Jamie, she vowed to enjoy each day of her vacation. She would deal with the heartache later, the way she always did. Alone.

*   *   *   *   *

Back at Clark's place the next day, she and Jamie read and played games during the hours Clark was flying. In the evening, when Jamie was asleep, she and Clark had a long talk. Impersonal topics helped to hide her feelings. They discussed the hunting season, Jamie's school, and Esther's church steeple. Clark brought her up to date on the technology that now permitted people to conduct their business electronically in remote places such as this. Most importantly, they talked at length about trusting God, a renewed experience for them both.

"I've believed in God all my life," Clark said. "But after I lost Lillian, I got it into my head that church was for women and children. Figured I'd send Jamie to Sunday School with one of the Chadwell ladies. But Eunice and Rebekah set me straight. Said children need parents who believe enough to act like it. Eunice told me about one of those funny things we call Henry's parables. Said I couldn't love God with all my heart unless the rest of my body went along." He chuckled again. "And she's right, of course. So I go with Jamie now."

Darcy felt a weight lifting from her mind. "I have a friend in Elko who told me something along the same line. She was right, too."

Clark grinned. "Friends have a way of doin' that."

"Doing what?"

"Bein' right. Especially the ones who love you enough to tell you the truth, even when you don't want to hear it."

Darcy nodded in agreement. Then, having covered every subject except his pending marriage, they studied the book of artifacts.

"What does Bert think of the burial cave?"

He leaned back in his chair. "Haven't told him about it yet, or the artifacts, either, for that matter. Not sure he wants to know. You see, what we call the Anasazi, some Navajos call 'the Ancient Enemy.' They have a special feelin' about them. A mixture of respect and fear, I think. Been taught to shun those old ruins as places of bad spirits. I don't want to offend him with my ignorance. Need more information before I tell him. That book you gave me will come in handy."

"But he was praying there at the pillar. He must consider it a sacred site."

"More of a historical site. A landmark and restin' place along the old tradin' route. I doubt he knew about the burial cave. It's probably been covered with rocks for centuries."

He shifted in his chair. "I bet Harley Willis didn't know about it, either. By the look of the rocks around Jamie's mine, I think it was part of an older landslide. Jim wouldn't have allowed Jamie near the place if he knew what was in there. Jamie says Jim cleared some rocks off the flat area in front of the cave, and called it Jamie's mine. I suppose the slide that killed him and Sarah was the one that opened the shaft to the burial chamber. Anyway, I've been readin' up on a federal act that protects Native American graves. I sealed the entrance to keep animals out, especially the two-legged kind."

His voice lowered to a coarse whisper. "Lady, if you and Jamie had been in there when that tremor hit..." His voice almost choked. "I'd never have forgiven myself. Never would've gotten over it."

Darcy, reliving her frantic prayer for Jamie outside the cave-house during the rockslide, didn't hear Clark finish. When she showed no response to his remark, he cleared his throat and continued. "Had a land surveyor locate the boundaries. Then I posted it against trespassin'. Lots of hikers and ATV's around nowadays. I've checked around very discreetly about the pots in those pictures you took. Some of them could be Hohokam—that was a prehistoric native culture in southern Arizona. At any rate, they're very old."

He leaned back in his chair. "I've looked into the legalities of ownin' artifacts. Harley Willis must've known what was happenin' when he bought those two sections of land. The original claim was a section, so now Jamie owns nearly two thousand acres, includin' that meadow. That tremor must've shook somethin' loose underground. There's more water out there now. Could be good cattle range in a few years. And his property joins mine."

Darcy looked puzzled. "I thought it was illegal to dig artifacts."

Clark answered, "It is nowadays. Accordin' to the Federal Antiquities Act, it's against the law to dig artifacts on public land, but not on private land. Artifacts command a premium price, especially in Europe. They're sold on the black market. That's why the U.S. Treasury Department keeps such a close eye on the market. As we all know, wealth invites crime. Most crime in this area involves poachers or rustlers or pot hunters."

"Are there still a lot of buried pots?"

Clark shrugged his shoulders. "Accordin' to the BLM, there are literally thousands of sites along the Utah/Arizona border, especially around the Four Corners area. When the early settlers started clearin' the land, they unearthed countless sites. The government protects those sites now. There's a story been goin' around for years now about a rancher—up around Kanab, I think—who uncovered a shaft with people buried in a sittin' position. Thought it could be Montezuma's treasure, hidden there when all this area still belonged to Mexico. Didn't want the government tyin' up his property as an archeological site, so he filled it in. Lots of people still lookin' for it."

He fumbled in a drawer and handed her a flyer. "This comes from the Archaeology Advisory Group. All about vandalism and theft of historic sites. Stiff penalties for buyin', sellin', even transportin' items taken from those sites. Local folks know that anyone seen around here with a shovel or a backhoe on public land had better have a good explanation. And anyone sellin' pots better be ready to prove they came from their own property. That's why I check out my clients before I fly 'em around out here."

Darcy read the flyer. "Does this mean that Jamie could become wealthy by digging and selling the artifacts on his own land?" Her old suspicion reared its head. "Will you help him develop the site for pot-digging, since it's located on private land?"

Clark tilted back in his chair. "What some folks call pot huntin' is often nothin' but grave robbin'. No excuse for that kind of greed. Imagine how we'd feel if someone dug up our relatives for money. I'd like to think that he'll see its value as a historical site, or a Native American cultural site. Maybe somethin' like Walnut Canyon or Wupatki on a small scale. For his age, he's pretty sensitive to the idea of the mesa bein' a sacred site, because his sister was buried there." His forehead bunched into wavy lines. "Does he know that cave was a burial chamber? He hasn't mentioned it."

She pondered. "All I told him was that it was someone's private place. He didn't know it was a grave, but he'll figure it out. He doesn't know about that cache of old pots in the cellar, either. But he knows about the few pots a badger dug up. And about his dad's mine, of course."

He was quiet only a moment. "The cellar is buried under that last slide. Next summer I plan to take Jamie to some of the national parks and monuments, like Mesa Verde and the like. There's a great museum up in Blanding, Utah. He can learn that some things are more important than wealth. But for now, the pots are as safe buried in the cave as anywhere, until he gets old enough to decide. You and I are the only ones who know about them. And if Jim actually got any gold from that mine, I'm sure it's buried, too."

As they discussed this idea, Darcy was surprised at the secure feeling his plan gave her. In Harley Willis's words, Jamie had something more precious than gold or artifacts. He had love and wisdom and guidance. How different were Clark's ideas of guardianship from Aunt Belle's. She thought again of Grandmother's lovely things that Aunt Belle had appropriated, save for those few that Grandmother left in Judge Collins's care, to be given to Darcy when she came of age.

"Let's have some more tea," she said. As she poured the tea from Aladdin's lamp, she mentioned her Grandmother's boarding house. "Grandmother was widowed young and left with nothing but a big old Queen Anne house. We lived in a small town near the Allegheny and Appalachian mountains."

Darcy began to reveal more than she had intended about her childhood.

"She often entertained the town's most distinguished citizens. Back then I thought she was a social climber, because that's what Aunt Belle said she was. Then much later Judge Collins told me what she was really doing. Her boarders were mountain girls from motherless homes, girls with academic potential but poor social skills. They attended a vocational institute in the town, but that boarding house was their finishing school. They learned the skills that most upper-class girls learn from their mothers. The judge thought

I already knew that. But Grandmother had never explained it to me."

Even as she spoke, Darcy felt the pain of her misjudgment of Grandmother. "I learned later that the dinner parties were actually interviews, rather like secret auditions for college scholarships. Judge Collins and a group of businessmen provided opportunities for under-privileged students. Some of those girls went on to advanced degrees as a result of Grandmother's influence."

Clark's gaze never left Darcy's face as she told about her grandfather's eighteenth century English calendar watch. "Judge Collins wrote to me after I graduated from college. He told me Grandmother had left the watch in his care rather than including it in her estate, which would be my inheritance. It was to be sold when I came of age. She feared Aunt Belle would try to steal it from me. She was right, too, because much of my inheritance was spent on fancy improvements to Aunt Belle's house. When Judge Collins found a buyer for the watch, it more than paid off my student loans and my first car." Darcy didn't mention her investments that she had kept secret from Cal. She shrugged her shoulders. "But in the long run, it was good for me to earn my way by working in the real world. Grandmother's world wasn't exactly the real world, you see. Her heart was still in England with her Aunt Louise."

Clark leaned forward. "You should write a book about your Grandmother. Her story is inspiring, and you can tell it better than anyone else could. Folks should be able to read it."

His suggestion took her by surprise. At times she had been tempted to write a book of her own, as opposed to those ghostwritten for others, and had once mentioned it to Cal. His only concern was the potential for a bestseller or for profit. Clark, on the other hand, saw her writing as something of value in itself. Yes, Grandmother's story should be told, and what better way than in her own granddaughter's book?

"Thank you for the suggestion," she answered tentatively. "Yes, I think I will."

For a moment they sat quietly. Darcy sensed, but could not explain to herself, a warmth and wholeness she felt when those fond memories of Grandmother replaced her harsh old ones.

Clark pondered, then added: "Someone else I'd like to see you write about is Bert. Interestin' man. No formal education. My mother taught him to read after he was grown, but beyond that he's self-educated and an expert in native rituals and customs. Bert and Clara are Christians—what some Navajo call the 'Jesus Road'—but they respect the old ways and the people who still practice them."

Darcy couldn't keep from asking. "Why was he praying at the rock pillar?"

"He doesn't consider it prayin'. More like chantin' or singin'. His ancestors weren't Christians. Only way he can honor them is through their old way."

"Is the chanting a modern Navajo ritual, or an old one?"

"I'm not sure. My guess is, Bert thinks more about the reason for the ritual than the method. That's his way of lookin' at things. Pays more attention to attitudes than behavior. Says attitudes are the cause of behavior."

He grinned. "Once I asked if his ancestors heard his chant. He said the dead aren't the ones who need to hear. It's like he's caught in a time warp. I'm surprised he's a Christian. Still wears the traditional Navajo hairstyle." He laughed. "It's easier than wearin' short hair. Don't have to get it trimmed all the time."

That simple explanation made Darcy's thoughts spin. *I judged Bert by his hairstyle. I'm as bad as Aunt Belle was. Bert's right! Attitudes do cause behaviors, both good and bad.*

Struggling between her laughter at Bert's quip and her guilt and confusion, she decided to steer their conversation to a lighter subject. She closed her eyes and rubbed the teapot mischievously. "If this were really a magic lamp, what would you wish for?"

Hearing no answer, she opened her eyes and looked across the table at Clark's face. He was staring at the ceiling, eyes squinched, as if studying her question. Her gaze played over the craggy eyebrows and the wayward hair that fell over his eyes. There was something about those deep-set eyes. Something about the way they held her gaze. More than the shape or color, it was the kindness and the tenderness they held for Jamie. Nothing was missing. They were perfect. Out of those eyes flowed the affection she had longed for her entire life.

But it would never be hers. *He knows how I feel about him. He knows! But he's marrying Rebekah. I don't want him to know I'm in love with him. Or what a fool I am.*

Her mind was searching for words when, unexpectedly, Clark reached across the table and covered her hand with his. She felt his warmth. "Darcy." His voice was a coarse whisper.

A matching warmth welled up in her chest and spread through her body. She couldn't breathe. Then, jolted by her physical response to his touch, she yanked her hand free. Deep inside her chest a door slammed. Something recoiled.

How can he touch me that way and say my name that way when he's planning to marry Rebekah? Does he expect me to be happy for him? To congratulate him? I can't congratulate him if I haven't been told. And I don't want to be told, don't want to pretend I'm happy about it.

She stood up and spoke quietly: "I should go back to Eunice's. I can't keep her up late." She had her coat on and was starting out the door, her voice ragged in her throat. "I'll take my truck, so you won't have to waken Jamie." She kept walking. "I have something to do."

"Darcy, I'm sorry." The urgency in Clark's voice startled her. "I should've been more considerate. Should've known it's too soon." He followed her to the truck, his face a study in self-reproach. "Let's don't part this way. Let's don't let this hurt Jamie, or ourselves. Darcy...."

He didn't try to touch her again, not even her elbow. Darcy took a deep breath. Knowing how she must have felt, how dare he touch her that way, so tenderly, as though he actually cared! Was that the way he touched Rebekah when he proposed? *Was he about to tell me about his engagement to her? To let me down easily?*

An ugly thought crossed her mind. *Or, just maybe, was he putting a move on me?*

Her thoughts flared white hot. She remembered what Carol had said so long ago in college: "You look like a starlet, so men expect you to be a pushover." *Men!* The first thing that had attracted her to Cal was his focus on academics. So what, if later she learned that it was only his current role. Cal, for all his faults, was never promiscuous.

Confusion swirled within her. Her mind was beyond forming an explanation. A promise to come for breakfast and a perfunctory farewell was all she could manage.

The truck tires scattered gravel as she drove off. She was grateful that Rebekah and the others had left yesterday, and glad she had stayed upstairs, so not to see Clark's and Rebekah's good-byes. Now all she wanted, or needed, was to be alone with Eunice.

CHAPTER 15

Gulping mouthfuls of cold air, Darcy slammed the door of the truck at the Chadwell house. Eunice looked up from her reading and scrutinized Darcy's face as she walked in. "Dear, is something wrong?"

Determined not to make a scene, Darcy tried to regain her composure. "I think I'm just tired."

She accepted the older woman's invitation to join her. As they chatted, Darcy sought to turn the conversation to the subject that bothered her. She needed confirmation about Clark and Rebekah. No more guesswork. She would not mention her fall-out with Clark, and she must be discreet in ferreting out the truth from Eunice. She decided to take an oblique approach.

"Clark and Jamie certainly get along well together."

Eunice's eyes danced. "Yes, they do. We were grieved, of course, at Sarah's death. But we feel so blessed that we have Jamie, and that he has such a fine man to raise him." She paused, waiting for a response, then went on. "Clark has been lonely. We always include him in our family gatherings, but being a guest cannot fill the void of not having a family of your own."

Darcy stared at her lap. "I know." Remorse for her behavior toward Clark swept over her. *I'm such an idiot. If it's true about Clark and Rebekah, he was only trying to let me down easy. He wasn't making a pass at me. He's not that kind of man. And I made such a scene!* She was glad that in her rush to get away she hadn't left Clark's gift on the mantle. It would have been an undeserved, spiteful act. After all, they had been good friends, with much to share in memory.

Eunice's words handed her a perfect opening for the big question that bothered her. Darcy chose her words carefully: "Rebekah has been so much help to him and to Jamie."

"Oh, yes. Rebekah loves him. After her wedding..." Her hand flew to her mouth. "Oh, goodness, I'm telling secrets."

A heavy weight settled in Darcy's chest. That settled it! So it was true about Clark and Rebekah! Again, dejection and anger welled up inside her. *I shouldn't have been invited here. Yes, Jamie wanted me to come, but Clark should have known better. And why did he keep talking about how his house needed a woman's touch? Why didn't he just come out and tell me he was going to marry Rebekah, instead of trying this kiss-off routine?*

She managed a meek response. "I'm happy for her." Her smile felt like a mask painted on her face. She wanted to leave this room, but of course that would only make matters worse.

She decided to change the subject. Something else had been nagging at her, and she needed to talk with Eunice about it. Here was her last opportunity—she would be leaving in the morning.

"Eunice, something has puzzled me. Maybe you can explain it. Last June in Reno our choir bus broke down on a Sunday, and we had to wait a couple of hours for repairs. We were parked in a residential area, and it was a scorching day, much too hot to keep the students in the bus." She described the small air-conditioned church nearby, a stained glass chapel like Grandmother's.

"I went in and told the usher about our breakdown. The people were wonderful. They invited us in and the men set up extra chairs. Then they went on with their church service. The choir sang a song with a line, 'Pardon for sin, and a peace that endureth.' The minister said that no matter how religious we are, we can't find enduring peace if our hearts are filled with unforgiveness. What did he mean? I thought salvation and forgiveness were the same thing."

Eunice chuckled. "What a friendly church." She took Darcy's hand. "That line you mentioned is from one of my favorite hymns. It's called 'Great Is Thy Faithfulness.' You are a Christian, aren't you, dear?"

Darcy nodded. "Yes, but not a very good one, according to what that preacher in Reno talked about. I had so many grudges about people that when I grew up I forgot about God."

Eunice smiled and nodded her head. "Yes, that often happens, and it's unfortunate. But the important thing is that God didn't forget about *you*. He loves you and He forgives you. He loves us all, even with our faults. Or, as my grandsons say, 'when we goof up.' Our faith is based on His love, not on our own merit, and that is the source of our peace. That's what the Bible's all about, just trusting God."

There was that word again. *Trust.* Darcy mentally scanned her doubts. "But then, what about peace and forgiveness? I've recently come to a closer walk with Him, but I have to tell you—forgiveness doesn't come easy with me, and neither does peace. How can I ask for His forgiveness when it's so hard for *me* to forgive? And if God knows about our hidden secrets but loves us anyway, why is it necessary for us to ask for forgiveness? Doesn't He already know how we feel?" To her own ears, Darcy's questions sounded juvenile, the kind she should have asked when she was young.

Eunice nodded. "Yes, He knows. But He wants us to acknowledge our faults and ask for His help. If we deny them, we can't grow."

She leafed through the Bible on her lap. "I believe the minister was talking about Christians needing to forgive each other's wrongdoing in order to have happy lives. Here in Mark, 11:25, Jesus says, 'Whenever you stand praying, if you have anything against anyone, forgive him, that your Father in heaven may also forgive you your trespasses.' "

She laughed softly. "Henry used to say that we wouldn't think of moving new furniture into a dirty house, so how can we expect to move our nice clean souls into a heart filled with resentment? Condemnation is destructive, you know. It robs the joy from our lives. I think of it as plugging our spiritual access to God the way cholesterol plugs our arteries. It's deadly to our happiness."

When Darcy didn't respond, she continued. "You see, dear, 'leaving the past behind' is not the same thing as 'getting over it.' When someone hurts us, the damage begins. And every day we harbor that hurt, it compounds."

She added softly, "And forgiving others is only half the solution. Remember, that verse speaks of forgiving each other. We must also ask forgiveness from those *we've* hurt. It's very painful and difficult sometimes. Like the time Henry and I asked God to forgive us for the way we first felt toward Jim Granger."

She straightened in her chair. "We were very wrong about Jim. And we couldn't overcome our feeling until God removed the darkness we carried inside. But think of all those years when we didn't see Sarah and Jim and Jamie. All those wasted years."

Darcy was shocked at the idea of darkness in Eunice Chadwell. "But," she whispered, "How can we forgive or be forgiven by someone who is already dead?"

Eunice was slow in answering. "Folks have wrestled with that problem for ages. We can't speak to those who are gone. Perhaps if you write the offenses down, and pray about it, the Lord will help you find a way that is right for you."

"But something else still puzzles me," Darcy responded. "How can we be expected to forgive someone if we don't understand what caused them to hurt us?"

"Oh, you see dear, we don't have to understand. We all have our inner conflicts and we're seldom capable of fully understanding someone else's problem. God is the one who understands. Forgiveness doesn't come from knowledge or wishful thinking. It's a spiritual decision. It's something we do. It's our choice."

"Choice? You mean if we choose to forgive—even if we're still angry, or hurt—it still works?"

Eunice chuckled. "Yes, that's a good way to put it. And once we have done that, we must leave it with God. It's like that old spiritual that says, 'Gonna lay my burdens down.' "

She paused. "Love is based on trust, you see. We can't truly love God without trusting Him." Another pause, then, "It's the same in love between people. Trust is forgiving without understanding."

"Oh, yes, I see. But is there a ceremony or a ritual we're to follow?"

Eunice pondered only a moment. "A formal apology is sort of a ritual. But for those who are not living, well dear, I see no reason why we can't make our own ritual if it helps us to commemorate our forgiveness. It can't hurt, as long as our faith is based on God's word and not on the ritual itself."

Make our own ritual? Like Bert at the tall rock? Darcy stared into space; what a novel idea! After a long pause, she said, "Thank you, Eunice—you've been a big help to me. I'll ponder what you've told me. I'd better get to bed now. Tomorrow's a traveling day."

As Darcy climbed the stairs to the cozy guest room, she looked back and saw that Eunice had bowed her head.

* * * * *

Darcy tossed in bed. Her friendship with Clark and Jamie was destroyed. She should have left before Clark saw her looking at him *that* way. Grandmother had called that look "sheep's eyes" when she warned the girls not to mistake infatuation for true love.

She didn't want him to know how she felt, yet she wanted his love more than she could admit. Ever since the night he sang the song about the Buckaroo, she had wanted to be part of his life, to talk for hours and share his dreams. She wanted to give back a measure of the companionship he had given her—to give, not just take. To be joined at the heart, a real wife in every way. To hear him whistle every morning.

Wry thoughts now filled her mind. Yes, she had come a long way—in the wrong direction. Carol was right. Independence can be lonely. Especially when you're carrying excess baggage.

She jerked her thoughts back and sat straight up in bed, her eyes wide open and Eunice's words pounding in her ears: "Perhaps if you write the offenses down, and pray about it, the Lord will help you find a way that is right for you."

She also recalled something the minister in Reno had said, something about forgiveness being active, not passive. Something about an ax and "the root of bitterness." Was she supposed to chop the bitterness out? It was worth a try.

Digging through her suitcase, she found her ever-present writing pad and began to write. Long columns of short phrases took shape, a lifetime's litany of silent rage that burned like acid in her mouth. First was her long list of grievances against men. Not all men, just those who treated her as fair game for their lust.

Once finished with that, she started on Aunt Belle and her daughters, Brenda and Gayle. Anger she had preserved in her heart poured onto the paper. Darcy hated living with them after Grandmother's death. She hated the way they gossiped about everyone they knew, even their church friends.

Judge Collins once said that Belle and her little clique got more satisfaction from seeing evil people punished than from seeing good people rewarded. Darcy believed it. She tried to avoid the ones who considered no question too personal to ask. She cringed when they asked in a saccharine voice, "Why don't you live with your parents?" What was she supposed to say? "Because they don't want me?" In the end she retreated into her own world of studies and music. So tightly had she slammed the door against Aunt Belle's church that she closed God out as well.

Her friend Lydia once argued that the problem was not in Belle's church, but in Belle herself. "She has no true friends. Nobody likes to be around a person with a bitter spirit," she explained. "So people turn away."

Knowing that to be true, Darcy had tried to hide her own rancid frame of mind from herself. But it could not be concealed. It seeped out in her thoughts and dreams.

She recalled the way Brenda and Gayle made fun of the refinements Grandmother had taught her. She detested the way they mimicked her posture. "Miss America," they sneered, "You walk like you swallowed a broomstick." And when she was honored for her volunteer music lessons for disadvantaged children, they stole her satisfaction. "Goody Two Shoes, you just do it to get attention," they taunted. In the end, Darcy had believed them, and despised them for knowing it.

Venom poured from her pen onto the yellow paper. She loathed them for gossiping about Grandmother's illness, as though they had never heard of privacy. She hated the way Aunt Belle rolled her eyes and explained "the real reason" for everything Grandmother did. She was just jealous, Aunt Belle. Even when she smiled—which was seldom—the corners of her mouth turned down. She seemed to want everyone's lives to be as miserable as her own.

And Vegas! Why do people there assume that every blond woman who goes to Vegas—even on a college scholarship, for heaven's sake—is really just another wannabe starlet? And what about Cal? He knew better. Why did he want her to be glamorous? Why did he let Vegas affect him that way? What about his unattainable goals, his impossible dreams? What was he searching for?

And what should she have done differently?

There it was again, that scathing self-blame for not keeping Cal on an even keel. She could feel again the indignation that consumed her every time he started off on a new identity. The truth was hard to face. She had preferred anger to understanding or pity.

Now that knot of anger in her heart toward Cal was loosening, only to be turned inward toward her own mistakes. What arrogance to presume that she could change Cal! Who did she think she was? God? That's what Carol would have asked. What a pompous fool she had been, preserving her ugly memories like amber in her own heart, memories that spoiled her happiness as much as Cal did.

Had she been shaping herself into a replica of Belle? If Belle was pickled in her own vinegar, as Lydia had whispered, then Darcy was poisoned by her own venom. Was that what Clark saw in her? No wonder he chose Rebekah. Where was the inner beauty she wanted him to see? It didn't exist. Once again the angry pen touched the yellow paper. *Foolish pride!*

From the upstairs window Darcy looked across the distance to Clark's home. His windows were dark. Everything was dark. There would be no chance to talk privately with him tomorrow. She'd have to write him a letter of apology when she got home. Or call him. Would he forgive her? Did he know about forgiving without understanding?

An hour or so later, emotionally spent, she slept.

CHAPTER 16

Morning came too soon. Darcy hugged Eunice and gratefully accepted her invitation to call if she wanted to talk. As she drove to Clark's house, the muscles in her shoulders tightened with each bend in the road.

If tension had been issued a color, the air around the breakfast table would have been black. Jamie, seeming not to notice, prattled as usual, holding the silence at bay through breakfast and later on as they made their way to the truck downstairs. She was thankful for that.

"Bert says if I learn to ride Bucky real good, I can go on the cattle drive. And ride in Little Britches," Jamie said as they neared the truck.

"Little Britches?" Darcy had not the remotest idea what that was. But small talk gave her a way to pretend that nothing had changed. Everything had changed.

"It's a rodeo for kids." Jamie explained. "Can you come to the rodeo next summer? You can ride Midnight."

She looked at Clark's anguished face but avoided his eyes. "I'll have to check it out." She wasn't going to string Jamie along with promises.

Saying good-bye this time was much more painful than the last. She wanted to apologize to Clark for her behavior and wish him and Rebekah a wonderful life together, but the deep hurt she felt at losing him weighed too heavily on her for that. She needed more time to sort out her feelings. She could not risk the chance of falling apart and making a scene; she must maintain her composure and her dignity, as Grandmother had trained her to do.

After sharing a quick hug with Jamie and a limp hand-shake with Clark—barely letting her eyes meet his—she climbed into the truck and started the engine. She looked back at Clark. "I'll call or write to you," she said, then gunned the engine and sped away.

*   *   *   *   *

Darkness was coming on when Darcy settled into the motel at Provo. Eunice's words had played over and over in her mind all the way there. While she showered and dried her hair, she planned for tomorrow. The gas tank was full. Tomorrow was Sunday. There wouldn't be much traffic on Interstate 80 across the Salt Flat.

She settled into bed. Trying to squelch the memory of her disastrous holiday experience, she forced her mind to focus on what Eunice had said about forgiveness: "It's a decision of the spirit. It doesn't require our understanding. Our job is to forgive."

She wanted to tell Carol what she'd learned. She could almost hear Carol's comical response: "So you discovered you aren't God!" And she would be right, as usual.

Her thoughts turned to Cal. How could she expect herself to understand him? How much wiser was she than Cal anyway? She was as young and foolish as he was. Hadn't she made her own decisions by rejecting what she disliked instead of looking for what she liked? Hadn't she chosen college in Nevada just to get away from West Virginia? Why had she spent her energy resenting her negative childhood, when she could have accomplished more by letting it go?

New questions flooded her mind. Had she married Cal because she hated other men, who looked at her *that* way? No. She loved Cal—the original Cal, anyway, the one with his face in a book.

A tiny glimmer of insight began to penetrate her dark thoughts. She opened her wallet and stared at Cal's picture. She and Cal had needed each other then. Two young adult orphans in a big wicked city. "Poor little lambs," they called themselves. They had found refuge together. Sad to say, they both had brought their childhood pain into their marriage. They both sensed that the qualities they admired were missing from their lives.

In time their search for identity had led them in opposite directions. While Darcy probed for meaning that lay in the depths, Cal's attention was captured by the glittering surface. With the ragged edges of their disillusionment, they sawed away every connection they had established and ultimately failed each other. Maybe, in time, they would have met in the middle. Maybe she could grieve for that Cal.

After long minutes she retrieved from her suitcase the sheets of yellow paper and slowly tore them into confetti, tucking the tiny bits into her jacket pockets. She watched the weather report on television for the time of tomorrow's sunrise, then set her alarm for two hours earlier and slept fitfully.

* * * * *

The world was still dark when, long before daylight, she pulled out onto Interstate 80 to cross over the Bonneville Salt Flat toward Elko. Few headlights greeted her along the straight road from Salt Lake City toward the Nevada border. From time to time she glanced through her rear-view mirror at the eastern horizon until a faint glow appeared above the distant Wasatch Mountains. As night paled, the cobalt sky lightened to pink, with shimmering traces of gold outlining the low clouds on the horizon. An undulating string of geese honked overhead as she scanned the road for a turnout and stopped the truck. The icy western breeze stung her face when she stepped out, holding the shopping bag.

Shivering, she removed her jacket. From the bag she unfolded a white gauzy dress and pulled it over her jeans and sweatshirt. Fumbling in the bottom of the bag, she came up with a mother-of-pearl hair clasp. With her fingers she parted her hair from temples to crown and fastened it with the clasp. Her hands trembled as she unwound a framed photo of Cal from its white mesh wrapping and stood it on the hood of the truck. As the sky lightened, she dug in the bag for the silver-plated metal box she had brought from Vegas. Her fingers struggled to open it, and at last lifted out a tall cardboard container. It, too had a silver coat. For a long moment she held it close, then set it on the ground beside her.

The sun, though not yet visible, cast a rosy glow in the eastern sky. As she watched, it slowly appeared and the glow poured over the salt flat, washing the white earth in a pink watercolor bath, plunging the low places into violet shadows and highlighting the raised areas with glittering gold leaf. She had never seen a barren desert more beautiful.

The frigid air assaulted her throat with each breath. Her lips moved in a whisper. "Cal, I'm sorry that we weren't happy together. I'm sorry you didn't find what you needed. I'm sorry for the bad thoughts I've had. I don't fully understand what ruined our happiness, but my new friend Eunice told me I don't have to. God understands, and that's enough"

Again, anger and hurt rose in her throat as she recalled Cal's deathbed concern for his funeral services instead of a final message for her. She was determined to see this through. "I forgive you, Cal, for not saying good-bye. And for the other things that hurt me."

Still plaguing her memory were his attempts to change her. Whereas Grandmother had tried to equip her for a proper life, Cal considered her mere raw material to be molded to enhance his own identity. *Pygmalion in reverse,* she thought––and not for her benefit.

Her eyes stung, and her breath smoked in the icy air. She pressed her hand against her cold lips. "Cal, I forgive you for that. And please forgive *me* for not trusting you, for not knowing how troubled you were. I'm sorry I didn't get you the help you needed. I was so angry at you for trying to change me, that I didn't notice how frustrated you were with yourself."

A sob escaped her throat. "It wasn't all your fault. Forgive me, Cal. Please. I love you." From the left pocket of her jacket she pulled a handful of torn paper bits. The tiny confetti sifted from her hand and drifted on the wind.

At last she could grieve for the man she married, now that the anger had stopped plugging the flow of love from her heart. With some difficulty she opened the cardboard container and held it over the edge of the low embankment. As she gently lofted Cal's ashes into the stained glass morning, she heard soft plunking sounds and watched the glittering particles flutter in the breeze. Released with long denied affection, Peter Callahan now mingled with the rosy dawn and settled on that desert of alabaster salt—to her, a million generations of healing tears.

* * * * *

Her words to Cal, so opposite from her old feelings, now reminded Darcy of her Grandmother's penchant for painting her own version of reality. She didn't harm anyone, but simply saw things as she wished them to be. True, her clipped British accent had rubbed off on Darcy. What Grandmother had tried to teach her was to think before she spoke. Maybe it was her way of covering her true feelings with something more acceptable. Grandmother's words were always correct and gracious, though seldom affectionate.

"Grandmother," she began, "I didn't expect you to brag about me or exaggerate my good points, the way you did my father's. I just wanted you to accept me for who I was—just acknowledge my presence, that's all. I didn't know why you wouldn't, or couldn't, tell me about my parents. I think I understand, now, some of the pain you tried to hide from me. You wanted to prepare me for facing a harsh world. I admire and appreciate your motives, but it's been a heavy burden. I don't want to carry that load the rest of my life."

She took a deep breath. "You left good tracks for me. But I started looking at other tracks and got confused. Please forgive me for being so blind, for not understanding you. Forgive me for resenting your teachings, and the expectations you had for me. Forgive me for taking offense at your church and your cultured ways." A sob caught in her throat. "Please forgive me for saying I wanted to spend every Christmas with Ramon and Rosa. Now I can feel how much that hurt you."

She stopped to blow her nose. "Forgive my anger at you for dying and leaving me with Aunt Belle. Forgive me for thinking you were cold and uncaring, when you were carrying such a heavy load. It's true I had an unhappy childhood, but that doesn't excuse my horrible attitude as an adult. I'm going to write a book about you. A very special friend suggested it.

"And then there's my new friend Eunice. Her daughter, Sarah, went away just like your son, my father, did. She learned to forgive Sarah without understanding why she left; that is, until she learned why she had left. She said God is the one who understands. And now I forgive you for not saying good-bye. I love you Grandmother. Good-bye." She launched another handful of confetti.

"Mother and Father, please forgive me for being angry at you. For a long time as a little girl, I didn't understand why you left me behind. I didn't know until after Grandmother died. Judge Collins told me that you went to Europe on a vacation, and died in an accident on the Autobahn in Germany. He thought I knew that, but no one ever told me. Grandmother didn't tell me because she wanted to spare my feelings. I'm truly ashamed for being more hurt by what I thought was your rejection than by your death. Please forgive me." Another handful of confetti floated in the breeze.

Her chest relaxed, then tightened again. Once again she saw Aunt Belle's sarcastic expressions behind Grandmother's back. Once again she heard Belle's criticism that did not cease after Grandmother's death. Belle's tongue was always coiled and ready to strike. Again the bitterness tried to put down new roots. She forced herself to remember what Eunice had said about forgiveness being an act of the will. "Aunt Belle, I forgive you, and also your daughters. Please forgive me for not appreciating the home you gave me."

Her words, as dry in her mouth as the arid desert, became a catalyst as her last handful of confetti fluttered in the breeze. Tears scalded Darcy's cheeks as the yellow sun splashed the desert. The root of bitterness entwining her heart had begun to loosen.

Eunice was right when she said the power of confession and forgiveness comes from putting them into words. Rebekah was right, too. She said people, even the ancient ones, have always loved the sunrise. They were looking for a new beginning, a new chance for happiness, she said. She tried to recall Rebekah's words. Something like,"Weeping lasts all night, but joy comes in the morning."

She looked again at Cal's picture on the truck. Her heart was now being healed, but tender scars remained. Bouncing from foot to foot, she rubbed her upper arms in the winter chill, knowing full well the danger of being out here alone. It was too early for travelers, but it seemed eerie that no trucks had passed. What would truck drivers think of a woman in a gauzy wedding dress (over jeans and a sweatshirt) talking to herself in this God forsaken place?

No! She edited her thoughts again. God didn't forsake any place. He was present at Jim and Sarah's cave, and in the dark burial chamber. Perhaps her best glimpses of Him were at Henry Chadwell's bedside and later at his funeral. He was in the plain churches of Elko and in the formal one in Reno. Wherever she had looked, there He was. And now she realized that He had been there all along, even when she wasn't looking. It was like Eunice said, "God didn't forget you." As for Grandmother's church, those stained glass windows hadn't held Him in. Neither had they kept Him out.

At last her mind quieted. The deep layer of guilt and resentment that had rested on her soul like a dark cloud was gone. She felt alive and free. Free, but strangely empty; as vacant and lonely as the unused side of a double bed. What she needed now was God's guidance for her future. Maybe she should pray for it the way Jamie did, right out loud. She had to learn sometime, and this was the perfect place. Nobody would hear her, except God.

She took a deep breath. Her whispered words smoked in the icy air. She began, "Our Father...." But that didn't sound like Jamie's prayers. Too formal. She coughed and started again. "God, thank you for remembering me, and for loving me when I turned away from you. Please forgive me my horrid behavior. Thank you for giving me a new start. But, God, now I don't know what to do about Clark and Jamie. I promise to apologize to Clark for the awful way I acted when he touched my hand *that* way. I should have congratulated him and Rebekah. But, now, Lord, should I keep in touch with them? Or fade out of their lives? Please tell me what to do. Thank you, dear Lord. Amen."

She took another deep breath. At last, her shoulders relaxed.

"Ma'am, you shouldn't be alone."

Startled, Darcy whirled to face the voice behind her. Caught up in her prayer, she hadn't heard the approaching noise.

"Not in a place like this, at this time of day." the voice continued.

She stared at a young man straddling a purring white motorcycle. "What? I'm okay," she stammered. He didn't look menacing, but she knew very well that the worst ones seldom did.

His eyes swept over the crinkled dress she wore over her jeans and rested on the jacket flung on the truck's hood. "Is your truck giving you trouble? Are you out of gas?"

Before she could answer, his gaze slid to the metal box in her hands and the cardboard box at her feet labeled *Human Remains*. His expression saddened. Removing his white helmet, he dismounted and stood beside her.

"Someone very close to you?" He glanced at Cal's photo on the truck.

Darcy swallowed. She had no intention of telling this stranger what she was doing here, but the words came unbidden.

"My husband."

"I'm very sorry, Ma'am."

She wished he would leave. She wanted to stay here a little longer. A quick glance about told her there were no other vehicles on the highway. No one but herself and this tall blond man in a white jacket. Maybe he was a state trooper. She glanced at his jacket. No identifying shoulder patches.

He shuffled his feet. "What was your husband like?"

Darcy was shocked, not at the impertinence of his question, but at the emotion that welled up in her chest when she tried to answer. "He was a very good man, a dedicated student and music professor." Amazed at the invasion of her memories, she found herself listing Cal's virtues to this stranger. "He was interested in so many different things. Always trying something new." She nodded toward the photo. "He was handsome, but he didn't exploit his good looks. He turned down dozens of modeling offers."

She sounded exactly like Grandmother. And, she noticed, she felt no resentment or anger. Somehow she knew what he was going to ask.

"I gather this is your anniversary," he said. "How long were you married?" His eyes scanned that ridiculous dress she wore.

"This would have been our tenth anniversary." She didn't want to discuss it.

"Ten years...today?"

She merely nodded as fresh tears poured down her face. Hot salty tears for Cal. She covered her mouth with her hands. How could this young man know that *today* was their tenth anniversary? A no-brainer, of course—he had already guessed that by the wedding dress she wore.

His tone softened. "You loved him very much."

Darcy stiffened. "How can you tell?" *I mean, what makes him think so?*

"If you didn't, you wouldn't be out here at this hour on your anniversary." He paused for a moment, then reached for the cardboard carton. "I'd be happy to dispose of this for you."

She turned to look at the waste barrel nearby. "Thank you very much." As he bent to pick up the cardboard box, she whisked the gauzy dress over her head and rolled it up. In short order she stuffed the dress and hair clip into the box. Again she wrapped Cal's photo in her wedding veil and grabbed her jacket.

The young man walked back from the barrel, then once again straddled the motorcycle. "Are you sure you're okay?"

"I'm okay. Thank you so much for stopping. I'm ready to leave now."

As she opened the door of the truck he walked the cycle nearer. On its white gas tank gleamed an insignia—a pair of gold wings.

He said no more, but waited until he heard the truck engine roar, then waved and drove ahead. Darcy watched the cycle disappear into the turkey-platter smoothness of the desert, then pulled onto the road. Within minutes she met a long string of trucks. Unusual, she thought, that they were so close together.

CHAPTER 17

D arcy was hungry. After breakfast in Wendover, a small town near the Nevada border, she could be in Elko in a couple of hours. Hurrying into the nearly empty cafe there, she ordered breakfast.

"You came at the right time," the waitress said. "We've been overrun with truckers."

"That's funny—I was out on the Salt Flat and for a long time there wasn't any traffic, in either direction. Then it all came at once. It seemed odd."

"A truck overturned and spilled cattle on the highway back at Rowley Junction. You must've just missed it," the waitress said. "It stopped traffic both ways—right here in town and back at Rowley Junction. I heard it all on the Highway Patrol's short-wave. They radioed our local officers and told them to stop traffic here while they rounded up the cattle. We were swamped—the travelers pulled in here for breakfast while they waited. They got the all-clear only a little while ago."

Darcy stifled a grin. Was it a miracle, or some kind of sign, that she'd had the desert all to herself when she needed it?

Back on the Interstate for the last leg of her trip home to Elko, Darcy pondered what had happened out on the Salt Flat. There she had emptied herself of a lifetime of bitterness and resentment, all by simply forgiving those who had given her cause for it, as Jesus taught in the Lord's Prayer. She felt a spiritual release that she had never experienced before.

She couldn't decide whether or not she should tell Carol about her experience on the Salt Flats. She new Carol would get a big laugh about Darcy standing out in that bitter cold desert wearing her wedding dress and talking to herself. What would Carol think about that young man dressed in white with a white motorcycle ... and gold wings! She laughed out loud. Carol would think he was an angel. She believed in angels; after all, the Bible spoke of them. Sometimes they looked and spoke like ordinary people, Carol maintained. But while Carol tended to see them frequently, Darcy was a bit skeptical. She had a hunch that the public's fascination with angels was fueled as much by the marketplace as by spirituality. How then could she explain that young man and his uncanny message—the first voice she heard after she prayed for guidance? "Ma'am, you shouldn't be alone." *Shouldn't be alone.*

That brought her to the subject of miracles. Some of her friends saw a miracle whenever things worked out to their advantage. In Darcy's mind a miracle would have to be something that defied the laws of nature, like the sun standing still. So how would she classify a situation like a disillusioned city woman finding true love in the Arizona strip? Or a child who believed in God being rescued by a woman who had lost her faith? Or was it the other way around? Had God rescued her through Jamie? Had He led her to him? Did He deliberately put those boulders in her path in the desert?

Her mind reviewed the coincidences—if there were such things—that had changed her life. Skeptics might try to explain it all away. After all, this hadn't been a typical burning bush experience. She didn't actually hear the voice of God directing her to Jamie's part of the desert when he prayed, or when they were lost inside the burial chamber.

But what about Clark's just happening to show up in time to save Jamie from the landslide? For that matter, what about the bus that broke down beside that church in Reno on a Sunday, an event that ultimately had led to her new-found peace and forgiveness?

Yes, she reasoned, science and psychology could allay a lot of superstitions, but they couldn't bring the sense of rightness to her heart that this ritual on the Salt Flat had given her. No, this was just what she needed: a kick in her pompous ego, an ax to her root of bitterness, an end to the blame and shame that had plagued her for years. Henry Chadwell was right. The new Darcy couldn't find peace until the old Darcy was cleared away. It wasn't Cal or Grandmother or Aunt Belle, but Darcy herself who needed to hear her own apologies.

Now she remembered Eunice's words, "When God forgives us we must forgive ourselves as well." Or, as Clark had so eloquently phrased it, "Cut yourself some slack, Lady. Time to get out of the pool." So many friends had tried to help her see her strong points. Did they know her better than she knew herself?

Darcy saw her next step clearly now. She must let go of her habit of critical introspection, accept God's grace, and begin a litany of thanksgiving.

* * * * *

Hours later, Darcy looked at all the work she had accomplished since she arrived home. From the minute she walked through the door, she had tried to call Clark. No answer. She left a message on Carol's answering machine to let her know that she was home, then called Clark again. No answer. His answering machine was not turned on. Disheartened and needing to keep busy, she hung photos of Grandmother, Roman and Rosa—and Cal—on her bedroom wall. Then she hung pictures of Jamie and Clark on the opposite wall.

She made tea and called again. No answer.

She had promised to let Eunice know when she arrived home safely, and she decided to do it now before it got much later. Eunice's voice on the phone sounded as cheerful as ever. After Darcy's brief message, Eunice lowered her voice to an excited whisper. "Darcy, next week I'm going to have my first helicopter ride. I should say 'chopper.' That's what Jamie calls it. Just imagine, at my age! Clark is taking me to Denver. It's actually a business flight, but there's room for me. I'll be there for Rebekah's engagement announce-ment." She chuckled. "I'm afraid our secret wasn't very well kept."

"I'm thrilled for her." Darcy's words tasted like sawdust.

"We are too. They wanted to make their announcement at Christmas, but his parents couldn't be here yet. So we kept it a secret—as much as we could, anyway."

Darcy paused longer than usual. "Clark's parents? I thought his parents both had died. I don't understand."

"Oh, no dear, not Clark. Mike Donnelly. His parents are missionaries who just got back from Mexico. He helps them in their mission work. We've known Mike a long time. He and Dan were smoke jumpers together."

Stunned, Darcy managed somehow to finish the conver-sation. In broken sentences she managed to tell Eunice the whole story of her misunderstanding, beginning with Jamie's "I've got a secret" announcement to her, the whispers at the Christmas party, her reaction to Clark's touching her *that* way when she understood that he was to marry Rebekah, and finally Eunice's own words that night when she had said, of Rebekah, "Oh yes, she loves him."

"Oh, my dear," Eunice replied. "I am so sorry! I should have said she loves him as a *brother*. He's like family to us. What he did for Jim and Sarah, and now is doing for Jamie, makes us all just love him."

As Darcy listened, she was looking into the mirror of her own soul. Recalling her thoughts when Clark touched her hand made her cringe inside. That was not righteous indignation. There was nothing righteous about it. She needed to change the subject.

"Eunice, I need to tell you this. What we talked about the night before I left—about forgiveness—has changed my life. I am eternally in your debt." She went on to tell Eunice how, on her last night there, she had emptied her anger at Cal, Grandmother, her parents, and Aunt Belle onto the yellow tablet sheets, and how she had experienced the lift of forgiveness in her ritual out there on the Salt Flat.

"I can't begin to tell you how my burden has been lifted. Would you please pray for me that this healing will last?"

"I'll certainly do that."

"One more request," Darcy said, haltingly. "I need to apologize to Clark for the way I acted. I've been trying to call him, but he doesn't answer and his answering machine is not turned on. Please pray for me that I can find the right words when I do reach him."

"Yes, dear, I will pray for you. And I will also thank God for releasing you from your burdens. God is blessing you, and He will continue to bless you."

* * * * *

Again and again she tried to contact Clark, and paced the room when there was no answer. Trying to keep herself busy so she wouldn't fall apart, she opened the boxes in the china cupboard and polished the tarnished tea service lovingly, exactly the way she was taught, then placed Clark's and Jamie's Christmas gifts to her in a place of honor on the bookcase.

The sound of tires on the graveled street caught her attention. *I hope it isn't Carol. I don't feel like talking. And I smell like silver polish.* From her office window she saw a small gray pickup she recognized. It belonged to a mechanic at the airport. Its door opened with a screech. Long legs unfolded and someone stepped out. Someone tall and slender.

She was out the door before he got to the top step. "Clark...." She could say no more. Her throat was stuck.

"Darcy." It was the soft, warm, melodious voice that she had come to love. Her breath that had been held captive for hours came out in a rush. She held the door open and moved back as he stepped into the room. Why? This didn't make sense. Was something wrong with Jamie?

"What's going on?"

His mouth curved into that mischievous smile she loved. "I got lost." Before a laugh could escape her throat, his hands touched her arms. "Eunice contacted me in the chopper. I was over Utah, so it didn't take long to get here."

She moved closer. "Clark, I'm so sorry. I owe you an apology."

"No need to feel bad. Just a misunderstandin'. Eunice told me all about it. Let's forget about it and start over." His hands rested lightly on her arms. She didn't resist, but moved closer. His long arms went around her waist.

"No, please," she whispered. "I need to say this. I need to apologize out loud. I need to tell you about all the baggage I've been carrying around for years, baggage that I have now dumped, and to give you a chance to reject what you don't want to deal with."

And she did, standing in the circle of his arms, her face resting in the hollow of his collarbone—right where she had dreamed it would. She didn't make excuses. Her story was long, starting with her orphan years with Grandmother and then Aunt Belle, her years with Cal, ending with Cal's death and his crass rejection of her on his deathbed. She held nothing back: not her discouragement, her anger, her fear, or her cleansing ritual out there on the Salt Flat.

Clark held her gently, never interrupting while she exercised her need to trust him with her story. Their newfound intimacy calmed her heart.

Darcy stepped back. "Where's Jamie?"

"Stayin' overnight with Phil and Jimmy. He knows where I am, and why." He pulled her closer and lifted her chin in his callused hand. His gray eyes searched hers. "I have to tell you, it's not nearly as much fun at home without you." His lips brushed her hair. "I love you, Darcy. Been fallin' in love with you since the day you brought Jamie to me. I want you to marry me. We belong together."

"But we haven't even dated," Darcy squeaked. She didn't know why she said that. That wasn't what she meant. But her mind raced, stumbling over memories of mistakes she'd made. Shouldn't they think about this a while? It was so sudden, and hasty decisions had been her undoing more than once.

She barely heard Clark rambling about their first date. "Oh yes we have. Remember that day when you invited me to a lovely landslide?"

Darcy laughed, then moved closer to him.

"Okay. Let's try this," Clark said with a forced, comic drawl. "Would you kindly permit me to come a courtin', Miss Drucilla? And then will you kindly consent to be my wife?"

"Clark... I've made so many mistakes. Maybe we need time...."

"We've both made mistakes. Let's work it out together. Now's the time. I'm lonesome without you, Darcy."

God, please tell me what to say! Eunice's words interrupted her turmoil, something about love and trust going hand in hand. No! It wasn't too sudden. In the months since they met, she and Clark had shared a lifetime of experience and intimacy of the heart. Of course they belonged together. Of course she trusted him. Of course she loved him! The warning bells in her heart fell silent.

"You shouldn't be alone," she heard herself whispering to him. The words fell lightly from her tongue, as though she had rehearsed them a thousand times in her mind. "And I want to be your wife. I love you, Clark."

He must not have heard. "Darcy, Sweetheart, say you'll marry me." His lips touched her nose. He smelled like leather.

"I did, and I will. I want to be your wife." she whispered. "I love you, Clark."

His eyes opened wide in surprise, then closed. His lips were on her cheek. "When? How soon can we... be together?"

"After school is out. I have a contract."

He backed away. "What day is school out?"

"Sixth of June."

"Our weddin' will be June seventh." He was close again, kissing her forehead. "That's as long as we need to wait."

"By a minister." She kissed his shoulder. His jacket smelled like horses and gasoline.

"Dan Chadwell is an ordained minister." He kissed her eyebrows.

"In the Chadwell's church?" She kissed the hollow of his cheek.

"In the Chadwell's church, I'm sure. Jamie can be my best man."

She stood back and managed a stern expression. "Has that kid been praying again?"

"Reckon so." He kissed her eyelids. "Somebody has for sure."

"I'm glad. He says good prayers."

He kissed the tip of her nose again. His hair fell forward, tickling her eyelids as an eloquent silence surrounded them.

His arms drew her into a very close embrace. She was surprised by her physical response to his nearness. Her shoulders tensed. He released her. Again the gray eyes poured their message into hers. His voice became a gravelly whisper. "Darcy, we can wait." His lips brushed hers momentarily. "Trust me."

Cautiously they stepped apart, allowing the promise of fulfillment to enfold them in quiet serenity. Yes, she trusted him. Her shoulders relaxed and her arms circled his neck. Their lips touched, and touched again. Lips that fit together perfectly, the same way their hearts and minds did.

No fireworks. No "Hallelujah Chorus." The earth didn't threaten to spin from its axis. Nothing but a rosy glow that filled the emptiness around her heart. Nothing was missing. It was perfect.

In that moment, Darcy knew she would no longer be alone.

The End

Printed in the United States
79131LV00003B/130-501